Useful Girl

ALSO BY MARCUS STEVENS

The Curve of the World

USEFUL GIRL

a novel by

MARCUS STEVENS

ALGONQUIN BOOKS
OF CHAPEL HILL
2004

Published by
ALGONQUIN BOOKS OF CHAPEL HILL
Post Office Box 2225
Chapel Hill, North Carolina 27515-2225

a division of
Workman Publishing
708 Broadway
New York, New York 10003

This is a work of fiction. While, as in all fiction, the literary perceptions
and insights are based on experience, all names, characters, places, and
incidents are either products of the author's imagination or are used
fictitiously. No reference to any real person is intended or should be
inferred.

Library of Congress Cataloging-in-Publication Data
Stevens, Marcus, 1959–
     Useful girl : a novel / by Marcus Stevens.— 1st ed.
          p. cm.
     ISBN 1-56512-366-2
     1. Teenage girls—Fiction.   2. Northern Cheyenne Indian
Reservation (Mont.)—Fiction.   3. Cemeteries—Conservation and
restoration—Fiction.   4. Cheyenne Indians—Antiquities—Fiction.
5. Runaway teenagers—Fiction.   6. Teenage pregnancy—Fiction.
7. Mothers—Death—Fiction.   8. Montana—Fiction.   I. Title.
PS3619.T49U84 2004
813'.6—dc22   2003070808

10   9   8   7   6   5   4   3   2   1
First Edition

For Kelly who inspired us
with grace and love.

He had seen the skeleton of a Cheyenne girl dressed in an Army coat, disinterred when the railroad bed was widened. Her family had put silver thimbles on every finger to prove to somebody's god that she was a useful girl who could sew.

—THOMAS McGUANE, *Nobody's Angel*

Useful Girl

PROLOGUE

THE RIVER HERE bends and turns back on itself, eddying into a long, flat pool. Rose stands at its edge, one bare foot in the water, sending ripples like signals out across its surface. I take the moment as she's turned away to try to catch my breath and gather my thoughts. Though she's only six, I'm afraid of her questions, simple and hard to answer. I'm tempted to change my mind and not say anything. Act as if it were nothing. But she knows that we've come to talk—mother and daughter. We've walked up the bank of the Yellowstone to her favorite spot, away from houses and people, where she can dig in the mud with sticks and throw rocks in the deep green pool and watch the shadows of fish scurry away across the bottom.

I sit down among the cool stones of the riverbank and she turns toward me, expecting me to begin. I hold a letter in my pocket. It's from her father, and I fold and unfold it as I struggle with deciding how much to tell her, how much she can understand. When her eyes catch me fidgeting, I force myself to stop. I'm sure she senses more than I give her credit for. I've been underestimating her, too cautious with her happiness and her innocence. It's time to tell her the story.

She sits out of reach of my arms, and as she listens to me begin, she makes a pile of rocks as though accumulating evidence, as though all the parts of what I have to tell her might add up that way, one on top of the next, to some conclusion. She stacks with a steady rhythm, and when the pile tumbles, she picks them up and starts over. She watches my mouth as she listens, and I can barely hear my own voice above the river. With each mud swallow that dips and skims the surface of the pool, my thoughts scatter, as if taken in flight, too. But I keep returning to Rose and her patient expectation. I watch her child's imagination work as she thinks of how it was for me, when I was little more than a child myself, when I was only seventeen, without the experience to give me reason to trust in the future or to have a sense of the current of time, for better or worse.

When I'm done, when I've been quiet long enough that she knows I'm done, she walks down the bank of the river looking for driftwood and leaves me to my own thoughts, to the memories and the details I've left out. Part of this story comes from my own memories, part I have heard about since, the memories of others.

It begins with the spring my mother died.

CHAPTER ONE

SHE WALKED AWAY on a whisper in that quiet, empty part of night when it feels as if the sky is being held up solely by the soft breathing of sleepers. I was wide awake when it happened, though I didn't know about it until morning. And I didn't sleep until morning either. I lay in my bed watching the tree outside move almost imperceptibly in the wind and the shadows from the streetlight play across my ceiling. I listened to the rustling leaves and then to a dog moving on its chain and far away to a truck gearing down as it headed up the hill. She was gone, but there was no sound for her leaving.

As morning faded the sky and drowned the stars, I remember my father walking out into the yard, looking out toward the Yellowstone, the prairie and the mountains waking silently in the distance. I heard the screen door stretch on its rusted spring and I got up and watched him from my window. Then I knew she was gone. I don't know how. I don't remember being able to see his face, and I couldn't hear him, though it seemed he was talking quietly, speaking first to his hands and then to the silent horizon. He stood there until the sun found him and he turned away from it. I watched him until he walked back into the house, but he never looked up to see me.

My father seemed tiny from up in my room. Maybe it was because I'd spent my whole life looking up at him. He's a big man, and it was always like living with a giant. He'd shake the milk on the table whenever he sat down. He never said much to me, but when I was a little girl, he'd let me climb up onto his lap, which felt like climbing a mountain. He'd lean over me, with his coffee cup in his huge hands, and maybe say a few words to my mother about the coming day. And I'd rest my head against his chest, nearer the rumble of his voice, and never wonder if the world was unsafe.

I stood that morning in a big T-shirt at the doorway of my parents' room long enough to lose a sense of time. Mom was still in their bed. The covers lay over her and she was probably still a little warm. There was nothing to give it away, and yet the room felt empty. It's strange to think that there was something about her that I could miss from across a room, when I couldn't even see her face.

The doctors blamed her death on a congenital heart defect, and I think that's true. I think her heart broke, though it is hard to accept that it was purely a mechanical failure, that my mother was gone simply because she was betrayed by a muscle. As I imagined my own heart beating in the warm darkness of my chest, each beat seemed desperate, convulsive and inadequate. There were little bits of bone in her ashes and that's about it. And so little of that. The rest was water, I suppose, a little river.

Dad sat in the kitchen with his back to me, drinking his coffee. I remember listening to the clock tick. He held onto the warm cup with both hands, and he wasn't saying anything. I think he was afraid to speak. I think we both were. We were afraid to say something aloud that would make Mom's death real. And as I waited for him to move, I was thinking, *What if he doesn't know?* What if he'd gotten out of bed without ever touching her? He could be waiting for her right now to come in and begin her day.

As I watched him and he didn't move, I grew angrier. He leaned back and the old chair creaked and popped, and for a moment it looked as if he might be gathering his strength to get up. But he settled back in again, as though some new force of gravity held him captive. Once, my back was small enough that he could lay his hand across the whole of it. And now he couldn't even stand up.

"Why don't you *do* something?" I said, scarcely able to control my voice, to make it work.

He didn't turn. I felt my whole body burning.

"She's dead!" I yelled.

Dad stood up, nearly breaking that wooden chair. "I'm sorry, Erin," he said. "I know."

And then he turned and left me standing there.

IT WAS RAINING the day of the funeral, and there were too many people at the house, all crowded inside. With their voices appropriately hushed, they ate casseroles and Jell-O molds, salads with ranch dressing, cold pasta and little finger-whatever-foods. My grandmother, Dad's mom, sat in her chair clucking her tongue in disbelief so everyone was afraid to approach her. I sat on the piano stool a couple of feet away, and she allowed me to be quiet.

The whole time Dad circulated. I watched him nod as he was offered a few words from a banker from Billings and then from whatever business associate from the chamber of commerce who had shown up. Break down, break down, I kept thinking, lose control, go mad. But it was as though his shoulders were made of iron, and his eyes would never let go. His face was ashen and stony, but absolutely composed, not that different from normal, really. What a great trick he had perfected—one face for all occasions.

I remember thinking that someone should have been more openly upset, crying or yelling and sobbing. But instead we all mumbled and silently finished off the carrots and celery. Then Dad coughed softly into his hand, and for a brief moment stood alone in the middle of the room, his arms at his sides, his gaze lost. I could see his hands trembling. *Aloneness,* I thought, *that will get him.* And for the first time, I thought of running away.

"My son . . . " said Grandmother, and she cleared her throat. "My son expected it to be a relief."

Mercifully, someone approached Dad and he found refuge again in the man's firm handshake and matching expression.

"The funeral," Grandmother offered as explanation, then sank back into her chair and resumed her quiet clucking. She tapped her foot like an angry music teacher trying to enforce the beat, and with each tap the air in the room seemed to get thinner and my throat tightened until, finally, I had to go outside.

A few of my friends had come to the funeral, but most of them stayed only a little while afterward. My best friend, Jennifer, lasted the longest, but even she didn't make it that long. I was glad to be left alone. I sat on the back deck, where I wouldn't be found, and let the rain soak my black dress and the cold turn my legs red. Water poured off my hat, and my tears mixed with the rain, so no one could tell I'd been crying. When I'd had enough, I went up to my room and took off my wet clothes and put on my worn-out sweats and sweatshirt. I meant to go back down, not simply disappear, but I needed to find my breath first. I was afraid if I did go down with my throat that tight, I would only make a scene. I could just imagine the hands reaching for me, the sympathetic eyes and kind words, the feeling that the door was barred, escape impossible.

Aunt Kristine, Mom's younger sister who had come out from

Connecticut for the funeral, found me sitting on my bed. She knocked softly on the frame of the open door.

"May I come in?"

I nodded, but I didn't really want her to. I was afraid she'd been sent up to make me cry. Ironically, if there had been a theme to the family conversation that afternoon, besides the weather, it was the general concern that I had not cried at the funeral. I had not been seen crying by anyone. Somehow *I* was supposed to cry but *they* weren't, as if I, a child, a girl, should perform this sacrifice so that they might maintain their stoic self-control. Aunt Kristine sat down on the bed next to me, and surprised me with a grin.

"I think your Dad must know every rancher with cow manure on his boots in this half of Montana. It smells like a barnyard down there."

I smiled. I couldn't help it. She was hardly exaggerating. She caught my eyes and could see that I'd been crying. She laid her hand on my knee. "Do you think you can live with him?"

I shrugged.

"Like you have a choice, huh?" Aunt Kristine knew Dad well enough, what he was like.

I was afraid to try to answer her, and she didn't make me. We sat for a long time, and when I began crying again she scooted closer, and she held me and cried, too. She didn't move or say a word until it was dark in the room, and we could hear people downstairs beginning to leave.

"We should go down and see them out, don't you think?"

"I don't really know any of them. I think Grandma left already."

Then we heard a cough and the bellowing voice of my grand-dad, Mom's father. He was nearly deaf, so he shouted most of the time. He was having some trouble finding his cane. "Old Joe," he called it.

We smiled.

"Okay, so I do know *someone*. Do I have to go down there, really?"

"Well, unfortunately *I* do. The old crank is riding home with me." She laced her fingers in mine, and I stood up with her.

By the time we got downstairs, Granddad had found "Old Joe," and he was standing with the front door gaping open behind him. Gusts of wind blew inside and scattered wet leaves across the carpet. The rain came down in sheets in the streetlight beyond him. His raincoat whipped at his legs. His damp, gray hair stuck on his wrinkled face. For a moment he looked panicked, as if it had just occurred to him for the first time that Mom was gone, as if he had meant to yell for her to help him and then realized his mistake. I watched his hand slip slightly on the wet handle of the cane. Then he caught me, saw what I saw. He tightened his jaw.

The screen door rattled so loudly in the gale that he had to shout. "I'm leaving. It's high time for this house to get back to normal!" And he turned and shuffled out into the night. He'd completely forgotten that he wasn't going anywhere without Aunt Kristine. She hurried after him.

I tried to wave to her from the door, but she had her hands full getting him into the car. When I shut the front door against the wind, the house was empty except for me and Dad. He was sitting in his chair as if he was ready to turn on the TV, as if everything were suddenly alright, as if the hurt would go away now that all the people were gone, no longer reminding us of her. But then he looked over at me.

It rained for so long after that, I lost track of the days and weeks. There was mud everywhere and the Yellowstone became swollen and brown. A hundred-year flood, they said. It was too cold for the grass to green up, and the plain was gray as the sodden sky. I got used to my windows beaded with rain. I began to prefer to see the world that way.

CHAPTER TWO

I THOUGHT EVERYTHING would change after my mother's death—that it had to. I guess I wanted concrete evidence that the world was as shaken as I was. I expected months of painful healing—a year of *significance*, at least. But what came instead, as the rest of our neighborhood went about its business, was an ice age of grinding numbness. Nothing in my life changed. I blamed the place where we lived. I blamed my father's house, with its relentlessly mowed lawn, and our perfectly manicured, immaculately planned subdivision called "Riverview." The durable siding and aluminum-framed windows of the houses looked to me like fake, frozen-forever smiles. The bright white paint hurt my eyes and made my heart ache. All of it seemed so impervious to change. But that was just its shell. Someday we would be startled to realize that it was actually falling apart, just as I was surprised by my own face reflected in my bedroom window—that same perplexed expression I can remember on my mother's face sometimes.

The rains stopped abruptly. June passed almost dry and by July the grass on the hills was brown. You could see it in the yards of some of the neighbors' houses, too, where the sprinkler systems weren't reaching the edge of the lawn, the dryness creeping in, curling up the sod. I stared out at the burnt hills, and wondered if I had the nerve to go out. I prayed for the rain to come back, for the excuse to stay indoors protected by glass.

But Aunt Kristine was back in Sheridan to get married; she was moving onto the family ranch. Granddad had been carted off to a rest home in Laurel, where he had a younger sister who could look in on him. His collapse was so sudden that he'd been unable to offer a fight. He handed over the ranch to his one remaining daughter, and the hydraulic lift slowly levitated him in his wheel-chair into the handicap van.

Aunt Kristine's wedding was to be the first family gathering since Mom's funeral. I could hear Dad whistling downstairs, shuffling through his closet, looking for his one suit. I was supposed to be getting ready, too. He'd wanted to skip the wedding, but since we *had* to go, he decided we would head down early so he could stop by the job site on the way. There was no use in trying to point out to him that it was anything but "on the way." It would add an hour, at least. His construction company had a contract to pave a section of state road down south of the Northern Cheyenne Reservation. It was a big job for a small outfit like his, and he was in over his head, afraid to let it out of his sight even for a day. Besides, he lived to work. I'm convinced that his only reason for keeping fishing gear in the garage was so that he could complain about having no time for it.

He was yelling up the stairs that it was time to go long before I was ready, and I heard his impatient boots on the front steps as I grabbed a brush and a hair scrunchie from the bathroom on my way down. He had the truck pulled out of the garage, idling, and was sitting on the driver's side with my door open, waiting for me. I barely got it shut before he backed out of the driveway. He was not one to be late, not for anything, even something he'd rather skip.

As we crossed over the bridge to the freeway, I looked out across the Yellowstone. In the main channel the river surged around a rock that was about the size of a small house. The waves piled up on it, green and brushed with white foam, as if confused to encounter it there. Then the river relaxed into a run along the riff-raff, squeezed uncomfortably between the pilings of the bridge, and fanned out thinly over a riffle downstream. Many times since Mom died I had waded out in the middle of that gravel bed where it was only knee deep and let the water wash around my legs, pushing gently, as if encouraging some weakness, looking for it, offering to wash me away.

We followed I-94 to town then south on I-90 to Hardin, up out of the Yellowstone bottom, past wheat fields and stretches of bunch grass and sagebrush. From up on the bench I could just make out the Pryor Mountains to the north, faintly blue at the rim of the yellow plain. Dad took the exit for the Little Bighorn Battlefield and accelerated as we headed up the grade past the monument gates. I caught a glimpse of the parking lot shimmering with rows of motor homes, and beyond that the battlefield, now a hayfield, where the Indians had been camped. I knew the monument pretty well. We must have come here a half-dozen times on school field trips, and at least once with visiting relatives for the reenactment at the end of June.

This stretch of road through the Crow Reservation to the Cheyenne had been recently improved, wide shoulders and fences set way back on the easement. There was hardly any traffic. I could feel Dad's foot press a little harder on the accelerator. This finished project must have reminded him each morning just how far behind schedule he was, despite working Saturdays for weeks now. He looked particularly uncomfortable dressed as he was — the white collar of his shirt chafing, the unfamiliar tie lassoed, pulled tight around his neck.

The dress I'd picked, dark and mostly gray, wasn't a lot better. I'd found it already ironed, hanging in a bag in Mom's old closet. I liked its plainness, its potential for camouflage. With all those aunts and cousins and the groom's family visiting from back east, my best hope for the wedding was to disappear. I couldn't handle any more sympathy or attention. Dad and I tended to stand out, provoking the inevitable questions. *Where's the wife? The mother?* Without her, we were an inexplicable pairing, two unconnectable dots.

As we approached the town of Busby at the border of the reservation, there were more pines on the crumbling yellow sandstone bluffs, and even a couple farms laid out in the bottom. Dad's face was set in a scowl. I could tell he was thinking about the run-down houses we were passing, their blistering paint and dirt yards, the laundry out on lines, rustling in the breeze like flags or banners of poverty. He didn't like what he saw, what it seemed to say about the people who lived here. Many of the houses were surrounded by the wrecks of old vehicles and not just a few but scores of them, junkyards with trunks and hoods flung open, collapsing into the landscape. Tepee poles leaned against the roofs, basketball hoops teetered over courts of plain hard dirt, sweat lodges with shredded plastic tarps dotted the backyards among the swing sets and bright plastic play sets. Most of the old trailer homes and simple dwellings looked like they must have been part of a government housing plan years ago. One sat up on a hill with its windows and door recently boarded over with plywood that had spray-painted on it the green letters NCHA, Northern Cheyenne Housing Authority. A few were new and well kept, at least as nice as the average Montana ranch house, but he did not seem to notice these among the clutter and chaos of the rest. Dad liked order. And this was not that. He liked Riverview, odd as it was, stranded by the river across from the freeway with not a town or other subdivision in sight. He liked his acre of mowed grass and trim landscaping with its carefully placed boulders, his relatively new house, the bonus room, the three-car garage. He didn't grow up on a ranch, but he was familiar enough with the crumbling outbuildings with their own car and truck graveyards. He knew the sour smell of manure that wafted through the house downwind of the corrals when the snow melted. I know Dad had no romantic illusions about life in rural Montana. The reservation seemed the same to him, and worse. It seemed aimless and poor. He'd been driving this route all summer to get to the highway project. He saw the unemployed, the wrecks, the mangy dogs, the poorly kept houses. And not much else.

"You'd think with all the federal money they pour into this place, they'd have done *something* worthwhile."

I shrugged and kept quiet. He wasn't looking for anything more than a "yes sir," anyway. He saw what he saw.

As we approached Lame Deer, we passed the brand-new sign for the Charging Horse Casino and Bingo. "Now who the hell would drive all the way out *here* just to put a buck in a poker machine? Must be where the Indians go to blow their unemployment checks," he grumbled. "That's tribal sovereignty for you, right there. Make your own laws so you can have a casino. Did you know Uncle Claude has a place over up on the Flathead rez, private property, but he can't even hunt on it without their permission."

I shook my head. I didn't know.

We came into Lame Deer down the hill from the West. There were very few people on the street, just an older woman waiting by the grocery store listening to the tribal station on her car radio, and a couple of kids teasing a dog in the parking lot. Two guys unloaded a flat tire from the trunk of their car and wheeled it slowly behind the new Conoco station, the Cheyenne Depot.

South of town the road began to lose elevation, the hills dried out, the dirt became redder and scraggly cottonwoods replaced the pines. When we hit the newly paved section, black with new red shoulders, the rumble of the tires quieted to a soft whine, and the road was suddenly perfectly smooth. Dad relaxed.

We crossed the Tongue River on a new concrete bridge. The water was low, a shallow channel among the weeds and silted banks that occasionally found a deeper hole. Finally, as we made a wide curve to the west, we began to see the signs for road construction ahead and the pavement ended. The flagger started to wave us down to stop until she recognized Dad's truck. He hardly waved back at her as we passed, though she seemed to want to tell him something.

Not a truck or grader was moving when we found the road crew. Dust drifted across the road. The workers were all standing around, knotted in a group beyond one of the graders that was stopped with gravel piled up in front of the blade. Something wasn't right. Dad frowned and slowed down abruptly. It almost looked as if they were on a break except they seemed to be staring at something on the ground.

"What the hell?" Dad jumped out of the truck. I climbed out to follow and could hardly keep up with him. Nobody had seen us coming, and they stepped aside quickly as Dad pushed through.

It was eerily quiet. The only sound was the wind whistling through the grass and sagebrush and the ticking of the grader's engine cooling. I moved around so I could see what they were all looking at.

One of the workers, an Indian, was kneeling in a shallow hole. Everyone watched silently as he lifted melon-sized stones out one at a time until he had a large pile. Then he began scooping out handfuls of the sandy soil.

Somebody finally said something. "Come on, why're ya being so damn careful? Just pick it up."

I couldn't see what was in there yet, but I could see Dad's face, a look that was all too familiar. It was the face he made when he thought something wasn't being done right, the way he looked at me, too, sometimes, as if I were the embodiment of some kind of error, some manufacturing mistake, a crooked road with the wrong camber. The Indian continued to dig carefully, unaffected by Dad's impatience. He looked young, maybe nineteen or twenty, just a couple of years out of high school. Even kneeling he seemed tall and gangly, his lean arms powdered with a pale reddish dust. He took off his gloves and laid them next to him. Gently, he brushed away the dirt from what looked like a wool blanket, rotten and faded blue. He worked slowly, seeming to caress the dirt as he prepared to lift the covering away. I looked up at Dad again, who seemed ready to jump in and take over.

Everyone was expecting the same thing. A body. But when he lifted the shroud of disintegrating wool, there was no body left, only partially mummified remains, reddish-brown bones the color of old varnish, and brittle, papery skin still stretched thinly over parts of the chest and the arms and legs. The skeleton was small — a child. He pulled the blanket away revealing the skull with wisps of hair clinging to it. I found myself drawn to the infinite black holes of each eye socket, which seemed to stare up at the blue sky.

"Cheyenne," he said quietly and lifted a dried, twisted moccasin with a worn pattern of beads. "A girl."

A girl. A shiver spread across my skin like a breath of snow.

"Shit." Dad's voice snapped in the silence.

The Indian boy looked up at him, angry. But Dad had already turned to the man next to him. "Get your grader. Let's cover this back up."

"You sure about that, Jack?" The man eyed the Indian who still had his hands on the blanket.

"What do you mean?"

"I mean . . . " He lowered his voice and turned away so that the rest of the crew couldn't hear him. ". . . I'm not sure what the legal requirements are in a situation like this. We might have to report it to someone."

Dad did not hesitate. "Cover it up."

The man shrugged then pulled on his gloves and climbed into the cab of the grader. A cloud of black smoke drifted from the exhaust as he stepped on the throttle to charge the hydraulics.

The Indian looked down at the child's remains as if he might pick her up in his arms. He pulled the covering away. What was left of it didn't really look like a blanket, more like an old woolen coat. Her small hand was drawn into a fist as if she had been trying to hold on to something. Then I saw the black, tarnished thimbles. One on each finger.

"You," Dad yelled. "Get the hell out of there."

The Indian ignored him. He stayed where he was as the rest of the workers moved off. He carefully laid the coat back over her, and began speaking to her, softly chanting something that sounded like a prayer. His hands rested on the coat and his eyes were focused on her. I found myself watching him instead of the remains, listening intently to his faintly audible voice drifting away. At the end of each phrase I could just make out the refrain Ma'heo'o, Ma'heo'o—a prayer to the Great Spirit. He got up and pushed a little dirt with his boot over the girl's remains. When he caught me staring at him, he didn't turn away. He held my eyes long enough that I began to feel uneasy. The wind blew his hair across his face, and he brushed it back, allowing himself an easy smile. Suddenly, I realized how odd I must have looked there on the side of the dirt road, dressed in my formal dress. He looked back at the bones then took his shovel and walked off.

The ground began to tremble as the grader backed up to maneuver and drop its blade in front of the girl. Wrapped in those folds of decaying wool she looked tiny and vulnerable. The grader pushed forward; dust and dirt and rock filled the hole. I imagined the crush of stone on my own chest, and then she was hidden again. For the millionth time I thought of Mom's death, alone in the night. Did she open her eyes? Did she know? My grandmother tried to reassure me that most people die alone, even when someone is nearby. Her own father had died when she was in the room. She heard a cough, and when she turned to ask what he had said, he was gone.

The crew walked to their trucks, ready to quit for the day. I was left standing there alone. Dad stared right at me for almost a full minute before he spoke. "Why don't you wait in the truck? This will take a second."

I got back in, brushed the dirt from my dress and watched Dad in his suit talk to each of the crew. Dressed that way he looked like an FBI agent and each man nodded seriously. The last one he spoke to was the Indian kid, who didn't look him directly in the eye but didn't look away either. He stood there stoically as Dad seemed to make subtle threats. Finally, he offered a nod and Dad left him alone. I was struck by how calmly he waited while my father walked away and climbed back in our truck.

The grader finished its work and then moved down the road. Dad seemed angry as he pulled away and drove past the line of crew vehicles.

"I want this kept quiet," he said, without turning toward me.

"It's kinda spooky," I said, knowing he wouldn't like it, but I couldn't help myself.

He looked at me like I must be nuts. "What?"

"That skeleton, that girl buried out there." My voiced dropped. "All alone."

I felt the truck slow down. Dad turned to me. "If this gets out, it will cost me plenty. Understand? I can't afford to stop work while they figure out that some Indian died a hundred years ago from god-knows-what. If we hadn't dug it up, nobody would've known the difference."

"Sure," I said as nonchalantly as I could.

"Just forget you ever saw it."

The clouds, which had been building all morning, were now almost black on the horizon, and soon cars coming from the other direction had their headlights on, and they were wet with rain. As we approached, the squall defined a perfect line. The road was dry and then suddenly it was flooded. The windshield wipers worked hard, slapping back and forth. Soon my arms were covered with goose bumps from the cool air of the defrost Dad had turned on to keep the windows from fogging. It was always amazing to me that you could sit right next to him and suddenly he would just not be there—not far off, like he was thinking about something, just not available. We both stared down the road and thought our separate thoughts as the windshield wipers timed our silence.

When the sun burst out of the clouds, the warmly lit rain and velvet-blue hills seemed unreal, as if painted for my benefit. I couldn't get those bones out of my mind. My heart pounded as I thought of them. I closed my eyes and the skeleton stood up before me, reorganized its joints and became a girl. I looked out at the plains, through the rain, and I imagined glimpses of her. Running. And then in darkness, someone wrapping her in that coat, laying her on the ground. I thought of all the nights and days that had passed as she lay there for a hundred years.

CHAPTER THREE

I'M SURE DAD had almost forgotten about the girl by the time we arrived at the ranch. The sun was out. The county road was damp enough to keep the dust down and the air was clear. He parked out by the irrigation ditch in the shade of a crumbling cottonwood. Most of the guests seemed to be there already and rental cars nearly outnumbered the local ranch vehicles. He sat for a moment after he turned the engine off. Maybe he was thinking what it would be like to have Mom here, how much easier it would be to follow the path cut by her bright smile at occasions such as this, rely on her for the niceties and introductions.

"Come on, Dad. We better get going."

He took a breath. "Yep." But he didn't move.

"Or we could leave now, and tell them we got a flat tire."

For a second he looked tempted. He considered it. "That would only make us late."

"Maybe it won't be that bad," I suggested.

He turned to me with a look that made me laugh. "It's a wedding not a hanging," he said and opened his door. I got out my side and waited for him as he straightened his tie in the side mirror. The sun was already getting hot again. The cars steamed and the freshly mowed field smelled richly of timothy hay. I walked a step behind him. Both of us took a deep breath as we rounded the corner, back of the house.

On the white tablecloths, the centerpieces with stargazer lilies looked hastily restored, water stains drying where the wind had upset them. Some lights hanging in a grove of aspens glowed faintly in the afternoon shade as they swung gently in the last puffs of wind that had followed the storm. There was enough room to the ranch, acres of hay fields and cow pastures, to wrap a blanket of quiet around the gathering. Everyone seemed at home, pleased with the summer day and their place in the world. Aunt Kristine's new family stood apart from the house, drinks in hand, looking up at the mountains.

Aunt Kristine was not out yet. Her groom, Mark, was laughing with some friends. His black suit looked tailored for the city, but he had on new cowboy boots. He pointed out where the renovations of the old house were to be with great sweeping gestures and chopping motions of his hand that indicated where part of the original building was to be demolished.

As I wandered among the tables, I was swarmed by my much younger cousins, the oldest only ten. At first they expected to include me in their game of tag, but when they saw my dress, my shoes, how "old" I looked, they raced off, yelling as if I had been transformed into some kind of monster. The boys' white shirttails were hanging out, already grass stained, their jackets left behind. The girls' bows were undone, their hair falling. It looked like fun.

My granddad had been positioned where he would need to be for the ceremony, which put him off at a distance from the group, and he sat hapless in his wheelchair. No one was willing to approach him. His reputation was well established, and sitting there, stranded in the direct sunlight, I'm sure he thought he had a damn good reason for being pissed off.

He ended up falling asleep during the actual wedding. I sat next to Dad who did not move, as though he were being punished. My aunt looked beautiful in cool white under the stand of dark-green spruce trees. I was too far in the back to hear her voice well, but I noticed that she held Mark's hand through the whole ceremony, and that's where his eyes rested.

Dad took his turn ahead of me in the receiving line. When he got to Mark, he looked uncomfortable. As critical as he might have been among friends about this city slicker with new boots, in person Dad was intimidated. He shook hands stiffly, mumbling his congratulations and then came up with a fake smile before moving painfully on. He stood apart. I'm sure everyone just thought he resented the slip of fate, the slight off-timing that had cost him this ranch. If Mom were still alive, she would've got the ranch; it was the obvious scenario. At least Dad was from Montana; simply by birthright he ought to know better what to do with it. Now it was to be managed by my aunt's new husband, a man from Connecticut who ran a business in outdoor clothing, fleece and Gore-Tex, a man whose livestock experience before the last couple of years was getting bit firmly in the ass by a horse at a dude ranch when he was a teenager.

I reached for Aunt Kristine before she saw me. Her arms were cool, but her cheek, when I kissed it, was flushed.

She held my face with two hands. "Don't leave without talking to me."

I nodded and promised, though I really wanted to take off right then. Mark hugged me as though we'd never met. We'd actually spent half an afternoon once playing pool. I beat him twice, and we had a good laugh. Now, just like Dad, I mumbled something awkward, which I was glad Mark missed as he greeted the next guest.

I walked away from the end of the line, away from the voices, the exclamations and congratulations. I looked down the line of suits and dresses and realized how few people I knew. Most of the guests had either come in from out of town for the wedding, or they were new to Sheridan, moved in over the last few years. The family I did know were all on my mother's side, and they treated Dad and me as if they felt they had to make a special effort to include us, to make sure we "belonged" even though now, without Mom, we pretty much didn't. Dad finally latched on to one of the few locals he knew, and launched into the usual conversation about this year's sudden heat wave and the beginning of fire season.

I stood around trying to pick a destination, but the thought of each potential conversation made my stomach turn. Eventually, I wandered over by the open bar, snuck a beer and headed out to a hayfield on the far side of the aspens where I could sit by myself for a while. The freshly cut alfalfa was laid out in windrows. Crows and magpies hopped from line to line chasing insects. The rich, humid smell of the hay made my head hurt as I sipped the beer and listened to the dull throb of the music. This was just the kind of event my mom had loved. She would've managed to get Dad out there, too, at some point, shuffling his feet cowboy style, rigid from the waist up, accidentally spilling a grin. I thought of her in a flowered dress sitting at the edge of the dance floor, her hands resting in her lap, a beaming smile. It amazed me how the ache of her passing could still seize my heart. I constantly reexperienced her death as something about to happen.

For a while I watched an eagle climb the thermals over the shoulder of the Bighorns. With each turn it made I took a breath, and with each exhale I let the thoughts of my mother go until I was surprised to find myself thinking of that Indian who'd dug up those bones, how he'd stood there that extra moment, looking back at me. I felt my neck getting warm. There was something about him, how unafraid he'd been with my father, and his face, which seemed more confident than any of the boys I knew. And maybe it was his voice, too, the way he gently lifted the girl's hand, the way he said the quiet prayer for her that made everything else seem so unimportant.

Ahead of me, through trees half consumed now by brush, fallen cottonwood branches and uncut grass, was the old homestead. It was a hand-hewn log building that Granddad had put a new roof on sometime in the late eighties. When I was a kid, I used to go there when we played hide-and-seek. Even if someone thought to look in the old cabin, they could never find me among the mess of old furniture, books and pictures coated with layers of dust and cobwebs. Sometimes I stayed long after the game was over and they stopped looking. I remembered most the smell of old books and wood smoke.

I finished the beer, which was probably the first whole bottle I'd ever had to myself. My head was buzzing as I wobbled over to peer through the cabin window. It was too dark inside to see. I knew the door wouldn't be locked, but I had to push hard to get it open. My eyes adjusted slowly to the darkness; the only light came from the narrow gap of the door and a couple small windows. I took a deep breath to try to steady myself. It was a bigger mess than I'd remembered. Even more junk had been piled in there since Granddad had moved off the ranch. There was an antique typewriter and suitcases stuffed with newspapers and everywhere stacks of books, almost all of them histories. He'd always been a big Indian wars buff. There was an old Colt Army officer's–model revolver in a holster on the desk, badly rusted, and a saber which I found accidentally and painfully with my shin, sending it clattering across the floor. Underneath a stack of photographs was the chair he had always sat in to smoke and read and where he used to bounce me on his knee when I was little. It still smelled of his pipe tobacco. I sat down and picked up one of the books—*The Fighting Cheyennes* by George Bird Grinnell and then under it Edward S. Curtis's *The North American Indian*. I flipped through the pages and could just make out the photographs, images of Native Americans with long peace pipes and headdresses, the cigar-shop chief most people still thought of when you said Indian. There was something tragic in the photographs, too, an awareness that the subjects were part of something already gone, as if that were the point of the pictures, to be a kind of epitaph.

A thin crack of light from the door shone like a beam onto a loose, unframed photograph on the floor next to the chair. I picked it up. The image was a copy of an old daguerreotype—a U.S. cavalry soldier stoically posing by his horse. Even in the dim light his eyes were startling. I recognized them. Though I knew it couldn't actually be my grandfather, he had those same eyes. I turned it over; on the back was written: Judson Ira Brennan, b. 1835, Granby, Missouri, d. Sheridan, Wyoming, 1887. I turned it over and looked at him again. He looked to be in his forties, about my dad's age.

When I put the picture back down, the slice of sun had moved. It was now glowing on a stack of three leather-bound journals, one of them left open. They looked newer than most of the stuff around, the pages not yet yellowed with age, and they were covered with a shaky scrawl in black ink. Dates and names. Descriptions of fighting. Lots of references to a General Crook. I figured these must be Granddad's notes. I'd heard he'd tried to write a family history of the early homesteading days and particularly the period during the Indian wars. On the last page I saw the name again, Brennan, my mother's maiden name. The unfinished paragraph read: "Captain Brennan retired from the U.S. Army in

1879. Moved to Sheridan, Wyoming back onto the home ranch with his younger brother, Vail, and sister-in-law Edith."

I closed the journal and started to put it back, covering the old photo. But then, instead, I picked them all up and took them with me. Something made me want to have them. I don't know why. I might have figured that I'd take them out to Granddad sometime at the rest home and ask him about them. I brought them out to the parking area and put them under the seat of Dad's pickup.

I ran into him on my way back to the party. He was walking around outside the house, looking it over. He could have been thinking that this is where Mom grew up, that one of those upstairs bedrooms could have been hers, a window where she once leaned to look out across the trees at the sunrise. But he probably wasn't thinking that at all, more likely he was just looking over the changes Mark had in mind for the remodeling project.

"Do you think we could sneak out yet?" he asked, craning his neck to see a certain pitch of the roof. He turned to me with a hopeful grin.

"Sure, Dad," I said. "Just let me go tell Aunt Kristine."

I found her amid a gathering of girlfriends. I didn't know any of them, and I felt funny walking up to interrupt. I stopped at the periphery of the group and waited for her. As I watched her laugh with her friends, I wished I was her. Not *like* her, I wished I *was* her, with everything laid out ahead of me like a brightly lit road.

After a minute she noticed me and excused herself. She wrapped her arm around my waist, and we walked out to where Dad had pulled the truck around. He gave her another stiff congratulations and then climbed in without looking back. I don't think he heard himself let out a deep sigh. I leaned forward to wave, and I could just see her eyes, still bright across the distance of the lawn and driveway. I felt like a prisoner being taken away in an orange suit.

We headed out to the county road that bent at right angles around section lines, out past the grain silos intermixed with the imposing headgates of new five-acre ranchettes, then up onto the empty, windblown benches of the working ranches, and joined the freeway north. I put my headphones on, skipped the CD ahead, and let the music fill in over the rumble of the truck.

Chapter Four

Dad used to tell a story about a bull elk he found up in the Beartooths trapped under an avalanche. He was hunting alone when he happened across just the tip of an antler poking out of a scree slope below a crumbling rock face. He lifted rocks for an hour to uncover one antler that was almost as thick at its base as his arm before he found the elk's battered head, an eye still frozen open. His fingers were raw from lifting the splintered stones, and he sat and stared for a long time at the pit he had made and the beautiful curve of the antler that extended out of it. Then he pushed a few of the rocks back into the hole to cover the elk's head and left it that way. He didn't make it out until hours after dark. That story gave me a terror of avalanches as a little girl. When I thought of that pit of rock, that battered antler reaching out, and then the glassy eye of that elk under the last stone, I thought of my own body trapped that way—splayed, moved and broken at the whim of stone and then relentlessly held there.

Summer days only made my sense of claustrophobia worse. They felt supernaturally long, as if the sun's arc were actually distorted, the earth tilted over more than normal. By nine, the sun was so high in the sky, you'd think it was almost noon. Dad had decided I was the perfect person to take over what used to be Mom's job, the bookkeeping for his business. I stared at a gigantic pile of invoices, trying to decide if I could get through half of them before lunch and then take a break. I picked one up, started to enter it into the computer, but I couldn't face it.

I ended up doing the dishes. I dipped the plates in the scalding rinse water and watched the cat stretch out in the cool shadow of the garage. The sun burned the yellow tile by the sink, drying the soapy water. It was so quiet I could hear the air circulating in the house, whistling under the doors.

When Mom was alive, on hot summer days like this, we used to go to the pool in Billings. I swam my hair green and laid my wet face on the warm, cracked cement, breathing in the damp smell of it, watching in extreme close-up the water spread in a dark stain away from my wet hair. We didn't talk a lot, but some. I got to say most of the things I needed to say as she listened with her eyes closed, the skin of her thighs turning splotchy red in the sun.

A banging on the door made me jump and I nearly dropped a dish. My heart was pounding as I caught my breath then went to the door and picked up the FedEx package. Dad's business did not get many express packages. When we did, it was something important. I looked at the sender's address: Boise, Idaho—an out-of-state bid that he had worked hard on. He thought he had a good shot at it, and we needed the job. I was tempted to open it, but instead I laid it on the couch by the front door so he'd see it when he came home.

The pile of invoices still lay on the desk, untouched, so I decided to clean house next. After a couple of hours I made it into the living room. The FedEx package with its bright letters, its urgent message, still rested there on the arm of the couch. If it was great news, if it was a contract, Dad would be thrilled to get it. I tried to imagine how crazy he might think it was for me to drive almost two hours to bring it to him. If it *was* good news, though, he might be glad I'd come. I just wanted to get out of the house. But then I felt the pang of another idea. And once the thought crept into my head, I couldn't shake it. It was more than just the idea of *seeing* that guy again, that Indian who worked for Dad, more than the minor thrill that he might stop what he was doing and look at me, like that, again. I guess I also wanted him to know, just for the record, that I wasn't some silly girl in a ridiculous dress.

As I backed Mom's car out of the garage, the seats felt cold in the bright sun. I wasn't used to driving her car yet. Her lipstick was still on the dashboard, and it rolled from one side to the other with every turn until I reached the freeway. After an hour and a half, I made it to Lame Deer and after that the landscape seemed to empty gradually, abandoned to the insects buzzing in the midday heat.

I left the new pavement and a mile or two later came upon the flagger in exactly the same place she'd been the previous week. She waved me by and I slowed the car for the gravel detour. They were making progress laying down the new road bed at this corner. Everything looked different, but I still recognized the spot where they had reburied the Indian girl. I could still see a patch of rock that didn't quite match the color of what was around it. It was subtle, though. If you didn't know it was there, you'd never notice.

Dad was farther down the road, though most of the men were already quitting for the day, dusty and tired. I parked behind a grader and took my time getting out of the car and walking down the road. I watched each of the workers getting into their pickups, but I didn't see the guy who'd found the bones anywhere. Of course not. What had I expected? I felt stupid.

Dad looked up puzzled as I approached.

"I thought this might be important," I said, handing him the package.

He opened it without saying a word to me, read for a moment then looked up, disappointed. It was the last thing I expected. "Long way to come for nothin'."

"You didn't get it?"

"They've changed the specs. They want another bid." Starting over did not seem promising. He waved the package at the road. "Looks like this job is going to have to be made to pay somehow." As he shook his head, I had to remind myself that it had nothing to do with me. He stood there for a moment longer. "Well, I gotta get back to work. See ya at home," he said and headed back toward the graders. I half expected him to kick the dirt like some kid who just struck out at a softball game.

I looked again for that Indian guy as I walked back to the car, but there were only a few of the equipment operators finishing up. It's amazing how silly something like that turns out to be, something you've worked over and over in your head, when you actually connect it with reality. There was nothing to do but go back and start into the pile of invoices

After I got back on the pavement, I rolled the windows down and let the warm air blast through my hair. I waved as I passed the flag woman, and I saw her wave back. She must have been wondering what I was doing, driving all the way out here just to turn around. *What's the difference, anyway,* I thought, *moving or sitting still at home, going forward or doubling back.* A dust devil spun along the shoulder next to me catching up debris in a dizzying dance. I was just getting up to speed on the new pavement as the road curved near a bend in the Tongue River. I casually followed the course of the stream as it wound among the cottonwoods. A few hundred yards upstream someone was sitting on the bank.

I let my foot off the gas and slowed down so I could get a better look. The smell of the river's muddy banks wafted in through the open windows. It was miles from any house. As I got closer to the river I could see it was a man, by himself, and there was a dark blue car parked on the shoulder, the door left open. Then my heart jumped. He was a long way off, but it *did* look like it could be him.

Some brush along the side of the road interrupted my view so I pulled off and parked at a turnout on the shoulder behind the blue car. I got out and walked back to where I could see, aware of the sound of my footsteps popping on the gravel. I still couldn't tell if it was him, but whoever it was hadn't moved. I looked back up the road to see if anyone was coming. My face felt hot. This was not something I wanted to get caught at, but I had to get a little closer to be able to see. I climbed cautiously down the bank but still couldn't get a good view. I had no choice but to push on through the brush. Thorns caught on my clothes and scratched my arms and I almost turned back, thinking what a dumb thing this was to do. I stopped to catch my breath, and though I couldn't see him yet, I thought I could hear him. I was sure I caught the hint of his voice cutting through the soft gurgling of the small river.

I took a few steps out of the brush where I could get a glimpse down the bank. It was him. He was sitting on the root of a fallen tree that lay half in the water. He had no shirt on, his hair lay over his shoulders, shiny black against the deep color of his skin. And then I heard his voice more clearly.

He was singing.

I could only just make it out, a faint chant, reaching across the short distance, a spell borne on the warm breeze that mixed with the smell of mud and wet leaves. As I listened, I expected him to look over, to catch me spying on him. When he didn't, I began to move closer, keeping a couple of cottonwoods in the line of sight between us with the idea, I guess, that I would hide if he turned around. But he didn't. He kept singing until I was close enough to see the long muscle of his shoulders and arms as he leaned back on them. He must have been swimming. His hair was still wet.

Then he stopped. I took a careful step back to get out of sight behind a tree, but the sound of my movement made him turn, and he caught me. There was no pretending that I just happened to be walking by. I stepped out where he could see me. "You were singing," I shouted lamely across the intervening distance of fifty yards or so, as if that offered an explanation for my sneaking up on him out here in the middle of nowhere.

He stood up. He was almost as tall as Dad.

"I'm sorry to bother you." I stumbled, "I just . . . heard you singing."

That made him smile. I walked up the bank so at least I didn't have to keep shouting.

"It's a hot day," he said as I got closer. I didn't know whether he meant it as the reason for his singing, or for why he had his shirt off. I know I was staring at his stomach and he must have noticed. He picked his T-shirt up out of the grass. He moved with a casualness that made it seem as if he thought it was perfectly normal that I just happened to be walking by down the bank of this river.

"It sounded good."

He pulled his shirt on, briefly hiding his face.

"Nice day for a swim," I said. I had to think of something to say. Standing there dumb while he dressed was unbearable.

"Just cooling off after work."

We both stood there silently for a moment. Then he seemed to be waiting for me to start walking back to the road. I turned to go back the way I'd come.

"This way's easier," he said and climbed a livestock trail that cut up the bank. Up on top, it was flat and open, no brush to scramble through. He held up the barbed wire of the fence for me so I could duck through.

"What are you doing all the way out here? On an errand for your Dad or something?"

"Yeah, something like that," I answered, as if that were the real question. I walked behind him as we cut back across the pasture to the car, wishing I had just stayed home. When we got back to the road, he shut the door he'd left open, then came back and leaned against the trunk of his car. "My name's Charlie White Bird."

"Erin," I said, then added my last name awkwardly, "Douglass."

He looked down the road. "It was illegal to bury those bones like that, you know," he said abruptly.

"It seemed wrong," I said lamely and tried to look away. But he held me with his frank gaze, not letting me so easily off the hook.

"What would you have done?" he asked.

I wasn't sure whether he meant, if I were in his position, finding the girl, or in Dad's. I picked the easier scenario. "I don't know. What *were* they supposed to do?"

"Call the sheriff, or the BIA police on the reservation."

"But it's too old, don't you think? I mean it's obviously not a murder."

He didn't say anything to that, as if to suggest the question— how much time has to pass to make a killing not a murder? I felt I had to answer. "She could have just been sick. Who knows, right?"

"They're still supposed to call the police," he said and sat on the trunk of his car. He didn't seem to be in any kind of a hurry to leave.

"Do you think she's the only one?"

"Seems like it. The way we got everything dug up around here. If there was anything else we probably would have found it."

I looked nervously back down the empty road. Dad would be coming by any minute. "Where is everybody? Shouldn't they be going home by now?" I asked as casually as I could manage.

"They graded the rest of the road yesterday. I'm sure everyone'll go that way back to Billings from now on," he said. "It's shorter."

I was suddenly aware of my hands, wishing I had a way to hold them that felt comfortable.

"They're all gone by now."

That was a relief, but I really needed to get out of there. I didn't really want Dad beating me home, either. "I gotta go."

He didn't move, which made it hard to just walk away. "What's the hurry?"

"No hurry, I just . . . you know . . . should probably get home."

"Could you help me do something first?" He said it the way he would to an old friend, a natural question.

"Sure . . . I mean, I guess. What?"

"I was thinking we should put some rocks to mark the spot where they buried her. So we don't lose track of where it is." He hopped off the trunk of the car as though it was already decided.

"I don't know. Seems like they wouldn't like that." *They* meant Dad, and I knew *he* wouldn't like it.

"So?"

"Won't they just tear it down?"

He shrugged that off and started walking toward his car. "Meet me there. It'll only take a minute."

"I don't think I should. Really."

He stopped at the door of his car. "Do you think they should just run a grader over her and that's it? It's okay? Nobody knows? Nobody cares?"

"Of course not, but . . . "

"So meet me there." He got in his car and shut the door. He had it started and was heading back down the road before I had a chance to respond.

I got in Mom's car and fumbled with the keys. I had to turn around if I was going to go help him. If I just went straight, I could go home the way I came. What were the odds that'd I'd ever see this guy again, anyway? Practically zero. He didn't need my help to put some rocks on her grave.

I started the car. He was far down the road already but I could still see him in my rearview mirror, which meant he could still see me. It would be pretty obvious to just drive off, like saying I thought what Dad had done was right, or that I was afraid of him. I put the car in drive and pulled forward a few feet, still trying to make up my mind until I was too far onto the road to make a U-turn. I looked back just as Charlie disappeared around the corner. I had to back up again to get turned around, and I caught up with him where the pavement ended. The flagger was gone.

Charlie drove slowly on the dirt road. The gravel rumbled under my tires. When we finally got to where the road crew had been, they were also gone. Trucks and graders were parked on the side of the road.

The fan continued to run after I turned Mom's car off, cooling the engine, its hum emphasizing the quiet. Besides that and the snapping of grasshoppers jumping over the road and some kind of small bird flitting about in the sagebrush, it was silent. Charlie was standing by the spot when I reached him. He already had a big rock in his hands. He kneeled down and laid it gently on the spot. My stomach was in knots. He didn't say anything but got up and went looking for another rock. I stood there for a moment, my hands shaking. Then I started looking, too.

It took us half an hour to build the cairn. None of the rocks from the construction pit run were really big enough so we had to look off the road in the grass, prying them out, brushing off the insects that clung underneath. My hands were raw by the time Charlie took the last rock from me and set it on top. "We'll see how long that lasts."

"It's just gonna piss them off."

"Yeah, but what are they going to do about it?"

"They'll knock it over. They'll assume you did it."

He shrugged. "You thirsty?"

"Yeah."

He went to the trunk of his car and got a bottle of water out of an ice chest. He sat on his hood, and offered it to me. I sat next to him, but not too close, and took a long drink. I handed it back to him, and he leaned his head back and his Adam's apple bobbed as he drank. Water spilled down his chin and neck. When he finished he wiped his face and then caught me grinning at him.

"Thirsty?"

"Yeah. I guess so."

The afternoon sun lit the grass and the sagebrush with a warm wash of light. A truck approached in the distance. Instinctively, I stood up.

"Don't worry. It's just some farmer," Charlie said, reading my mind. Still, I took a couple steps away from the car, and neither of us said anything until the truck had passed.

The dust settled and the warm, thick air of the afternoon wafted generously between us. I should have left then. It was an obvious opportunity, but I didn't feel like going. I sat back on the hood of the car. A magpie flew up out of the grass and beat into the wind with rolling wings of black and white that looked like waves, like the grass that undulated beneath it in the breeze.

"*Mo'é'ha*," he said. "That's the name in Cheyenne." He rolled his hand in the air imitating the way the magpie flew. I watched the bird until it dropped into the grass again, pouncing on some hidden prey.

"Have you lived on the reservation your whole life?"

"Off and on." He looked at me and I looked away. "I live with my uncle now, great-uncle, I guess . . . Uncle Leonard's pretty old. Mom thinks it's a good idea to have someone out there with him. His place is pretty far from town. I like it 'cause I don't have to live with my three sisters."

"Where do they live?"

"Near Busby. Mom works at Chief Dull Knife College. My oldest sister just graduated from there. These days my dad's in Seattle most the time. He does heavy construction work."

"What about you?" I asked.

"Huh?"

"Are you going to college?"

"Nah, I don't think so." He said it in a way meant to cut off the subject.

A puff of wind made me shiver.

"It's getting cold," he said and reached over as though he was going to lay his hand over mine, but instead put it down an inch away.

My attention fixed there, and the wind died just as I spoke again. The sudden hush had the effect of making my words sound much more important than I intended. "My mother died a few months ago."

He looked over at me.

It surprised me to be telling him this, a complete stranger. But I did, I told him the long version, from the beginning. Sometime during my story, he moved his hand onto mine. I cleared my throat. I looked down at his hand and prayed he would keep it there. It felt strange to be out here alone with him, so far from anything else, but it also felt good.

"My dad said a weird thing right after."

"Yeah?"

"He said, 'I'm sorry,' like it was his fault. Then he just wouldn't talk about it. Everyone tried to act like it was all just normal again." I took a breath, stopping myself. "Anyway I don't know why I told you. I think I'm getting used to her being gone now, or at least I feel like I can accept it. It's okay." Then I felt dumb for saying that. If it was so okay, why was I talking about it?

He lifted my hand, making small circles in my palm with his thumb. I kept talking mostly because I was afraid he might stop.

"My mom was . . . " I started. Then I didn't really know what I wanted to say, what it was about her that had made her different. Would it even seem that way to someone else? But he was listening. I could say anything.

"It's like she knew she wasn't going to live that long. Like she was always saying good-bye for real, you know, for good. I can't get thoughts like that out of my head."

He held my hand, still.

I can't imagine what he saw when he looked at me. But when I looked into his eyes and then at his lips as he spoke, my heart was racing. I thought that, more than anything, I wanted to kiss this boy, this stranger. I could feel the idea surge through my body as if I had nothing to say about it. I didn't know anything about him. But I knew I wanted him to kiss me. I was intensely aware of the quiet—no sound of the river, no trees to gather the breeze, no traffic. Then I could tell he was thinking the same thing.

He leaned over and the heat of his body seemed to burn all the oxygen from the air between us. He kept my hand. And his lips were warm, too, and the taste of him made me dizzy, and I was glad when he took my shoulder with his other hand to steady me and kissed me again.

As he leaned away, I was shaking. It wasn't cold, though it was starting to get late. I prayed my heart wasn't pounding so loudly that Charlie could actually hear it. I tried to concentrate on breathing. It wasn't as if I'd never been kissed before, but it was never like that.

"I should go."

He didn't say anything, but he still held my hand. I thought he was going to kiss me again, but then he didn't. He let go and slipped off the hood of the car. I took the cue and slid down, too.

He turned his lights on so I could find my keys, which I thought I had tossed on the seat. I found them on the floor by the center console. I got in and started the car. When I rolled my window down, he reached in and let his hand drift lightly over my hair to my shoulder. He seemed as uncertain about what had just happened as I did. I drove away, and when I looked in my rearview mirror, I saw him standing by his car fading away in my taillights. The landscape ahead of me was invisible beyond the reach of the headlights, and I followed the dirt road to the pavement on faith.

I DECIDED TO stop by Taco Bell on the way home so I'd have something to show for being so late, as if I might have gone there for dinner and got so caught up in the ambience of the place I just had to hang out for an extra two hours. I waved the bag at Dad on my way in, but he hardly noticed. He didn't see the point of fast food that wasn't a hamburger. He had the table covered with paperwork, the FedEx envelope at his elbow. Since Mom died, he'd started using the dining room as an office. The computer was at one end, his calculator at the other. We often sat there in the evenings like mismatched bookends working in silence. The whole house was changing, slowly, subtly losing Mom's presence. Any suggestion of her had begun to retreat, the way dust does, to the corners. She was in the closets, in the landscape painting still hanging in the living room above the unused fireplace, in the fading curtains, in a couple of candelabra still sitting at the corner of the mantle. But in the rest of the house, she was disappearing. Dad didn't like clutter, and not much else in interior decorating really mattered to him. He organized using the principle of elimination. I wondered as he hauled out to the garage unused chairs, throw pillows and vases, and then end tables, how long it would be before the whole house was completely empty.

"Did you eat dinner, Dad?"

He shook his head and flipped through some more paperwork.

I tried again. "Should I try to find something?"

He looked up, but it took him a minute to register what I'd said. His face was still twisted with the frustration of working on the bid. He shook his head, as much to chase his thoughts away as to say no, gathered the papers in a pile and stood up. "I'm going out to the shop for a while. I'll find something later," he said, which could have meant anything from some packaged frozen dinner to a bag of microwaveable popcorn.

I got up and dug through the freezer to see if I could find something for him anyway. In the back I spotted some homemade stew frozen to the shelf, something Mom had made and put away for a night when she wanted a break from cooking dinner. Under a thick coating of frost her neat handwriting gave the month it was made as March, a month or less, maybe even just a couple weeks before she died. It was solid as a rock and cold enough to burn my fingers. It would have been warm when she put it there. I almost threw it away. But then I thought of how upset that would make her if she knew. She hated waste. She was the type who saved two tablespoons of leftover spaghetti sauce.

The hot water I poured over it to get it out of the Tupperware felt good on my hands. I put it in a pan on the stove and it sizzled and popped on the red-hot electric burner. As I went out to feed our dog, Sadie, I smelled the pan begin to scald before the stew had started to thaw. When I was younger, while Mom cooked dinner, I would have been out in the shop with Dad, holding the end of the tape measure or a board that he was sawing. We used to have something to talk about, or at least he put up with my chatter and acted interested. There was no way I could go out there anymore. He'd think I was being weird. Sometimes I half-thought it was because I had developed breasts. He couldn't pretend I was a boy anymore. I think he made a conscious effort to avoid spotting any new curve that might challenge his preferred image of me as a cute little neuter-sexed girl. He didn't seem to think there was anything odd at all in the lack of boys calling or of requests from me to stay out late on Saturday nights. I was more useful to him with no boys attached and no imminent claims on adulthood.

When I came back in from feeding Sadie, the stew had splattered all over. It was burned on the edges but still frozen in the middle. I lowered the heat and put a lid on it.

THAT NIGHT I lay in bed unable to sleep. The streetlights of Riverview were bright enough to light the hills in an artificial yellow glow like a crippled sunset. I stared up at the ceiling, imagining Charlie's hand running through my hair, his fingers grazing my neck. I felt the bed falling away, as if lifted in a stiff wind, a storm out of my control, and twisted the covers in knots trying to fight my way to sleep.

Finally, I gave up and turned on the light at my desk, a dim bulb that barely lit half the room. Granddad's journals still sat there. I hadn't touched them since I'd brought them home. I picked one up and flipped through the pages. There were long descriptions of battles and raids, flanking and firepower, marches and rations, and weather—an entire army that acted as if it were on a big outdoor vacation, fishing and hunting, staging horse races. Then I came upon the description of a battle that stopped my skimming and drew me in. A dawn attack on a Cheyenne camp, horses stampeded, women and children running for cover, a desperate and scattered defense. Retreat. Refugees.

I closed the journal quickly as if that might stop something that had already happened. I looked up at the window, which in the darkness reflected just my face, hovering like a ghost, and I had the sickening feeling that I knew what had happened to that Cheyenne girl, or an idea anyway. The part that mattered. It came to me as a tale, a story my mother might have told me as I fell helplessly asleep.

▲ ▲ ▲

SHE WAS SWIMMING underwater, deep in a pool where the water rolled over old river rock, her dark brown eyes like mirrors, her black hair pulsing in the cold water as her arms pulled her toward the surface of the pool. She broke into the air with a laugh, looking up at the sky scattered with clouds and lined with cottonwoods, green with spring, suddenly alive with the sound of the wind. She swam to a sandy bank and lay out in the warm May sun. The chill of the nearly frozen river melted away, and her thoughts were about nothing, just the color of red on the inside of her eyelids lit by the sun.

At nine years old she was not supposed to be so far from camp alone. She sat up brushing the sand from her skin. Her dog lay a few feet away on the bank watching her patiently. His tail began to wag when she looked his way, shaking the play travois she had harnessed to him. She'd already loaded it with driftwood, thinking that if she came back with firewood maybe her mother wouldn't mind as much. She started off away from the woods, deciding on an alternate way back. At first it was easier leading the dog across big gravel banks of the stream, through clouds of mayflies dancing in the warm afternoon air.

But the sun bewitched her, led her thoughts astray, and she

walked a long way down the bank before she realized that she'd gone too far and the winding river had bent almost directly west, away from camp. She studied the bank, looking for a way to cut off some of the distance she had wandered, but everywhere it was thick with willow, hawthorn and chokecherry. She had no choice; she pushed into the thorny brush, pulling the dog behind her.

The travois made it almost impossible for the dog. He inched along, whimpering, the harness tangling up constantly in the brush, until she realized that she had to abandon the load or they would never make it through the thicket. She dumped the sticks and pressed on. In some places the snow was unmelted, up to two feet deep, shaded by the brush. It was cold and damp and smelled of mold and rotting wood. She looked up at the sky for a bird to show her a better way, but there were only the clouds beginning to gather color from the ending of day. Eventually, she cut loose the travois, too, which had taken her hours to make. Now she knew she would be in trouble, coming back with her clothes torn, with nothing to show for it, having lost the travois to boot.

"*Nenvoo 'sešétse oeškéso,*" she said. *Show me the way, dog.*

The dog whined and headed off through the brush, pushing with his nose, getting through much more easily without the travois hanging up on every root and branch. He ran farther and farther ahead of her as she crawled to get under the hawthorns, until she could no longer see him.

"*Oeškéso, oeškéso!*" she yelled after him.

Suddenly, she stopped and pulled her hand back with a jerk as if she'd accidentally touched a cold snake. But the snake was a frozen hand with a blue woolen sleeve. She screamed and scrambled back but couldn't get far in the thick brush. She could it see clearly now—the body of a white man, a dead soldier who she had almost crawled right over. He was still mostly covered with snow and just beginning to thaw. His eyes were open, a thorn jammed under one of his eyelids; his mouth was frozen open, too, around a thick, swollen tongue, surrounded by the sparse, reddish whiskers of a young man. Covering his body was the matted fur of a buffalo robe like one of the dead animals she saw every spring, elk and deer that hadn't made it through winter. He was the first white man she had ever seen this close up.

She jumped up and ran, caring nothing anymore about the thorns or her clothes as she clawed through the bushes. Finally she came to the slope of the floodplains where the brush gave way to grass and big cottonwoods. She spooked the grazing ponies as she ran for her mother's tepee at the edge of camp. The blue smoke of the cooking fires curled up into the orange sky. She hardly even noticed her dog running behind her.

Chapter Five

THE GRASS STILL smelled like Weed and Feed two days after Dad sprayed the yard. I didn't believe him when he said it wasn't toxic. Jennifer and I put on our shoes to walk across the lawn. We each had a glass of lemonade, singing with ice, and a plastic green-and-white folding lounge chair. The blue sky looked patriotic above our white house with its red shingled roof. Beyond the border of the subdivision, the hills were brown and dull, the weeds unkempt, the grass tinder dry and scattered with rust-colored rock. When Jennifer came over it was our ritual to drag our chairs to the corner of the yard where we couldn't see another house, nor be seen, and sunbathe, staring up at the rocky bluff that had been the bank of the Yellowstone however many million years ago.

She set her glass down next to mine. "What are you doing to-morrow?" she asked, as if I needed a calendar to keep track of my social schedule. I didn't answer. I knew she would continue anyway. "'Cause I'm going into Billings."

I thought I knew why. She was being casual about it, but she wanted me to come. The rodeo. A particular young cowboy whom she'd yet to name. I took a big gulp of sour lemonade. "I can't go."

"Why?"

"I have to do some stuff for my Dad."

"On a Sunday?"

I shrugged.

She was angry. To calm her down, I asked her what was the big deal about going to Billings. I knew she would go on for a while about this new boy she'd discovered. Her plan was a double date, her and the mystery cowboy and some unknown friend of his and me.

I closed my eyes and held an imaginary conversation in the gaps of her rambling in which I told her about the boy I'd met from the reservation, the real reason I couldn't go with her. I was meeting Charlie. Dad was home when he called. I guess Charlie would have just hung up if he answered. We had no plan, just meeting up in town. It sounded as unreal to me as it would have to her. It had the potential to change everything, or maybe it already had. *I was meeting Charlie.* The thought echoed in my mind as I squinted in the sun to look over at Jennifer and imagined her bright red lipsticked mouth frozen in an "O", her blue eyes wide as she processed her shock. *An Indian? From the reservation?*

Jennifer's plan would be a good excuse, if I needed one. "If I get done, I'll meet you there."

"Promise? You can show up late, no big deal."

"Jeeez. Yes, I promise. But anyway, if I don't make it you'll see, it'll be better without me."

She pondered this. It was difficult for her to adjust her plans; she'd worked them out in such precise detail. She turned her head away from me, closed her eyes and tilted up her chin, the faintest hint of sweat beading on her upper lip. Then I saw that she was smiling.

I CLOSED MY EYES and when I opened them there was Charlie's face. Each time the sun came out from behind the clouds, it lit his eyes and made his face glow. I'd met him at Costco and we'd left Mom's car in its huge parking lot. We drove out of town, found a small park, a place out of the way where we could turn on the radio and watch the clouds build in the distance and then move in on us. Fat drops of rain crash-landed on the windshield and pretty soon the windows were fogged. The world felt no wider than the reach of Charlie's arms. There was nothing to see out there anyway. He caressed my hair and my arms, and we kissed for hours. We kissed the way you do when it's new, like there's nothing else, like you've invented something nobody else knows about, until your lips feel thick and your face numb. The rain stopped and the sun soaked the roof of the big car. Sweat beaded up on Charlie's neck and made him look like something I wanted to eat. We sat together that way long enough that our skin stuck, long enough that it made my stomach queasy.

On the drive back it felt good to be sitting apart, the air rushing in, drying my hair, blowing much needed oxygen into my face. I drifted into a place free of time. My dad, my mom's empty house, did not exist. It was as if I had skipped all that, and, like my aunt Kristine, I had a future—at least for the duration of that drive back into Billings.

We were in the left-hand turn lane, ready to pull into the parking lot, when a car across the intersection started honking at us. I looked up. The driver was waving at Charlie, but Charlie was trying to act as if he didn't see him. He lurched the car forward and made the left turn the second the green arrow came on.

"Hey," the driver shouted at us as we raced by, raising his hands as if trying to figure out why Charlie wasn't acknowledging him.

"Do you know those guys?"

Charlie looked over his shoulder. "Yeah, I guess so. I just didn't feel like running into anyone right now."

He circled around to the back of Costco, and we waited to see if they would follow us. "That guy who was driving is Teddy. We've been friends since I don't remember. We're like third or fourth cousins." He stopped as if trying to decide if he wanted to tell me any more. He turned the car off and rolled his window down. "He's been living out at Pine Ridge in South Dakota. Last time I saw him was before he left." He shook his head. "He's a hot-head, one of those guys you know's gonna end up out at Dawson County or in state prison in Deer Lodge."

The rows of cars before us shimmered in the heat.

"This one time we were in town, really late, like two in the morning. We got stuck at this stoplight, and when it finally turned green some Billings kids ran the red and cut us off. We just about had a wreck. He jumped out of the car before I could stop him and started pounding on their hood like it was some kind of drum. He really scared 'em. They thought they were about to get their asses kicked by a couple drunk Indians off the rez. Anyway, that's what he wanted 'em to think."

Either Teddy didn't think to look for us behind Costco, or he didn't bother. Charlie drove me to where I'd left my car. I got out without kissing him. The parking lot was busy and it didn't seem like a good idea. I walked around to his side and leaned on the window. "When do I get to see you again?"

"I gotta work this week."

"Me, too," I nodded. But I was thinking, *That's only eight hours of the day. What about the other sixteen? How do I get through those?*

"Don't worry, I'll find you," he said and then he drove off. With so many people around I think he didn't want to hang around too long.

I WOUND MY WAY home through Riverview's meandering paved streets. This strange bit of suburb looked like it had been dropped out of the sky. Around us the landscape was still wild— pasture and rimrock, the prairie and distant mountain peaks. We weren't even a town. Everyone worked or went to school in Billings. We had no community building, no common park, no center. Yet on nights when everything was dark around for miles, and the sound of the Yellowstone drowned out the buzz of the sparsely trafficked freeway, it seemed as though we should be a town, a village, a camp, a clan. After all, it was just us and the darkness.

I decided to come in through the front door, so Dad wouldn't think I was sneaking in, but he was asleep on the couch, the TV blaring. The new digital satellite dish was a real boon for him. He'd found a channel that ran only Westerns. *She Wore a Yellow Ribbon* was his favorite movie of all time; he was a sucker for John Wayne's simple speeches, simple western truths.

I tried to sneak by, but the creak of the bottom stair betrayed me. "Where have you been?" he asked, fighting his way out of sleep.

"Nowhere," I said. "Didn't you get my note? I went to the rodeo with Jennifer." I started upstairs, turning away to help disguise the lie.

"Erin, come back down here, I need to talk to you."

I stopped a few steps further up where I had to lean out to be able to see him.

"Do you remember those bones we found out at the job site?"

"I was supposed to forget."

He frowned. I tried to appear disinterested, as though I had to think hard to remember. It was one of those times when I realized that there were some benefits to Dad's cluelessness, that he wasn't the kind to be sensitive to what my face might be trying to tell him.

"Somebody's been putting a marker on the spot. We take it down and it's up again within a few days."

"Creepy." I caught my breath.

He looked at me as if he suspected something, but I'm sure I was just reading into his expression, a sudden awareness of just how frightening his reaction would be—if he did know about my part in it, or about Charlie, any of it.

"Is that all, Dad?"

As I walked upstairs, I'm sure he was trying remember if he'd been like that when he was a teenager, so oddly disconnected. Imagining him as a teenager was impossible.

I sat on my bed and waited for it to get completely dark. Soon I saw the lights of the house that spilled out on the lawn going off. I heard Dad shut his bedroom door. I snuck downstairs past his room, found the cat and went to sit on the front steps. I stared out at my neighborhood as the Big Dipper wheeled slowly across the sky from right to left.

I looked down the street at the rows of different, but almost the same, houses, with different, but almost the same, cars parked in their driveways. Once upon a time, a prairie fire would have changed everything here, left a charred plain traced with orange worms of fire, eating the last of the green life, and for a hundred miles scarcely an animal would be moving.

It had to be Charlie putting that marker back up.

CHAPTER SIX

HOT AIR OOZED though the car windows smelling of exhaust and melting asphalt. The heat was putting me to sleep. I'd just nod off and then someone would rattle by with a shopping cart and startle me back awake. Meeting in parking lots wasn't particularly romantic, or comfortable, but it seemed best to leave my car where it wouldn't be spotted by someone I knew. I was even wearing sunglasses, a lame disguise, and I peered over them to watch the weary parade of people moving in and out of the grocery superstore and waited for Charlie to show up.

A woman walked by, herding her three young children, all of them dripping a trail of melted ice cream cones as she frantically tried to keep them focused on the project of getting safely from the store to the car. She was yelling by the time she pushed the key fob and then broke open a package of napkins to wipe their faces and sticky hands. But once they were in and the doors were shut, the oversized SUV whispered them all away, its dramas hushed. I could still see her yelling, but I couldn't hear it.

I think I was half dreaming again when a couple loading groceries into the next car woke me. By the time I focused on what they were saying, I was only able to catch part of a sentence.

". . . now that's an idea right off the reservation."

The man turned and caught me watching him. He must have been puzzled by my expression, my look of embarrassment. I was glad that Charlie wasn't there already.

The man smiled politely to get me to look away, and I turned back to the too bright parking lot burning in front of me. It was just a casual, dumb comment. So casual that the man would never have thought twice about it. He would never consider what it must be like to overhear people talking that way if you were from the reservation. Even if you never heard anybody say something like that, you'd know that's what they thought. You'd know about the stupid jokes my aunt Elsa made when she'd had a little bit to drink, and terms like "prairie nigger" that my family used so casually. I'm sure Charlie knew. Maybe he'd even heard about the Crow kid my cousin Danny and some friends had beat up after a football game in Hardin. They burned his car to a pile of melted rubber and steel. Or maybe that wasn't a big enough deal to have made it to Charlie, maybe it was too unremarkable. Nobody was prosecuted. I guess the Crow kid had been drunk, too. He kept quiet, anyway.

By the time Charlie showed up, I wanted to be as far away from Billings as I could get.

"What about your uncle's place?" I suggested. "Show me where you live."

"He might be around."

"Is that okay?"

"Uncle Leonard?" Charlie shrugged. "Sure. He already knows about you."

About you. It sounded funny, but also good, that for Charlie there was something to tell.

As we drove through Lame Deer, I slumped down below the dash. "Feel like you're smuggling me in?"

"Yeah, that's right. They don't allow white girls on the rez." He laughed. "Keep your head down so I don't get in trouble with the BIA cops."

When we got to the wire gate at his uncle's place, I made him stop to kiss me before we went up the hill. Uncle Leonard lived in a blue trailer perched near the top. There was a big drift fence next to it that Charlie said was there not so much for snow, as it was to keep the whole place from actually blowing away. I followed him up a set of rickety stairs to the small porch. The lights were off inside, and it took a moment for my eyes to adjust. Something had been left cooking on the stove, and the air was damp and fragrant, sweet with onions.

"I'll go see if Uncle Leonard's here."

Charlie went in the back, and I looked around the room. Photographs covered the pale-blue walls, a young man in a World War II uniform and someone else in Vietnam, and there were lots of pictures of an old Cheyenne man with a fiddle. It had to be Uncle Leonard. Alongside an elaborate, feathered headdress hung some beaded pants and next to them, a crucifix. On top of the TV were a bunch more pictures of family, graduation pictures of a girl who looked a lot like Charlie, and a couple school portraits, one that could have been Charlie at about fourteen. I picked it up to get a better look. It was funny that he looked so familiar already, even in an old photograph, as if I'd known him a lot longer than I had.

Charlie's uncle came out of the back, walking slowly just ahead of Charlie. His face had a doughy look as though he might have been sleeping. He reached a hand out to me, and when I gave it to him to shake, he held onto it. "You call me Uncle Leonard, okay?"

He looked older than I'd expected. He had on a western shirt with snap buttons and cowboy boots. He wore his hair in a long braid, and the weathered skin of his face made him look ancient. He sat in a chair next to the TV, and Charlie brought him some water. He drank the whole glass while we watched. I found out later he had diabetes. He set the glass down and closed his eyes, and I thought for a moment that he might fall asleep, but then he opened them again and looked directly at me.

"Charlie says you found some old bones. He says he thinks it might be a Cheyenne girl."

"Charlie found them, really."

Uncle Leonard nodded slowly and seemed to be thinking about something. He had such a slow way of talking you'd get the idea he might just stop in the middle of a sentence and never finish. "I've been trying to think whose tribe she might have belonged to. Maybe she was with one of the tribes at the Little Bighorn or Rosebud Creek. There were a lot of fights around the time of Custer. But there was nothin' right there, by the Tongue River."

"What about the Battle of the Butte, Uncle Leonard? That's close," offered Charlie.

"No little girls at that fight." He laughed.

"Maybe she got away," I suggested. "Maybe she died after some battle." My heart was pounding. I didn't know why, maybe I felt a bit guilty, a bit white.

Uncle Leonard seemed to be think about it. He didn't say anything for a couple minutes. Charlie was quiet, too. Then Uncle Leonard cleared his throat. "I heard a story from my grandfather once. It was after all the fighting was over, when Chief Dull Knife and his people escaped from Oklahoma, after they got some of the Tongue River country back." He gestured with a sweep of his hand at the window. "My grandfather said that his father, whose name was White Bird, went south to find some of his family, to make sure they were buried the way they should be. He went by himself, so nobody knew where. I think some people thought it was dangerous to go alone since a lot of the white men around were still mad about Custer. He might have found her to bury. Maybe she was his daughter or a niece."

I'd never thought of it that way, that it could be so personal for him, or for Charlie. Charlie leaned his back against the old TV cabinet. He looked relaxed, and I found myself wishing I could sit there with him. "Maybe she just got sick and died on her own," he said. "Maybe it was a long time before all the fighting. Maybe it was after. How do we know?"

Uncle Leonard rubbed his hands together, and he was shaking his head. He seemed pretty certain.

"She shouldn't be buried under a road. It doesn't seem right," I said looking over at Charlie.

"Just think how much is covered with asphalt these days," Charlie said. I could tell from his tone that he wasn't going to tell Uncle Leonard about the marker. He stood up. "We're going for a walk, Uncle Leonard."

I waited by the door while Charlie brought him another glass of water.

We walked down the hill behind the house, past an old water tank, rusted and filled with algae, surrounded by thistle. We picked up a stock trail that cut up to a thinly forested hill and finally out onto a rocky bluff. You could see for miles to the south and east. I sat down next to Charlie and wrapped my fingers in his.

"Don't you think she ought to have a name?"

The question caught him by surprise.

"Especially since she might have been part of your family."

"I don't think she was. That's just what Uncle Leonard wants to think."

"But it's possible."

He shrugged it off.

"What was that word you taught me, the name for a magpie?"

"*Mo'é'ha.*"

"That could be her name."

He smiled. "Then it would be, *Mo'é'ha'e.*"

I tried to pronounce it, but it was hard to get the rhythm of it right, the subtle stops and accents. It came out as Mo-eh-ha. I couldn't get the sound at the end, which he said was an aspirated vowel, silent, really, just a breath. He pointed in the distance, and began naming all the battlefields we could see from that spot, the famous fights and those forgotten—all the places where Mo'é'ha'e could have been fatally wounded.

I looked out across the bluffs and imagined her leading her dog along the ridge just out of view of the open plain. For miles around it would have been just the two of them, small as ants. Most of her story I could never get from Granddad's journals, beyond the facts and dates. Uncle Leonard or Charlie could guess at it, fill in a part of history remembered by the Cheyenne, but ultimately I would never know anything factual about her, more than what could be deduced from the dust of her bones and the location of her burial. But maybe that's why it seemed important to give her a name and imagine her story. If I didn't, what would there be? Not even a memory—only a nameless secret hidden under the black asphalt.

▲ ▲ ▲

SHE WAS HEADED for an outcropping of rocks at the summit of the bluff where she could wait for a party of warriors to return. Her uncle, *E-vóhpo-ve'keso,* the warrior called White Bird, would have been among them. As she searched, the heat danced in the air, making the shallow hills of the plain shimmer like water. Her eyesight was exceptionally good, and she was proud of it. In the long distance, she could see a group approaching. They were too far off for her to make out any detail, but something seemed wrong. She was afraid that someone might be hurt, slowing them down. Through the winter and spring a fearful tension underlay even the best moments as it became habit to worry about the constant threat of the white soldiers.

The group disappeared behind a hill, and then she saw way off to the south another group, the warriors she was looking for. They were instantly recognizable because of the way they moved, quick and light, and now they were riding fast to intercept the first group, which she realized must be a party of white men, probably miners. The warriors would meet them somewhere near the bluff where she was waiting. They skirted the hills, keeping low.

When they did meet, with nothing around to provide any sense of scale, they looked tiny and inconsequential. The miners pulled their wagons into a defensive circle, while the warriors wheeled around them like birds, flitting in close and riding away. At first it was like a dance, something choreographed, even a game. Then Mo'é'ha'e began to hear gunfire, only the tiniest pops like the sound her ears made coming down from the mountains. Even from a distance, she could sense the fear in the knot of wagons. The miners knew they were outnumbered. As the Cheyenne left the first attack, still running hard, one of the wagons was burning and the group of men inside the circle was focused on one of their fallen. Angry and afraid, they wasted ammunition shooting at the Indians as they galloped out of range.

One man tried to escape. He ran out into the plain, stumbling on the rocks scattered in the grass. He had a pistol but wasted his shots on the warriors' first approach when they were still too far away. They charged after him whooping and laughing and pulled their horses up short. He was looking for a fight, a grim last stand, but they nearly fell off of their mounts in their gaiety. They struck him first with coup sticks and clubs, and then they drug him behind their horses, taking him back and circling the burning wagons.

Only one of the warriors was hit. His horse stumbled as the man fell, and galloped off on its own out into the plain. It ran just far enough to feel safe and began grazing unconcerned with the fate of its rider. Mo'é'ha'e prayed that the man struggling to get up from the ground was not her uncle. She heard the Cheyenne's war chant as they attacked again and broke the circle. They chased another miner out across the grass until he fell, and they ran over him with their horses. His body bounced a few feet in the air like a rag doll. They pulled their horses up and danced on him until he was as limp as an old buffalo hide that had blown away with the wind.

The wagons were smoldering by the time the warriors began taking scalps. She saw them pause over the still shapes on the ground and could guess what they were doing. They lifted their prizes into the air with a whoop. One of them used a horse to pull over a wagon that had not completely burned, dragging the breaking pieces, scattering the prairie with a litter of white man's things. By the time they were done with their work, the wagons looked like the remains of a buffalo jump, scattered with bodies and junk.

Inside the circle of smoking wagons, among the dead and scalped and the garbage, too small for her to see from her overlook, next to a charred wagon wheel a boy about seven years old, maybe eight, sat mutely crying. He held his legs tightly and kept his face buried in his knees. For a while he went unnoticed by the warriors as they scalped and plundered. Then one of the Cheyenne picked him up with his free hand like a bag of flour. He put the boy on the back of one of the white man's horses and then got on his own. The boy held on to the mane of the spooked horse as it hopped and turned on its lead.

Mo'é'ha'e left her lookout on the hilltop. She hurried to a place near the camp where she knew the warriors would stop to paint themselves for the victory march into camp, holding their scalps aloft on tall poles. She ran fast, jumping deadfall and weaving through the sparse pine. She hid in some thorny brush, and waited while a mountain jay scolded her from a low branch overhead. Then she heard the horses approaching. First she saw White Bird, who was unhurt, and then the white boy being led behind. The boy sat alone on the horse, surrounded by the warriors who stopped to paint their faces and bodies in black soot. His face was covered with ash and smoke from the fight as if he, too, had been painted. Mo'é'ha'e wondered who he would have been traveling with. A father? An uncle? Someone desperate, certainly, to have brought a child along. Someone now killed. The boy had gone a long way inside himself, his soul hiding in its most secret corner. Mo'é'ha'e recognized the dullness in his eyes. She remembered it in her mother after her father was murdered. And she expected her mother's eyes would be bright with revenge this time.

She ran back to camp trying to beat the warriors to secretly tell her mother that they were coming and about the boy her uncle had taken. She just made it before the barking of dogs warned the camp anyway, and they gathered to see what the war party had to show. They rode into camp to a trilling from the women. The one injured man defied his wounds sitting on the back of another's horse, shaking his fist in the air. In the middle of them, numb with terror, was the boy, and Mo'é'ha'e was surprised because her mother's eyes did not shine when she noticed the boy, but looked sad. The very same kind of sad.

White Bird left his wife and two sons digging through some of the spoils he had brought, and rode up to Mo'é'ha'e's mother, Sweet Rose Woman. The boy was slipping on the barebacked horse as it trotted to keep up. White Bird jumped off his mount and walked the captive horse and the boy to her, handing her the reins, making a present of them. It was a formal gesture for a brother and sister who usually were more inclined to laugh and tease, a generous gift, but also expected of him. It was his responsibility to take care of his sister and especially her daughter. She thanked him ceremonially, but then she smiled. White Bird was a good brother.

Mo'é'ha'e did not take her eyes off the boy, but he wouldn't look at her, even when she walked right up to him. She shouted at him in Cheyenne to look at her, but he just turned away.

"*Enanahe, ka'eskóne,*" her mother said gently. *Let the child be.*

Mo'é'ha'e moved to the horse's head, pretending to give the animal her attention, but she kept her eyes on him until her mother lifted him down.

CHAPTER SEVEN

I WOKE TO the sound of voices downstairs, and went to the window to see who it might be then momentarily panicked. It brought back the memory of that morning when the county sheriff's car had parked just where it was now, after Dad had called to tell them about Mom. I listened from the top of the stairs, trying to figure out what it could be this time. Dad sounded worried about something, but I couldn't tell what until I walked to the bottom of the stairs, holding onto the handrail and taking a big step to skip that last tread. It took me a minute to recognize the other voice. It was Tom, Dad's old buddy who was a Yellowstone County sheriff.

"Okay Jack, this is how it was *supposed* to go. You find some human remains, you stop work immediately and take precautions to protect the site. Doesn't matter if you know for sure that it's a hundred years old, you treat it like you just found a crime scene."

"But what if I didn't know the law?"

"You have a contract with the state, you're supposed to know. Anyway, ignorance of the law is no excuse. If it's on state land you call the state, whoever you're working for, or you call the sheriff.

The coroner has twenty-four hours to get out there and report to the state archeologist whether it's a criminal or an archeological discovery."

"In the meantime, I can't work, right?"

"Right. But the state archeologist has a time limit, twenty-four hours, to report to the State Burial Board. It doesn't always happen quite that fast, but they're supposed to do it quickly."

"Then what?"

"Then whatever tribe claims it, probably the closest, usually reburies it as near the site as is feasible. They generally don't like making a big thing about it."

"Don't they start digging around for more artifacts?"

"I don't know. Probably not."

"Or they start arguing over whose it is."

"Huh?"

"Cheyenne, Crow, Lakota . . . "

"I don't think that happens much."

"But it does happen."

"Yeah, I guess it must."

"More time not working."

Tom didn't respond.

"Anyway, as it is, I already broke the law, right?"

"Yes."

"I'm already losing money on this job, Tom. Every day comes right out of my pocket. And what if I get my hand slapped, or worse? Is it a felony? What is it?"

"It *could* be a felony. I'm not sure what would happen."

"I need state contracts, Tom. I don't need a black eye over something like this."

"But there are a few people who know it's there, right?"

"The only one who might talk is that Indian kid. If I get rid of the bones, it's his word against mine. He could just be pissed off because I fired him."

"I doubt it would ever come to that. They don't convene grand juries over something like this." Tom paused. "But tampering with physical evidence could only make it worse, Jack. That could get serious."

They were quiet. Tom was letting it sink in. I moved as quietly as I could upstairs and sat on my bed shaking. It was easy for Dad to fire Charlie to keep his secret, or dig that girl up who'd been buried out there a hundred years. It was true—who would know, who would find out? I looked out the small window over my bed, with its yellow-flowered, lace-trimmed curtains Mom had sewn for me years ago, and watched puffy white clouds parade across the blue sky as if they had something to celebrate.

Half an hour after Tom left, Dad told me he was going out.

From my window I could see part of the yard and the door of the garage swinging open and shut in the wind. I sat on my bed and listened to the sounds in the house, the wind pulling at its joints, creaking in the rafters, rattling the windows. I tried to calm down, but I couldn't let go of the feeling that at any moment the wind sucking through the house would catch a door and slam it shut. I didn't know what to tell Charlie, but I was meeting him at the mall that afternoon. I'd have to tell him something, at least warn him that Dad was planning to fire him. But I wasn't sure how to do it without telling him the whole thing, and for some reason I felt a little guilty about what Dad was going to do, as if somehow I were responsible.

I closed my eyes to force myself to not think about it, but then all I could see was his hands and his eyes. Sometimes I felt like I could live in his mouth, his tongue and his breath. But I also knew it would be a relief not to hear from him again, not to run into him by accident somewhere. It would be a relief not to look in the mirror and wonder if by magic he saw something more perfect than I could ever hope to be. But no matter how hard I tried not to think of him, he stormed my unconscious. I couldn't chase him from my dreams. I can look back, now, and see that there was a moment when I could have stopped falling in love with Charlie. There was a moment when it was still possible, before I could no longer turn back. And it would have been easier.

WHEN I GOT to the mall on King Avenue by the A-1 Auto Parts, Charlie was replacing the fuel pump on his car. He had the hood open in the middle of the parking lot, his tools spread out on the warm asphalt. I watched him finish and wash his hands with some soap, the kind that cuts grease and melts like butter in your hands. Then he rinsed them with a jug of water that splashed all over his sandals.

"I think my dad went out and dug her up."

His face clouded over. I knew he was thinking the same thing I was. We blew it. We should have left it alone.

"I never thought . . . " I said.

He shrugged his shoulders. "Figures."

"I think we should go find out."

He didn't answer right away. He just started putting away his tools.

"You got enough gas in your car?" I asked.

"I think so."

The distance we covered in that hour and a half would have been at least a two-day ride a hundred years ago—two fires, two meals, two nights. Dreams and stars. Space that yielded only slowly. It was a long way to go to see what we knew would be there—the marker scattered, the ground roughly dug up and pushed back into place. We didn't have to dig to know she was gone.

I don't know why it felt like we had messed up, that we had failed her. "I'm sorry," I said under my breath. "Let's get out of here. But I don't want to go home."

"Okay."

We got in the car and he reached over for my hand. I sank way down into my seat. "Where are we going?" he asked.

"South," I said. "As far as we can. Until we run out of gas."

He leaned back in his seat, and the dust billowed behind us like chalk from a chalkboard, erasing everything. After a while I could feel the grit in my teeth. It didn't take long before it was dark. The road lay out before us, long and nearly straight, and it felt as if nothing mattered. It seemed perfect, to run as far as the gas would take us, though the gauge was already on empty.

I laughed and we laughed. What a stupid thing to do. We'd be stuck—an underage white girl with a reservation boy. They were going to kill us.

Antelope and jackrabbits leapt from the ditches. We made a wide turn to the east as the crescent moon lifted above the horizon. And we kept going. That gauge sat on empty for a while before the old engine began to starve and sputter. Charlie swerved back and forth shaking up the tank to get more gas to the engine, and it found new life for a few seconds before it was gasping again.

The engine quit. We coasted like a glider in the clouds, only the sound of the wind, the tremendous momentum of that steel Pontiac carrying us on. We had just enough speed to get off the road and then down into a gravel pit. Charlie didn't use the brakes and the car rolled to one end, up a slight incline, and then back up the steep road leading down into the pit, and then back again, like a pendulum. We were both laughing so hard I nearly choked. Eventually the car settled in the lowest spot on its own. The pit was twenty feet deep at least, and you couldn't see out except for the sky full of brilliant stars.

"They'll never find us here," he said.

"Oh, no. We're safe, now," I said with mock seriousness.

After a bit, we got out and sat on the hood. Charlie turned the headlights on then gathered some rocks and handed a few to me.

"A buck on who can hit that old rusted can," he said.

"A buck, huh?" I looked over at the can in the headlights.

"Go ahead, you can throw a couple first," he said like any boy would, as if I needed a handicap because I was a girl.

"Nah, you go. I want to get an idea of the range."

He threw his rock long, missed the can by fifteen feet at least. He shrugged it off. He hadn't expected to actually hit it. Close would have been good enough.

I balanced the rock in my hand, getting a feel for its weight. Charlie looked at me as though I must be joking. But when I threw my rock and it glanced off the can, catching an edge, he laughed.

"I can't believe it. It never happens on the first throw," he said. "Never."

He threw his next rock wide too, clattering in the gravel, and not another rock out of ten or twenty came closer than my first throw. Eventually he turned the headlights off to save the battery. We sat there on the hood next to each other for a long time as our eyes grew more accustomed to the faint moonlight. It shone on his bare arms, and his neck and cheeks. It shone in his black hair.

He slipped off the hood and stood in front of me. His hand touched my face, warm and callused. His fingers caressed my cheeks and pushed through my hair. I let my eyes fall shut, just to feel his hands on my neck and shoulders and then gently on my breasts. It made me dizzy. And his man's hands came back to my face and his thumbs softly pushed open my mouth, and he kissed me.

And how it happened wasn't clear even as it was happening, but our clothes were off, and I was pushing into his arms, trembling but not cold. I could feel his shoulders and his bare chest and stomach against my tummy and his narrow hips between my legs. It hurt just a little to begin with and then it felt like water—sun-warmed water. And I was falling—falling until suddenly he caught me with my eyes open to his shining eyes.

We slept all night in the big backseat of the Pontiac with the doors wide open for air, a tangle of limbs. I woke often, delirious in his arms and smell. I kissed his sleeping face softly, without waking him. I stopped as soon as he moved, and then started again when he was dreaming, until I drifted away with him.

Day came and Charlie and I slept in the hot sun for hours as it arched over the gravel pit. I woke late. Charlie was up, and he looked like he had been for some time. My legs were stiff and sun-burned from the calf down where the sun had found them through the open door of the car. It felt strange to be naked with Charlie, in the daylight like this, with my eyes open. His body was hot, his muscles tense; my skin stuck to his thighs, and his penis was hard again. His smell was strong, and his arms held me tighter with greater tension this time, and he pushed inside me longer, until we were both breathing hard.

We lay there, uncomfortable, as long as we could—until it was sweaty and impossible.

"We gotta get up."

Charlie laughed. And it made me laugh, too. Finally, he got up and began dressing. He leaned in through the open door of the car, silhouetted against the white gravel, and it made my naked body tingle for him to be looking at it so frankly, but I didn't want to move.

"Do you see your legs?" he asked.

"I know."

"Do they hurt?"

I tried moving them, peeling them off the seat.

He winced and gathered my clothes and began quietly dressing me.

"What are we going to do?" he mused.

"Starve to death."

"We'll probably die of thirst first."

"True." I swallowed.

He rubbed my feet before he pulled the socks over them and pushed on my boots. He reached out his hand and helped me out of the car. It was hot.

I picked up another rock and sent the can clattering across the gravel.

"You should play ball."

"My dad . . . " I started. "The same man who will be throwing pieces of our bodies into the reservoir tomorrow night—he taught me. He didn't want me to throw like a girl."

Charlie didn't say anything, and we both just stood there, thirsty and hungry.

"I guess I'll go up and hitch into town, and get some gas," Charlie said.

"Let's go together."

"What, and spoil your dad's fun by letting someone else chop us up?" he laughed.

He was right.

"Then I should go for the gas, Charlie. I'll get there faster."

"No."

"Yes."

He could tell that I was right. "What're you going to tell your dad?"

"I spent the night at Jennifer's."

"He'll buy that?"

"I might not have to tell him anything. Who knows if he even noticed that I didn't make it home?"

A truck went by on the road past the gravel pit, but the driver didn't look back to see us. "There's not a lot of traffic on that road. It might take a while."

"I'll be alright."

He kissed me, and I stopped once at the top of the gravel pit and looked back. He was throwing rocks at that can, and missing every time.

CHAPTER EIGHT

I NEVER THOUGHT it would be so long before I saw Charlie again. I figured it would be a day, maybe a couple at the most. I know that's the longest I thought I could stand to wait. Dad had bought my story, and things had gone back to normal, except Charlie was gone. Uncle Leonard said he'd left with Teddy, gone to some place in western Wyoming. Maybe I should have expected it. Maybe it was the normal thing for a guy to do, under the circumstances. He hadn't wanted to sit around and wait for Dad to fire him. He had plenty of reasons to want to get away, and I guess I was one of them. I was scared, too; I don't think I knew what I wanted to happen any more than he did. But I thought if I could just see him, I would know.

The first week ground by with agonizing slowness. Each day the sun seemed to get stuck midway across the sky, stubbornly refusing to get on with it. Nights were worse because I couldn't sleep. I held my hands in tight fists as though it required some effort from me to move the clock each tick forward.

By Saturday afternoon I was in a foul mood. Dad had set himself up on the lawn chair in the backyard. He had the barbecue smoking, and a cold beer freshly open. He raised the can when I appeared on the back porch as if he were about to offer a toast. "I've got sausages on. Grab a chair." He waved toward the garage. I stared back in disbelief.

Reluctantly, I went to get one. I was afraid I knew what he wanted to talk about. I was sure that our neighbor, Mrs. Gibbs, had been spying on me, noticed my unusual comings and goings. Everyone had "concerns" about a teenage girl who had her own car, very little of her father's attention and no mother's guidance. It took me a minute to find the lawn chairs folded up behind a pile of U-Haul boxes that we'd put some of Mom's old stuff in. I was just about to grab a chair when I noticed a new box. It was covered with dust, but not garage dust, more like dirt. When I looked closer, I could see that several boxes had been moved to make room for it, then piled back on top. The dust on them appeared recently disturbed. I lifted the old U-Haul boxes off of it.

"Are you comin' with that chair?"

"I just found them, Dad," I yelled back.

I listened to see if he'd decided to come in, then I quickly opened the box. Inside was the faded blue wool coat. My heart drummed heavily in my chest as I pulled it back to uncover the bones. Dad had done a careful job of packing her up. The thimbles were still on the fingers of her right hand. The heavy scent of earth flooded the room, dry and ancient. It caught in my throat and stole my breath. I never imagined she would end up here among all of my mother's things. As I stared at her small and fragile remains, it occurred to me how wrong I had been, thinking I could imagine this Cheyenne girl alive. Whoever she had been, her life, what she had truly hoped or dreamed for, was beyond anyone's reckoning.

"Do I need to come in there and help you?"

"No, I got it. I'm coming."

I touched one of the thimbles, and it felt colder than I expected, like a dark kernel of ice. I quickly folded the wool coat around her, shut the box and piled the old U-Haul boxes up over it, just as it had been. I almost forgot to get the chair on the way out.

"I should have turned on a light, I guess," I said as I walked over to him, but I didn't sit down right away. I was still too shook up. I never expected him to do that. I thought he would just move her, bury her somewhere else, but to wrap her up and hide her in the garage. Why?

He shook his head. "Earth to Erin." He held out a sausage impaled on his fork.

"Dad, I'm not really hungry."

"Suit yourself," he said. He took a sip of beer with a look that dared me to be rude enough, blatant enough, to walk away. But I couldn't think of a single subject to talk about that didn't require me to lie. A gust of wind pushed the garage door slowly open on its hinges. I sat down in the chair.

"It's a beautiful day."

Something had him in a rare good mood.

"I'm surprised you're not out with your friends," he said.

"I don't have any friends, Dad." I gave it my blackest reading possible.

"What about Jennifer?"

"I don't know what she's doing today. She's got some new boyfriend." As soon as I said the word "boyfriend," I knew it was a mistake. Wrong subject.

"Oh?" For a second his brain seemed to be ticking. If Jennifer could have a boyfriend, could I?

"It's nothing, you know, some rodeo bum." I decided to change the subject before he put it together. "How's work?"

"We should be paving that section of road in a week or so. That will almost get us back on schedule."

That's why he was so pleased. The road would be paved over soon. The box was hidden in the garage. A veil of smoke rose from the barbecue. I stood up feeling a little queasy. I had to get away.

"The sausages are going to burn," I said and headed back toward the house. I didn't look back until I got to the door. The sausages burst into flames, and Dad scrambled to put them out with a spray bottle.

I didn't stay in the house. I kept going. I walked out the front door to the sidewalk, down the street to the bridge over the Yellowstone. I stood at the exact center of the bridge and looked down at the water rushing away from me downstream, which gave me the sense that I was moving, not the water. I could feel myself slipping back, losing ground. I could run, but it would be like running on a treadmill, getting nowhere.

When Charlie finally did come back, he called at night. Dad answered the phone the first couple of times it rang. I heard him swear on the second hang up. I waited by the phone in the kitchen after that, and I got it before half a ring. Dad was still in the dining room shuffling papers. I whispered a hello, and then I let Charlie talk. He said he wanted to pick me up at the Target parking lot in the morning if I could get away. I wished it was safe to say more. After waiting almost two weeks, I needed to hear enough to know what he was thinking, have at least part of a normal conversation. But it was impossible. I thought I heard Dad push back his chair.

"Okay, I'll be there," I whispered quickly and set the phone down as quietly as I could. I hurried to the sink and turned the water on. There weren't any dishes to do, so I dumped in half a can of Comet. I wanted to be busy doing something if Dad came in. There was no way to guess what Charlie was going to have to say. It was hard not to think that he was planning to call it all off. He'd been gone so long. I was desperately afraid of losing that easy feeling of sitting next to him, talking about nothing at all. I brought the sink to a brilliant tone of white as I waited for Dad to come in to question me, but he never did, and I didn't quit until the cleanser started to hurt my hands.

CHARLIE WAS WAITING for me when I got there, sitting in the front seat with his car door open, as if he might have been waiting awhile. He said he'd always wanted to take me out to this buffalo jump near the border of the reservation. It wasn't on anybody's map or list of official archeological sites, but Charlie knew the rancher who owned the land through his dad. We went through half a dozen gates to reach a long, high bluff that broke abruptly into the surrounding prairie.

I sat next to him in the shade at the base of the sandstone cliff. The yellow dirt felt cool under my palms. He said the buffalo bones under the ground were five feet deep in some places. I shifted my hands on the uneven dirt. I tried to listen as he told me how the jump worked. I tried to keep myself from thinking that he owed me an explanation for where he'd been, that that's what we'd come all the way out here to talk about. Instead he told me about the buffalo runners who specialized in finding and luring the buffalo into the trap, their strategies and the difficulties getting it all to work just right. He hadn't touched me yet, though he was sitting close enough to put his arm around me.

"Once they were in the trap, where there was no way out, they had to get the buffalo to stampede, scare 'em enough that they'd be running too fast to turn back."

It felt like my heart was pounding that fast—too fast to turn back. On the surface he acted as as if everything was normal, that he didn't think anything had changed, but I wished he'd say something to confirm it. I looked up at the sandstone cliff, which was at least a hundred feet high, where we were sitting. It was terrifying to imagine the buffalo falling, one-ton animals, bellowing and then hitting the rocks with a force that would shake the ground. Finally I couldn't wait. When I spoke my chest felt tight. I couldn't get a complete breath.

"So where'd you and Teddy go?"

He turned to me and took a breath, too, before he responded. "I'm sorry, Erin. I should have called, but I was afraid your dad might answer, and then I'd get mad and be tempted to say something stupid."

I could just see that, Charlie introducing himself over the phone, chewing Dad out for digging her up. I knew for sure that telling Charlie about the box in the garage now was a bad idea. What would he do if he knew Dad had actually stolen the bones?

"Anyway, I did something stupid enough. I told Teddy. I even showed him where. He thought I should've called the cops."

"Do you think he would?"

"Nah." He shook his head. "I don't know. I hope not. What's he going to tell them, anyway?"

I closed my eyes so that Charlie wouldn't guess from my expression that there was something more to it now, something someone *could* tell the cops. Then he took my hand and he started talking. I could tell immediately from his tone of voice that it was going to be okay. At least for now. I could feel my breath come more easily, as he told me about his trip up into the mountains.

SOMEHOW TEDDY HAD got a job, and it'd been easy for Charlie to talk himself into going along. All they had to do was ride along this natural gas pipeline where it crossed over the mountains, flag any leaks or damage, and mark them on the topo map. The trip was supposed to take ten days. It didn't pay Teddy much and it didn't pay Charlie anything, but it was a good excuse to go get lost for a while.

They had no mule or spare horse to pack, so everything they brought had to fit into a couple of saddle bags. They weren't allowed to bring alcohol. The company was pretty strict about that, especially since they were Indians. So all Teddy had was a hip flask of Wild Turkey stuffed in one of his socks. Neither of them had given much thought as to what to pack, and they hadn't brought nearly enough food. Even though they started out eating only one meal a day, halfway through the ride they were down to a ration of two candy bars, one in the morning and the other as late in the day as they could hold out. Soon Charlie started wishing he had some kind of rifle or handgun. He said he was hungry enough to try barbecuing one of the many pikas they passed, chirping at them from up in the rocks.

They didn't have a tent or sleeping bags either. They slept on beds of pine needles and when it rained, under sheets of plastic. By the sixth day they were up high enough in the mountains that it felt like it might even snow, and Charlie said it was blowing so hard he couldn't hear anything, not Teddy who was always singing, not the pikas, not the mountain jays or squirrels, just the roar of the wind and his own teeth chattering.

But the next day the sun came out, and they didn't ride at all. They found a wide flat rock out in the sun and slept despite their aching guts. Teddy dug out the whiskey, and they shared it as they watched the shadows grow across the narrow pass. It wasn't much, but on an empty stomach, Charlie was drunker than he'd ever been. He swore he could feel the rock he was laying on changing shape.

"Joe Fights Last says you have a scholarship. Some place in Colorado."

Charlie lay back and stretched, trying to get a firmer grip on the rock, which seemed to be leaning steeply toward the canyon.

"Yeah, so?"

"How come you didn't tell nobody?"

"Turned it down."

Teddy took the flask back from Charlie, tilted it way back to get the last of the honey out of it, sucking it with his tongue. "Bull-shit."

"We should have brought food."

"Too much trouble."

"Are there any more candy bars?"

Teddy dug around in his bag for a moment. "Nope."

Charlie shook his head.

"Think of it as a vision quest, brother."

"Yeah, but all I can see is your ugly face."

Teddy laughed. "So you're leaving then, huh?"

"What?"

"Yeah, going off to that white college, bringin' your pretty white girlfriend. Gonna go get your white man's degree in B.S.?"

Charlie sat up, blinking to keep from blacking out. "What the hell are you talking about?"

"Hey, I don't blame you." He grinned sarcastically. "No, good for you, bro. You'll make a good white man."

"Shut up, Teddy." Charlie propped himself up on his elbows. Teddy had a mean smile. Charlie said he felt like he had to explain himself. "If I go anywhere, it's going to be to work with my dad in Seattle."

"I don't believe that shit. You're too smart."

"So what's with you? Why are you so worried about what I'm gonna to do?" Charlie lay back down and closed his eyes. He stretched his hands out and dug his fingernails into the rock to steady himself. Most of his family *wanted* him to go out in the world, like a modern warrior, make some kind of success. But it was a huge step after living in the remote, close community of the reservation to go as far as a city like Denver, to become just one Indian among thousands of white students. Maybe he was afraid, too, that if he went away like that, he might not want to come back. Or if he did, maybe he would feel stuck on the outside, get hassled for thinking he was somehow different, or special. I guess the last thing he needed was Teddy's advice.

The granite under his head was warm even after the sun had fallen behind the peak. The whiskey hummed in his brain. At some point he must have thought about us, too, about what had happened; he must have wondered, as I did, why he'd run off like this, letting me find out from his Uncle Leonard that he was gone. Somewhere in his gut he must have known that Teddy had a point. Going off to college with his white girlfriend made an improbable picture. He had to be thinking about the fact that the end of summer was a few weeks away. His head pounded with hunger and the whiskey. He thought he'd rather stay, even if he starved, rather than go back and face choosing what to do.

"This is ours, man. All of it," Teddy shouted. He stood up unsteadily and pointed out at the plain that stretched out from the foot of the mountains, reaching for more than a hundred miles to the blue edge of the sky. "Not the fucking reservation, man. We are warriors of the plains. *Hoka-hey!*" He said it from his heart, not sounding the least bit drunk. He lifted his hands to his mouth and sang out across the horizon.

I THINK CHARLIE liked the buffalo jump for the view, which stretched out before us to an extraordinary distance. It gave us the illusion that we could see what lay ahead of us, that we knew what would happen next. And even if that wasn't true, believing it was enough for now. I didn't think I wanted anything more. I told myself that I didn't need any guarantees for the future—just the return of Charlie's easy smile. In my heart, I desperately wanted to believe what he had told Teddy, that he wasn't going anywhere. I leaned against his shoulder and soaked in the false promise of the constant landscape. For the first time in as long as I could remember, I didn't want anything to change.

▲ ▲ ▲

Mo'é'ha'e sat by the opening of her mother's tepee mending winter robes. Her fingers were sore from pushing the needle through the heavy buffalo hide. Several lodges away five of the older men sat in a circle and passed a pipe. She watched the smoke drift up into the flat gray sky. A gust of wind blew a faint dust on their dark-blue trousers and yellow beaded moccasins and tugged at their graying hair. She could guess what they were talking about. With the new grass everyone expected the white man's army to come and start a fight. It was what the generals had said they would do if the tribes refused to move to the reservations, even though it was January, the middle of winter. White Bird stood near them, listening, offering only a few words. The white boy sat by his feet, his eyes cast down. He hadn't spoken a word in the week since his capture.

Sometimes when Mo'é'ha'e closed her eyes, she could hear her father's voice. She could imagine listening to him speaking with her mother in the lodge, telling her in a soft voice some of what the men had been discussing. She knew about his murder only from what had been told to her, but in the several years since, a vivid color had been added to the story by her imagination. They'd been camped near the Black Hills and he'd gone off to hunt by himself. Her mother didn't like the idea. Everyone knew that the army— Custer and his already infamous Seventh Cavalry—was in the area providing protection for an expedition of miners. But it was normal for her father to hunt alone.

It wasn't thought unusual when he was gone for three days. He could be out for a week. Mo'é'ha'e remembered her mother's face as she lay in her robes to sleep each night. She held her eyes open as if she were keeping watch, as if that way she might know what was happening miles away in the dark. Mo'é'ha'e had few reliable memories from that time except this one. Whenever she woke in the night, her mother was awake. After a week Sweet Rose Woman convinced White Bird to go looking for him.

Mo'é'ha'e's father had found the tracks of a herd of elk the second day out. He followed them until dark, and continued in the morning as soon it was light enough. By late afternoon he was at a mountain pass. As he got off his horse he startled a mountain goat with two kids. They clambered away in the rocks above him, but settled down to graze again once they were at a safe distance. He sat down on the warm stone of a table-sized rock and scanned the slope that fell away to a series of open parks. The sign he'd found was fresh, and he knew that the herd had to be bedded down within a few miles. The clouds building to the west of him occasionally blocked the sun, and the wind picked up, but the chill did not bother him. If he had to, he would spend the night. The elk were sure to be out in the open by morning.

He didn't have to wait that long. As evening approached, he saw the first cow elk come out of the trees. He was trying to decide whether to try for one now or wait until morning, and so he didn't turn when he heard the goats knock loose a rock behind him. And he may have heard the report of the rifle, or he may not, as he fell forward, shot through the heart.

White Bird found him still laying on the rock. His horse had run off, or had been stolen. There were moccasin tracks around his scalped body, suggesting that it was Indians who'd killed him. But White Bird knew better. White settlers had used the same trick years ago when the Cheyenne would visit the forts to get the annuities promised them by treaty as payment for the wagon trails that cut through their territory. Some of the settlers would put on moccasins and go hunting Indians. They had to cover their tracks because even if it was only Indians, it was considered murder, though nothing was ever done about it. White Bird lifted Mo'é'ha'e's father's body onto his horse and brought him home.

Mo'é'ha'e stared at the fire as the memories brought a shiver, then looked up at her uncle. As he spoke, he was looking off to the south where only the thinnest line of blue sky met the horizon. The north wind blew his loose black hair across his face. She was fiercely proud, but the burning sting of bile caught in her throat when she looked down at the boy. She knew why he was so quiet, better than anyone, and it made her angry. Could he really think of her uncle as a murderer? How dare he? Mo'é'ha'e returned her attention to her sewing, nearly breaking the needle with the intensity of her concentration.

The men spread the word that camp would move. Through the gray morning, while the tepees came down, belongings were lashed to travois and fires burned down and began to smolder, the boy sat in the dirt with his arms wrapped around his knees. Mo'é'ha'e's dog had curled up at his feet, its muzzle tucked between its two front feet.

Mo'é'ha'e's mother called her from where she was packing one of the horses. She had a bundle of dried meat in her hand and she tore a piece off and handed it to Mo'é'ha'e. "*Give this to the boy, he needs to eat.*"

Mo'é'ha'e frowned.

"*Do it, now, Mo'é'ha'e. Then come back and help me.*"

Mo'é'ha'e looked at the meat in her hand, trying to think of a way to avoid giving it to the boy, but her mother was still watching. She walked slowly over, the meat tight in her fist. When she offered it to him, he kept his head down and would not take it. She turned to see if her mother had seen the pointlessness of her errand, but she was not looking. She laid it at his feet, put her hands on her hips and said in words he could not possibly understand that she would take the food back if he did not eat it. When he did not respond, she grabbed it and gave the food to her dog.

CHAPTER NINE

THE SUN BAKED the asphalt streets and everything else smelled like burnt dust. Lying in the grass, looking up, I could almost feel the earth beneath me turning, rolling hugely through space, so that the tree branches swept across the sky and made me dizzy. Sadie beat her tail on the ground a few feet away, staring at a caterpillar inching its way across the yard. The sun soaked into my skin, and the distant sound of the river turning at the bend and the cicadas buzzing in the cottonwoods lulled me to the verge of sleep. I thought I could hear a little girl laughing so far away that the sound of it was almost lost in the breeze tripping through the leaves, and rustling the grass.

"Get a job!"

I looked up. Looming over me was Jennifer. Her face and hair looked made up for night, vibrating in competition with the green leaves and the blue and white sky. Her newly permed blond hair hung down in vivid, tight curls. All I could do was blink.

"We thought you might be dead."

In heroic defiance of gravity, I sat up. Just a few feet off the ground the air was cooler on my face. I looked past Jennifer's tanned legs. At the curb was the cowboy's truck and the cowboy. I knew his name now, Clayton. He sat in the cab, his head leaned back on the seat and hat tipped forward as though he might be sleeping.

Jennifer smiled. I had already heard all about him, in more detail than I really cared to. This was going to be her big summer, the big summer of Jennifer. "We're going swimming. You want to come?"

"Are you sure you want me to come?"

She smirked. "Yeah. Clayton thought it was a great idea."

I could feel gravity pulling at me again, and I wished I could think of an excuse to skip it, but my fuzzy brain was moving too slowly. "Alright, okay. Let me get my suit."

"You don't need a suit."

"Yes, I do, Jen."

I didn't have to look hard to choose a bathing suit. I only had one. I couldn't remember the last time I had it on. From my window I could see the truck parked out in front. Jennifer was already in the cab with Clayton, scooted right up next to him on the bench seat, laughing about something. She'd told me that he was staying at a motel in Billings, that'd been their getaway, but he was leaving soon, this time for weeks, or it could be months. She thought she was going to run away with him. But Jennifer wasn't going anywhere. Her dad, who was the Billings city prosecutor, would have half the county arrested and tortured trying to find her. If he knew about the cowboy, she'd be in solitary confinement until her skin started to mold.

I climbed into the truck next to her. Clayton smiled at me, an arrogant smile, as if he'd figured something out, something he knew about and we didn't. I rolled down the window and leaned out, trying to enjoy the warm wind. Almost immediately we were going the wrong way. "You missed the turn for the reservoir, cowboy."

Jennifer laughed.

"Ha, ha. What's so funny?"

"We're not going to the reservoir, Erin. Everybody'll be there."

"Yeah?"

"Clayton knows a better place."

"Great. A stock tank somewhere full of cow shit."

Clayton leaned over Jennifer. I wished he'd watch the road. "There haven't been any cows in there for a couple of years."

I rolled my eyes.

"Seriously, it's really nice." He gave me a warm look, as if he were my uncle or something, condescending. I tried thinking of him as one of my great-aunts—red lips, flowered dress, wearing an oil drum of perfume.

We turned off at a ranch road and Clay stopped at the gate. He sat there as if I was supposed to get out and open it. I didn't budge. Finally, he got out and opened the gate, drove us through, then got back out again and closed it. He did it all as if it was no problem, as if there was no way he was going to let me bug him.

The tank was in a pretty spot. There was a roll to the hills, and even a shady grove of cottonwoods to park the truck under. The new grass grew right up to the edge of the water, no mud or muck, and as promised, no cow pies floating in the water, which was blue. It was a spring-fed tank, not stagnant or muddy runoff.

I got out and leaned against the truck. Jennifer was already doing a kind of ballet spin past me, her arms outstretched, hair flying back.

"Come on, Clayton," she shouted, "Let's get in!"

Clayton leaned over the hood of the truck, resting on his elbows, watching her and not answering. She smiled and continued to dance. I don't know, there were times I wondered why we were friends, but right then, watching her dance, every time her face and bright eyes turned this way, I just wished I could protect her.

I shouted, "Don't you want to borrow my suit, Jen? I don't feel like swimming. Really."

She didn't answer but walked over to the edge of the pond, and with her back to us, she began to undress. I could see Clayton in the corner of my eye. He hadn't moved yet, and he was watching me, not her. When she was done and her clothes lay at her feet, he left the truck and walked past me with a stupid grin. She jumped in and yelled at the cold.

"Yeeow! Come on, Clayton!"

He undressed by the water, and before he jumped in he turned and looked back at me, his little white butt shining in the sun. He didn't react to the cold water, but swam calmly over to Jennifer. She circled around him, teasing and splashing water at him.

"Come on, Erin," she yelled. "Get in. It's great once you get used to it."

Instead, I waved at them and got back in the cab of the truck. I left the door open for air, leaned back and put my feet up on the dash. I don't know why I was invited along. I don't think it was to be a chaperone. I could hear Jennifer laughing and giggling in the water for a while, and then I heard them getting out. It was quiet and warm in the shade.

Jennifer practically put a billboard up in Billings just to make sure everyone, except her father, knew that she wasn't a virgin anymore, but I hadn't told anyone. I hadn't even told her. I also knew, in the moments when I could be truthful with myself, that it was a summer thing, that it had to end. At least I wasn't fooling myself about that.

THERE'S SOMETHING ABOUT a secret, a real secret that no one else knows, not another soul, that makes you feel invisible, wrapped in its cocoon of whispers. It makes you a stranger even with people who have known you since you were in diapers. I had missed my period by a week. No one had ever really talked to me about sex. Like everyone else I didn't pay any attention at school during sex-ed in the gym. I knew the facts, of course, but in a way that left plenty of room for denial. I told myself that what we did could not actually have gotten me pregnant. Not just once, not the first time. Even if it was possible, technically, it didn't seem right. *It wasn't supposed to happen.*

Still, I drove all the way to Laurel to buy a pregnancy test and got home only a half hour before Dad usually did. The directions said it worked best with first urination in the morning, as if maybe your secrets passed into your pee while you were dreaming. I couldn't wait. There were two tests in the kit, which seemed to put a lie to the claim that it was 98 percent accurate. I checked the driveway four times before I finally opened the package. A tiny corner of it fell to the floor, and I was careful to pick it up and put it with the rest. I peed into the cup provided and put five drops into the test. Plus means you're pregnant, and before you even do anything with it, it shows a minus, which says to me that most people take these tests hoping not to be pregnant.

I watched that negative sign without blinking, as if by staring at it, I could will it not to change to a plus. But it did change, slowly, like a dream, like something you can't really believe, because it wasn't there and then subtly, magically, it was. My hands shook as I stared at it, and it became clearer and more undeniable. Then I heard a car door slam. I knocked the package off the sink counter and was pulling my shorts up as I ran to the hall window to look out to see if Dad had come home sooner than he was supposed to. I peered through the window to see if the garage door was open. But it wasn't. I listened with my heart pounding for the door to open, for the sound of his keys rattling. Nothing. It must have been next door.

I went back to the bathroom and looked at the test again,

thinking for a second before it came into focus that I might just have been so shook up, so paranoid about it, that I imagined it.

But it was positive. And the one the next morning was positive, too. I sat on the toilet seat until my butt was numb, trying to think of who I could tell. But the answer was no one. Not a soul. Not even Aunt Kristine. I could just imagine telling her how I had made a stupid mess of my life before I'd even got started.

At first I was amazed at how clueless everyone seemed to be. I was so preoccupied with my secret I was sure you could see it in my face. When I looked in the mirror, *I* could see it. I couldn't see anything else. I guess I wasn't too surprised Dad didn't notice. He didn't even go in my room because he thought he might spot a bra or some of my underwear. As far as he knew I was still waiting, like Sleeping Beauty, for my first kiss.

I wandered through the house, cataloging in my mind the things I might be able to "borrow" without his knowledge and take to the pawnshop. I didn't know how much money I needed for an abortion, but I knew it had to be more than I had right then. One of Dad's guns would probably have done, easy to pawn, but he'd notice it missing. Besides the pawnshop might think I'd stolen it. There were still some china vases in the hutch in the dining room that Dad hadn't given away yet, but I doubted I would have been able to get much for them. In the room off the kitchen, which Dad had turned into a kind of storage area, was Mom's sewing machine. It was a good one, a few years old, but I remembered the argument she had with Dad over how much it cost. That would be worth something, maybe enough. The sewing machine was perfect. He would never notice it was gone.

THE NURSE WHO'D taken the urine sample left me in the room and shut the door, either out of respect for my privacy or to hide me from the other patients who might be walking by. I didn't think they could legally call my house. I had a couple of rights. After a few minutes a woman came in who was supposed to be a counselor. She seemed impatient. Probably because she was scheduled to be on lunch break already. She listed my options succinctly.

Adoption. Abortion.

When nobody came back to the room after a while, I got dressed and let myself out. I wanted to call Charlie, though I didn't know what I would say. With a short-lived burst of optimism I briefly thought I would be able to make it good news, that he'd be so excited we'd go out that very afternoon to shop for baby stuff. But my hands knew better. I'd found a phone down the hallway but they were shaking so badly I couldn't dial his number after three tries.

Finally I managed to dial my aunt, praying at one ring that she would be there and pick up, and praying at the next that she wouldn't and I could hang up, having settled with my conscience that I had tried to call. Then Mark answered.

"Hello."

I knew I should just hang up, quickly.

"Hello?"

"Hi." My voice seemed to come from somewhere outside my body. "It's Erin. Is Aunt Kristine there?"

"Erin, no, she's out."

I tried to think of a message.

"When are you coming down for a visit? We have the place pretty well torn up with the remodel, but I know she'd be glad to see you."

I let out a deep exhale, more than would make sense to him. "I don't know. Dad's pretty busy."

"Well, you're welcome on your own, you know, anytime."

I tried to say thanks, but there was something about hearing I was welcome anytime. I couldn't keep my voice from choking up. He heard it.

"What's wrong?"

"Oh . . . " There was no way I was going to tell him, but I couldn't think of a lie either. I breathed out again. How stupid it was, that I was going to start crying right now. What would he think?

"Are you okay?"

"Yeah," I managed. "I'm okay."

"I'll have Kristine call you as soon as she gets back." He sounded worried. "Are you at home?"

"No. But I will be soon, thanks."

I hung up. That was bad. She would call already thinking something was wrong. And I had known in my gut, as soon as she wasn't there, that I had been right. I couldn't tell her. Not yet, anyway. Not when I seemed so helpless. I felt on the verge of hysterical laughter. The sparse, undecorated hall of the clinic began to dissolve in a liquid way. The walls poured down. The glass of the windows spilled onto the floor. As I fled outside, the trees melted overhead as if they were made of wax and their color flooded everywhere, a school bus blurred across the street like the smear of a giant yellow oil pastel, and the black asphalt appeared to have an actual current to it. I stood on the corner for a while, afraid to move until the fear of being seen froze everything in its half-destroyed state, and I realized that I had to move. I dried my face with the hem of my dress and ran across the street, desperate to find an anonymous place to be. I fled to a women's room and for a while I stared into the mirror, as though the freak reflected there could actually tell me what to do next.

Eventually, I headed for the bowling alley. The drive gave me enough time to calm down and for my eyes to look a little less puffy and red. I knew Jennifer would be there practicing. She was on a team, and she took it pretty seriously. It had always been our place to talk, or the place where she talked and I listened. I guess

I figured listening to her complain about the cowboy would help take my mind off of everything else.

I bowled almost pure gutter balls, which was not normal. She got a spare and rushed back to the podium to record it in her neat handwriting.

"You're up!"

"Just put me down for another gutter ball." I leaned back in my chair, and took a sip on my 32-ounce Pepsi.

"No way."

"Come on, Jen, just do it. It's inevitable."

She laughed, but it wasn't at me. It was just a strange, change-the-subject kind of laugh.

"What?"

"Nothing."

She had been waiting for the subject of Clayton to come up on its own, and now she couldn't stand it. I decided I might as well make it easy for her.

"The cowboy?" I offered.

She looked around the alley as if someone might be listening to our conversation and moved closer. She rolled her eyes, and then she looked so happy that she really looked sad to me.

"When is he leaving?"

She gave me a desperate look, as if by some kind of fantastic magic, I might be able to change it.

"Tomorrow or the next day," she said bravely, but almost instantly she was crying.

"You shouldn't cry. It's the best thing that could happen."

"Huh?"

"It is. You knew he was leaving."

She stopped crying and shrugged, but then she was crying again.

"He was just the first. You wouldn't want to stay with him

anyway." She looked up at me mid-sob, and I said with convic-
tion, just the way she wanted to hear it, "No way."

She managed a quick nod, and I could tell she liked thinking
of it that way. She was toughening up. It was a funny thing to
watch, and it made me wonder if it was good. I felt worse for her
as she decided that maybe I was right and it was best, that she
wouldn't want to keep her first love.

"At least you aren't pregnant," I tried to say casually and re-
gretted it immediately. She sensed the subtle secret in it. She wasn't
sure, but suddenly she was thinking about me instead of herself.

"Why'd you say that?"

"You know . . . it's just a good thing, that's all."

She looked at me critically.

"Erin?"

And then I was crying, and she knew.

"Do you have something to tell me?"

"No. There's nothing." But it came out sounding hollow. I had
no strength to lie, or maybe I just wanted to tell her.

"Oh my God, Erin, are *you* pregnant?"

I answered with more tears.

"Who?"

"I can't tell you."

"You can't tell me?" She looked outraged.

I tried to think of a lie, but I couldn't give her a name, couldn't
make one up. I blurted it out. "You don't know him. He's a boy
from the reservation, he worked for Dad."

Her face fell flat.

"You can't tell anyone. I swear."

"What's his name?"

"Charlie. Charlie White Bird."

I don't know why I gave her his name. I guess I needed to tell
someone. She just nodded her head slowly. She could tell that I

was keeping the baby; she knew me, that I couldn't do anything else.

"Sooner or later, you'll have to tell someone."

I shook my head. It was stupid to tell her. And dangerous, too. I knew she couldn't keep a secret.

"Hey, girls!" the guy behind the counter shouted at us. "If you aren't going to bowl, go sit somewhere else. I need that lane."

Jennifer waved him off, then got up and bowled a strike on my frame, and she never said another word about it to me. I'd never seen her be so quiet. It surprised me to be able to feel in her silence the realization, which I think we both had, that our friendship was over.

Chapter Ten

I SAT CROSS-LEGGED on my bed until it began to get dark, thinking about the baby growing inside me. It had to be a girl. I couldn't see her any other way. Blue dusk dimmed the room until everything was soft, not hard or real anymore. I wanted to tell Mom about her, have a conversation that we might not have managed had she still been alive. I wanted to ask her what to do, maybe get her blessing to take the sewing machine and secretly end this secret. I guess sometimes we give the dead qualities of wisdom and compassion that they never had in life.

It got dark. I couldn't see my hands anymore laying useless in my lap. I knew my answer. I knew it, not because of some new wisdom, something I dreamed up that Mom would have said, but because I could not envision talking to my baby in this same way someday, an imaginary conversation with a girl who never was. I knew I would be haunted if I chose not to keep her, no matter what word the clinic counselor had used—embryo instead of baby, flesh instead of child.

Suddenly there was a loud bang as Dad let the screen door slam behind him. And he was shouting.

"Erin? Erin! Where the hell are you? The whole damn house is dark."

Out my window I could see the lights flooding the yard as he went through the house turning them all on.

"Erin!"

For a minute I thought about hiding, but he sounded determined. I walked to the top of the stairs.

"There you are." He looked at me as though I might be some kind of prowler. "Can you come downstairs? I need to talk to you."

I nodded. It felt like I hadn't seen him for a week. Certainly, we can't have said more than about three words to each other.

"And turn on a light for God's sake," he said as he walked off to the kitchen.

Passing the mirror I looked to see if there could be any evidence of the baby. Would Dad be able to see right through me? Or would I just break down and confess? The thought of it made me queasy. Maybe somebody at the doctor's office recognized me. Or maybe it was about Charlie, maybe Jennifer had already ratted me out.

Dad was sitting in the kitchen at the table eating a Lean Cuisine. I grabbed a bowl and some cereal for a snack. Even though I wasn't hungry, I wanted to appear normal. He was almost done by the time I sat down.

"Not much in these," he said to me, waving the empty plastic plate. I don't know why he bought them, but he was hooked; half his meals were Lean Cuisine.

He looked at me as though he was trying to think of what to say, except that somehow I was supposed to come up with it for him.

"What?"

His face hardened.

"Did you call your Aunt Kristine today about something? You got a message from her on the machine. She seemed worried."

My face must have gone white. He was figuring it out.

"Do you have something you want to tell me?"

My heart sank. *How? How could he know?* My arms went weak. I didn't know what to say; in a second I knew I would be crying.

His hands gathered into fists. He would never hit me, but the anger in his hands was terrifying. "I thought I talked to you about this. I thought I made myself absolutely clear."

He talked to me about this? No. No, he didn't talk to me.

"What?"

"Damn it, Erin." His fist hit the table and then I couldn't help crying, that sobbing kind that hurts your stomach.

He stopped. He didn't know quite how to react. "Who have you told?"

"No one, nobody knows." But I thought, *I'm close to telling you.*

"Somebody knows." He stared me down for a moment. "I got a call from the state archeologist and the coroner."

I caught my breath, and wiped my eyes with my sleeve. *What?* I tried to gather my scattered wits. He looked like an angry smear of charcoal, with his unshaved face and black hair.

"What's going on with you? I can tell something's up. You leave without explanation, you're gone half the day—and late at night."

"I don't have anything to do with this, Dad."

He scowled. He didn't believe me. "I told them that we didn't find anything. There *are* no remains. Somebody's just making it up to cause trouble. I don't know if they bought it or not."

"You don't think it was me?"

He reached for something by the chair. He set Granddad's jour-

USEFUL GIRL ▲ 97

nals down and opened them up to where I had been making notes about the Cheyenne girl. "What is this?"

This was like a fire drill for the truth. What would his reaction be to the real secret? I knew—I knew then. He stared at me intently, looking for a clue. I tried to keep Charlie and the baby out of my mind, so it didn't show on my face. Once the lies started unraveling, he was going to start putting the pieces together. Teddy was behind this, calling the sheriff, the coroner. I knew it.

"Those are Granddad's."

"That's not his writing."

"I don't have anything to do with it. I was just thinking . . . "

"I'm grounding you 'til you decide to tell me the truth."

"You can't *ground* me, Dad. I'm not twelve!" I couldn't help laughing. I glanced down at my hands and wondered if he could see that they were shaking. Charlie was coming to pick me up in less than an hour, meeting me down by the river. My mind reeled.

His eyes were blue flames. "I'm disappointed in you, Erin. You're hiding something. You're not to use the car for anything until I tell you different."

I tried to concentrate on breathing, to keep my emotions in the present moment, limit my reactions to what he was talking about.

"You better hope I don't find out on my own." He was so fixed on that Indian girl, he couldn't even see straight, even when it was right there in front of his nose. I almost spoke. I could feel the confession coming, but then he stood abruptly and the chair nearly tipped over. He picked up the microwaveable plastic dish from his dinner and took it to the garbage. Then he walked out of the room without looking back at me.

I was left sitting there, alone, my whole body covered with goose bumps. After a while I picked up the journals and took them upstairs with me. I stashed them under the bed, and then I went to the top of the stairs and sat down where I could just see

Dad, standing in the doorway of the bathroom, brushing his teeth. He always went to bed early, usually by nine-thirty. I think I would have told him, if it had gone differently, if he'd been able to listen. Now I knew I wouldn't. His face looked rough, and scratchy. His eyes stared ahead into nothing as he washed his face, the water dripping from his brow and chin. It's what he would look like if he ever cried. He spit and dried his face on the towel, then he walked into the bedroom where I couldn't see him, though he left the door open. I heard the springs on the old bed giving way to his weight and then his boots falling. For a long time, I saw his shadow on the wooden floor of the hallway. He sat there at the foot of the bed, and I could almost hear him talking, as if Mom was in there with him. His shadow wasn't moving. It looked small and weak, alone like that, laying on the floor.

▲ ▲ ▲

MO'É'HA'E WALKED IN the muddy ruts of the dragging travois, making a game of trying to stay in the line. Behind her, the boy struggled to keep up. His shoes were not made for this kind of walking. Mo'é'ha'e wondered why he didn't just sit down. Would anyone really try that hard to make him get up and walk? He could let the long line of Cheyenne disappear over the far hills, until the sound of dragging tepee poles was silenced. She could hear each of his steps behind her, and this irritated her, made her want to turn and hit him with the stick she carried in her hand. Couldn't he be quieter? Did he have to be so clumsy? Smell so strange?

Still, despite the boy, despite the rain and the muck and a chilly wind from the west, she was happy. Her uncle was with them again, and as long as the tribe was moving like this, he might stay. She could sit by his fire, listen to his stories and miss her father less.

Her dog ran ahead of her, bothering the horse pulling the

travois. It side-hopped out of line trying to kick the dog, to keep it off its heels. Mo'é'ha'e rushed forward to scold the dog before it caused a problem, before *she* got in trouble. She didn't want it to do anything that might upset her uncle.

They were headed north out onto the plains, looking for that particular fold in the vastness that held the Mussel Shell River, farther away from the wagon trails, the miners and settlers. The hint of green seeping out of the bottoms made the desolate, winterworn brown of the hills seem less threatening. Soon everything would be green. The buffalo would come with the return of the sun. She yearned for those long days when it set late on warm nights.

She heard the boy stumble behind her, and she turned and snapped at him.

"*Oneseamere 'hahste,*" she said. *Keep up, boy.*

Chapter Eleven

I snuck downstairs past Dad's room, shut the front door quietly and didn't let my feet fall with their normal weight until I was half a block away. Charlie was waiting for me on the other side of the bridge. I was half-tempted to sneak up on him, wade across the shallow gravel bar and then up the bank. I could see him standing by his car, but I knew he couldn't see me walking in the dark. I liked the way he leaned against the old car, looking down, drawing in the dust with his boot, letting his foot drift back and forth. Seeing him like that, relaxed and easy, it seemed as though it would be nothing to tell him. I almost felt like shouting it, but I didn't, and then my stomach tightened and I couldn't. Once I had, once he knew, then it would be real, and he'd have to react, and I really didn't know what I wanted him to do yet.

He saw me when I got to the bridge.

"Hey."

"Hey." He looked up at me and smiled.

I stood there with my hands in my pockets, feeling uneasy. His thoughts seemed far away.

"You okay?"

"Yeah, sure."

We scrambled down the bank to the river and sat on a beaver-felled cottonwood. There was enough light from the streetlight at the bridge behind us to cast a faint amber glow across the rocks, but the river was black, the hills opposite only vaguely definable against a field of stars. The air eddied around us, sometimes warm as if heated by the gravel of the bank, sometimes cool and damp from the river, smelling of algae and minerals.

Charlie could tell something was up. Maybe it was the way I looked at him. Maybe I was even trembling. I don't know. My hands were cold. He took them one at a time in his hands to warm them up.

"What's going on? You seem in a funny mood."

If I was ever going to have a chance to tell him, this was it. I took a deep breath, and I swear I tried. But then I couldn't. "My dad's pretty pissed off."

"What?"

"The Cheyenne girl."

He shook his head.

I told him, first about the call, the lie Dad told. And then about the box in the garage.

"Shouldn't we do something about it?" I asked him.

"I don't know."

Charlie put his arm around me and I scooted closer. I looked at the gravel at my feet. Each stone seemed carefully placed, just so. He changed the subject. He must have been thinking about it while he was waiting for me. "Do you think sometimes you could just leave everything?"

"Yeah, I could." My voice shook as I wondered if he was talking about this more than hypothetically. I deliberately stopped myself from saying more.

He shrugged as if that were the obvious answer for me. "I guess it would be easier for you. You belong everywhere."

"It might seem that way," I said, but I could see what he meant. What did anybody ever expect of *me*, a white girl, for my tribe, or even for my family? I could go out and be anything and nobody would care. Except I couldn't become un-white.

He touched my hair, not as something that wasn't quite right, that might be better another way, but as something perfect. He kissed me. My face flushed and my head spun. I reached for his hand and held it, and he laced his fingers in mine confidently. My body felt lit from inside, and all my muscles relaxed as if they had been tightly braced against a wind. I could fall, held that way. He put a strong hand on my shoulder to hold me and kissed me more intensely, taking me away from any other thoughts. I swear I saw the stars moving, almost spinning through the sky in great arcing streaks of light. It could have been any time, any night in the last five million years.

I let go of his hand and stood up. "Let's go get her out of my garage and take her down there and bury her where they can't find her. Once and for all."

He seemed to hesitate.

"What's wrong?"

"It's something an elder should do."

I let out a deep breath. "But how, Charlie?"

"I don't know."

"If we do it now, she'll be left alone. Nobody will ever know." He was quiet as he thought about it. He knew I was right.

"We can't just leave her in that box."

He took a breath. "Okay."

"I'm going to take Mom's car. We can leave it at Uncle Leonard's on the way down so you don't have to drive me all the way back out here, after."

He wanted to say it was no problem, he never minded driving, but it was more than an hour and a half down there. It was already past ten. "How are you going to do it?" He meant with Dad home.

"I'm going to be quiet."

I ran almost all the way back to the house. It was late enough that most of the lights were off in the houses, though there were a few TVs still glowing in upstairs bedrooms. A dog heard me and charged up and down his fenced-in run, barking, but no one came out. I slowed to a walk past Mrs. Gibbs's house, watching her windows carefully, but they remained dark.

I snuck into the backyard and Sadie came up to me wiggling her whole body with excitement. I let her in the garage with me so she wouldn't start barking and I shut the door before I turned on the light. It was a risk I had to take. My mind was so busy trying to think of what I would say to Dad if he showed up at the door that it was hard to concentrate enough to remember where I'd found the box. I had to get it as quickly as possible. The windows of the garage were in plain sight of Dad's bedroom. I hurried too much and knocked one of the stacks over. They tumbled down with a crash. I froze. Sadie was standing by the door banging her tail against it as if ticking off the seconds before I would be caught. I put the box in Mom's car, turned the light off and restacked the U-Haul boxes as best I could in the dark.

I waited for a while at the garage door to see if Dad had heard anything, or seen the light. I wan't sure how to get it open, either. The automatic door opener would be too noisy, and the lights would come on again, but I'd never opened the door manually before. I looked around in the dark until I found a red knob hanging on a string near the top of the door. I pulled it slowly half expecting to set off an alarm, but it made just a subtle click. When I tried the door, it lifted easily. I opened it slowly.

I put the Toyota in neutral and pushed it back out of the garage. It was easier than I thought. There was enough slope to the driveway that I was able to hop in and steer, and I got enough speed up to get it turned around and aimed down the hill toward the river. I set the brake and ran back to grab a shovel and shut the door.

Riverview was still asleep as I coasted down its darkened streets. I crossed the bridge, and I felt as though I could be leaving forever, as though I might never come back. Charlie and I could run away to another life. All I had to do was ask.

Charlie waved for me to follow and pulled out in front of me onto the freeway. I followed his taillights all the way to Lame Deer. When a car approached from the other direction his shadow would grow on the rear window and then drift across until it disappeared leaving just his silhouette behind the wheel. I kept myself awake by talking to him. I told him about the baby, that I was sure it was a girl. I talked about what we might name her, and what she would be like. I left out all the problems, the *where* and *how*, and focused on what color her eyes would be, her hair. I said I hoped she would look most like Charlie.

Uncle Leonard's trailer was dark when we got there. We parked my car and moved the box and shovel to Charlie's without speaking so that we wouldn't wake him.

Green-and-white mile markers floated by in the headlights as we left the reservation and crossed the bridge over the Tongue River. Light from the instrument panel glowed softly on his face. Several times I could feel myself start to tell him, now that he would be able to hear me, then my throat clamped down and I stopped myself. I reached across the seat and took his free hand. We came upon the orange signs warning of road construction ahead, and then the headlights picked up the collections of dump trucks and trailers. The pavement ended.

"I wonder if we can find it in the dark," I said. For some reason I was whispering.

It was hard to tell where she'd been; nothing looked familiar. We wanted a place not too far from her original spot, just far enough to be hidden. Charlie drove slowly but soon I knew we'd gone too far. "I don't know. You'd better turn around."

He made a wide turn and the lights swept across the sagebrush, flashing on the pink eyes of a jackrabbit. At a big turn in the road, I noticed a twisted, fallen tree sprawled at the base of a low hill.

"I recognize that tree. It was around here somewhere."

Charlie pulled off onto the wide shoulder and turned the car so that the headlights would help us to see. He got the box out of the back, and I grabbed the shovel. His boots popped on the gravel and we stumbled as we walked out across the shoulder of the road into the sagebrush. Charlie grabbed a handful of leaves from one and put it carefully into his shirt pocket. We jumped over a ditch filled with shadow so black that it could have been infinitely deep. The light began to fade behind us, and soon it was of little use. Way out over the horizon, a fat white moon was cresting and out in the distance a group of coyotes started up, not howling at the moon, but squabbling over something, maybe some dried-up prairie dog killed on the road. Charlie turned on his flashlight.

"I feel like some kind of grave robber," I whispered.

"You are."

The thought made me look around. The moon was still too low to bring any light, and the headlights were cold and hard in the darkness. We stopped by the tree.

"What do you think?"

"Seems good. It's farther from the road. It's not like anyone's gonna start digging around looking for her."

Charlie set the box down marking the spot. Moths fluttered in flashlight, throwing themselves against it, creating dancing shadows out on the dirt. For a long breath we both stood looking down at the patch of dirt that was going to be her grave. Then he took a lighter out of his jeans pocket. He twisted together a small bundle of the sage he'd picked and lit one end. White smoke twisted up in the beam of the flashlight as Charlie passed the burning sage in front of himself, and then me. It smelled sweet but aromatic, even medicinal. He picked up the shovel and started the grave.

"I'm going to run out of batteries." My feeble flashlight flickered but when I hit it with my palm it brightened up again.

Digging the grave was hard. The ground was full of big rocks and the shovel skipped across them, sometimes scarcely gathering anything. Other times, Charlie pried out a big rock only to reveal the larger one it had been resting on. Traditionally, he told me, Cheyenne wouldn't have buried this girl. She would have been left on a platform or under a cairn, even in a tree. But we had to hide her.

"I'll go see if I can find another shovel. Maybe they've left one out by the trucks."

"Take the flashlight. I can dig without it."

I found a grader parked a hundred yards down the road by a gravel pit, but there was nothing but an old pick with a broken handle leaning against it. I could still hear Charlie's shovel scratching and scraping against the dry ground. Because of the grader, I didn't see the approaching headlights until they were quite close. I ran around to the side where I could see Charlie, who was still working so hard that he hadn't noticed, either.

"Charlie, a car!"

He grabbed the box and dropped into the shallow hole to hide. There was nowhere else to be. There was no time to turn the headlights off, either. I could only pray that it was just some rancher driving home late, anyone but the sheriff.

Whoever it was slowed as he approached Charlie's car. He crept by, rolling his window down to look. The dim light of a cigarette glowed on the driver's side. He flipped it out the open window, and his headlights swept over the shoulder of the road as he took the turn. I saw Charlie's back clear as day, but if you didn't know he was there, he could be a rock. In a few seconds, the car was speeding away on Dad's new pavement. The whine of the tires faded as it disappeared into two small red dots.

Charlie started digging again.

"How deep are you going to make it?"

"I don't know. Deep enough that I can cover her up with a bunch of those big rocks. Deeper than she was."

"Let me dig some."

He handed me the shovel, and I started. Charlie had pried out the rocks and I was into a layer of sand. I made pretty good progress.

"That's probably enough," he said after a while and hopped up to get the box. "Hold the flashlight for me, okay?"

I took the flashlight. It trembled like a needle on a seismograph, recording every movement of my hands. He opened the box and carefully gathered the remains onto the wool coat.

"Let me help."

I climbed back into the grave with Charlie. We laid her carefully on the sand. The dark, fragile bones seemed to suck the light from the moon, as if they were not relatives of stone, but something vaporous, actually made of shadow. Charlie lifted the coat away from the chest, revealing a shoulder and then her skull.

"She's so small."

I couldn't help thinking of her alive, as if she might lift herself from the grave, and against a field of stars pull her skeleton back together, wrap the army coat around her shoulders and begin to dance, bent over, stomping, rattling those delicate skeleton feet, then standing and spreading her arms to the sky, spinning like any child who dances for the pure joy of dancing.

We lay the tattered coat back over her, folding it carefully to protect her. We were both so focused on what we were doing, it took us longer than it should have to realize that a car was approaching again, coming fast.

"Headlights," I whispered.

Charlie looked up. "I better get the lights this time."

"No, Charlie."

But he was already running toward the Pontiac.

"Charlie, just leave 'em!" I shouted.

All I could see of Charlie was his shadow. Then he turned the lights off, and it was dark until the white headlights of the approaching vehicle began to fill in. Charlie was caught out in the open for a moment. He stopped and turned, and I thought I saw him duck behind the car, just as a truck approached. Then the lights made a wide turn toward me, and I grabbed the empty box and dropped into the grave.

The hole smelled dusty and dry, like burned earth. I couldn't help thinking about that bulldozer pushing the rocks over the grave, and then the crushing weight of the tracks passing over, compacting the rocks into blackness. Even the dim moon was reassuring. Suddenly a brilliant light shone on my shoulder, making it glow. I tried, but I couldn't scoot in deeper without lying right on top of the bones. The truck stopped. I strained to hear.

The engine turned off, and I could hear the voices of two men. I couldn't make out what they were saying, but they laughed a lot, like they were drunk. I heard the doors of Charlie's car opening and closing. Then one of the men shouted.

"Hey! Where the hell are ya?"

"Allee, allee, all come free!" the other guy shouted and they laughed hard.

USEFUL GIRL ▲ 109

Then I heard their footsteps approaching the grave, heavy boots snapping on the gravel. The light still glowed on my shoulder. I pressed harder into the grave, feeling the bones through the ancient, dusty wool coat.

"Hey, look over here, I can see an arm."

"There's somebody in there."

I heard them stop maybe thirty yards away.

"Hey, you, come out of there!"

A rock pressed into my side, but I didn't dare move again.

"Maybe it's a body."

"Shut up."

"I'm going to throw a rock in there and see if he comes out."

"You better watch out. You don't know who the hell's in there. Where's your gun?"

"I left it in the truck."

"That's good," he said sarcastically.

Then the closer man laughed. He sounded big. "You're gonna try to throw that? You can hardly lift it."

"If I hit 'em, it'll kill 'em."

The bigger guy raised his voice. "Better get out of there or you'll be squashed like a bug." They laughed.

Suddenly a car horn sounded. I heard the big stone drop to the ground. When I looked up, the headlights were blinding. I could hardly make out the two men looking over at the Pontiac. They looked like a couple of coal miners on their way back to town.

Then the shorter of the two spotted me. "It's a girl."

"What the heck are you doing hiding in that hole, missy?"

The car horn sounded again. Charlie was standing by his car reaching through the window fumbling for the headlights. Both of the guys turned to look at him now.

"What the hell are you guys doin' out here?" I could hear the liquor thickening in the bigger man's voice.

"See that, Dean, it's a damn Indian." A realization of what might be going on came to them in that dull, exaggerated way it does for drunks.

"You been out here messin' around with this pretty white girl?" the one named Dean shouted.

Charlie ran, and maybe he shouldn't have. Maybe they would have left us alone. But I guess I would have run, too, out there like that, a million miles from anybody.

"Get him."

Charlie disappeared into the darkness. The bigger man took after him. He wasn't as fast. Charlie could easily outrun him. But the other guy started up the truck and tore off, bouncing into the night. His headlights picked up Charlie, who looked like a ghost lit up like that. Then they lost him again. I started running too. It began as a game, the two men acting as if it were a joke. Charlie was way out in front; the big man was falling behind gasping for breath. Then the truck crashed through the fence, stretching and popping the wire. He caught up with Charlie and nearly hit him as he slammed on the brakes. The driver started to open the door, but Charlie had already gained too much of a lead. Just as the truck pulled away to chase him, the big man tried to jump in the back, and he nearly fell on his face. He banged his fist against the truck bed and yelled so the driver would stop. He got in like an old Lab that can't quite make the truck anymore, breathing hard. They took out after Charlie again. I was running so hard my lungs burned and my side hurt, but I couldn't catch them.

They closed the distance on Charlie quickly. The headlights of the truck bounced across his silhouette. The truck cut him off and he veered to the left, to the north. And when I had to stop, I could see Charlie slowing down. The big man was standing in the bed of the truck as it circled Charlie, and he was laughing so hard I could hear him above the revving engine.

Then Charlie stumbled on some sagebrush as he dodged a turn of the truck. The big man jumped out and ran at him. Charlie had a rock ready, but the big man tackled him, knocking him into the dirt. He wiggled free, but the driver ran around the front and kicked Charlie before he could get up. He did it just to knock him down, to catch him. But that started it, the beating, and it was the last thing I could really see. It appeared to me as in slow motion, Charlie falling behind the truck.

"Leave him alone!" I screamed from about a hundred yards away. It stopped them only for a moment; they were too busy with Charlie to worry about me. He was making it worse by trying to get up, and they weren't laughing anymore. Charlie was getting hurt.

The door of their pickup was still open, the engine idling. I jumped in, and it took me several long seconds to find the gear shift, neutral first. When I hit the gas the engine raced though I wasn't moving. The little guy turned at the sound, and he was already running at me when I found reverse and slammed the gas pedal to the floor again. The truck flew back like a rocket, and I struggled to hold on. I wasn't looking where I was going, just at the two men running after me getting smaller in the headlights, and Charlie lying on the ground behind them. As they drifted away, the rush of the backward accelerating truck made me feel like I was falling, the way you do in a dream that wakes you in a panic.

When I hit the ditch, the sudden stop slammed my head back so hard that it cracked the glass in the rear window. For a second I was dazed, just listening to the wheels burning up in the dirt and the engine getting ready to seize. Finally, I let my foot relax on the gas pedal.

In the quiet I thought of the gun, the one the little guy said he'd left in the truck. They were about two hundred yards away still running toward me. *Under the seat. It must be under the seat.* My hand fished around. I found something metal, but it was just a pipe wrench.

"Shit."

I opened the door, and the cab light came on. I jumped out so I could see better under the seat. They were almost on me when I found the black handle and stainless barrel.

"If you wrecked my truck, I'm going to kill you, you dumb bitch," the little man yelled.

I looked up. He was closest, but he'd stopped running, and he was breathing hard. I had the gun in my hand, and suddenly my whole body felt weak. I didn't think I could use the pistol even if it meant my life. My hands were shaking desperately. The big man caught up, doubled over trying to get his breath.

"Okay, honey. Game's up."

I didn't know if the gun was loaded. I looked down to see if I could tell, but as I did, they both ran at me. Before I even knew what was happening, the gun was up, and there was a bright flash and an explosion.

They stopped immediately.

I pointed the gun at the big man's chest a few yards away. He looked scared. "Holy shit! You better put that thing down."

I didn't move. They both took a step backward. I tried to see beyond them, looking for Charlie but it was too dark out there. The little guy raised his hands up in front of him as if they might stop a bullet.

"Little girl, that trigger is light. Just be careful."

"I don't give a shit." I said it quietly and they backed off some more. If my face were lit, they would have seen tears. They would have seen that I couldn't see. I still couldn't see Charlie.

"What's your plan, darlin'?" The big man was beginning to feel brave.

"Charlie!" I yelled into the blackness, but he didn't answer. "Char—lie!"

The two men were trying to decide what they were going to do. They were still afraid to charge me. I walked away from the truck, keeping the gun pointed at the big man and began a wide circle around them.

"Where ya goin', huh?"

There was no reason to answer them. When they were closer to the truck than I was, they made a run for it. My arms were burning, and I let the gun point at the ground. They slammed the doors shut and the truck lurched forward and the tires spun as it pulled out of the ditch. They started to head at me, but when I raised the pistol again, they veered off. I heard the tires screech as they finally reached pavement, and soon, they were a small harmless light in the distance.

I found Charlie still lying on the ground where they beat him, curled up in a ball like a child.

"Charlie? Are you okay?"

He groaned and moved a little.

"They're gone."

He didn't answer, but his body relaxed a little.

I knelt next to him and lifted his head into my lap, brushed the hair away from his bruised face, and turned it gently toward the moonlight. His eyes stayed shut. The moon lifted in the sky like a blue balloon caught in the thermals, and soon its cool, white light brightened the night enough that I could see the mountains in the distance.

"Charlie?"

"Yeah," he breathed, and opened his eyes weakly.

"I'm going to get the car."

He nodded, and I lay his head as gently as I could on the ground. The sand felt soft and cool to my hand. It was a lot farther back to the car than I remembered, almost half a mile. The Pontiac shook as it started up. Its deep, slow engine was reassuring, and its belly dragged like an old serpent over the high spots and through the ruts left by the chase. Then I knew we were going to run away together, Charlie and I. We were going to drive off south somewhere and never look back. The thought of it was thrilling.

Charlie was sitting when I got there. He stood up stiffly, opened the door and dropped into the seat.

"You okay?"

He looked at the gun on the seat between us, and back at me again, and the way he looked at me almost made me cry. He put the gun in the glove box, pulling the hammer back onto safe with a gentle click, and slid painfully next to me on the seat. My mind raced to think of something to say, but it all sounded stupid. Charlie leaned his head back on the seat, and held his hurt shoulder. I followed the car tracks back out again, past the open grave and out to the paved road.

I started to drive away, but then I stopped, right there in the middle of the road. I couldn't leave the Cheyenne girl, not for me, not for Charlie, not even for Dad. I turned the car around and pulled off onto the shoulder next to her grave.

"I'll be back in a second." I kissed Charlie on the forehead, and he nodded weakly.

I felt exposed and vulnerable, kneeling by her out in the darkness. Two of the thimbles dropped out as I moved her more into the center of the grave. I picked them up to put back on her fingers, but my eyes were tearing and it was hard to see what I was doing. I gave up and simply wrapped the thimbles with her in the army coat, and then I carefully smoothed the rotted fabric over her skeleton and pushed the dirt and rocks back over her with my bare hands. Once she was covered, I used the shovel. I knew none of the right prayers, none of the rituals that Charlie might have performed. I simply did what I could. I put her back where she belonged.

It took half an hour to get the job done, and then to brush away our tracks. I kept reminding myself that there was no reason for anyone to come looking for her now. The road would be paved here long before Dad ever noticed that the box was gone.

Charlie was asleep when I got back to the car. I put the empty box in the trunk and locked it, then I pulled away slowly, trying not to wake him. After a while, I stopped thinking about the heating and the feeling in my stomach eased. I was thinking about the baby, and what to tell Charlie. We couldn't run away. My chest hurt to think about it. What if some Indian ran away with a teenage white girl? Would anyone make the argument that I was over the age of consent? Did anyone really believe in that anyway? That at seventeen I could legally decide for myself who to be with? I could just imagine my Dad choking on that one. He would not care that Charlie was really just a kid, too, or that we were probably in love. I looked down at the speedometer. I was going too fast. But what if when Charlie woke up, we were halfway through South Dakota already? Would he just smile at me, and we'd roll down the windows, and it wouldn't matter that we had nowhere to go?

A silvery light lay across his black hair, as though time had slipped, grayed it. I touched his face with the back of my hand, and he breathed more easily for a moment. I think if Charlie had been awake, it would have happened differently. We would have taken the big chance. But I couldn't choose on my own to do that to him. He was still asleep when I pulled up to Uncle Leonard's.

"Charlie," I whispered.

He didn't wake.

"Charlie. I don't know what to do."

He moved. I lay my head to his chest and listened to his heart beating. It sounded good, slow and strong, like the steady beating wings of a bird flying high across the sky. But his breath was syncopated, as if it hurt him even in his sleep. In the back was an old sweater. I lay it over him.

I watched him sleep, thinking of how close he was at this moment, how impossible my decision seemed. I kissed him on the cheek and pushed the car door shut, careful not to wake him. I drove out into the darkness toward the freeway, and the sky was filled with stars, all watching me. I looked south to the mountains and I rolled the window down, and breathed in the simple air. I knew what I had to do. And I knew I would not miss a soul.

Except Charlie.

Chapter Twelve

I snuck around to the back of the house hoping the door wouldn't be locked. The screen door popped and squeaked on its hinges, but the door was unlocked, and I slipped into the unlit house, following the wall with my hands through the kitchen. The dining room was light enough from the streetlights to see the clock. It was just after three o'clock. I took my steps carefully. I could hear Dad snoring in his bedroom.

While he slept, I packed an old brown suitcase that used to belong to Mom. The last thing I threw in were Granddad's journals. I kept looking over my shoulder at the door in case he suddenly appeared. But he didn't. When I left, I didn't take a chance with the stairs. I opened the window and tossed the suitcase out onto the grass. Somehow it held together. It was a longish jump to the tree, but I'd done it before. I slipped down the trunk.

The air was warm, even this late. I walked down Riverview's meandering streets to the freeway without hearing a single dog bark, as if I had already become invisible. I didn't know exactly when I decided to do it this way, where the idea came from. Not that I had it all thought out, beyond that night, but at least I knew the first step.

As I reached the river, the thought of Charlie sleeping in the car at Uncle Leonard's stopped me. I stood on the bridge where I could still see my house. They wouldn't let us be. If I stayed, once it got out, Dad wouldn't stand for it. I closed my eyes and saw over and over Charlie falling in the headlights of that truck. I knew I brought on those kicking boots and pounding fists, the bruised muscle and bone. I couldn't do that to him again. He was too beautiful to be hurt and humiliated because of me.

It didn't take long to get a ride hitchhiking. I wondered if I was making the right decision to leave the car. But my desire was to disappear. I didn't need a license plate tattooed to my rear end for any sheriff or highway patrolman to call in. I didn't have enough money for gas anyway.

It must have been ten blocks from the freeway to the Broken Spur Motel. My right arm hurt from carrying the suitcase and my fingers felt like they might never straighten out again. The motel sign cast a pink glow on the gravel parking lot. I drew my foot back and forth, mixing the pink dirt like paint with the yellow of the streetlights, looking for the courage to do what I was going to do. I needed a place to sit and wait. The Billings police would definitely hassle me for loitering at night outside a cheesy motel like this one. I ditched my suitcase behind a Dumpster and then I went in the coffee shop and splurged on some burnt decaf though it was scary to see even seventy cents go. I sat by a cold glass window and drank it, adding milk from the table to keep the cup full until it was cold and hardly resembled coffee at all.

A dog wandered down the street, stopping to look over his shoulder or to smell the air and then trotting a few steps forward before stopping again. As he came closer it was plain that he'd been on his own for a while, and it was food he was looking for.

He stopped at my window, and when he saw me looking, he wagged his tail.

I must have fallen asleep because the waitress woke me by refilling my coffee.

"Honey, if you're gonna sleep, you gotta get a room or go home."

"I'm almost done."

She walked back to her station as if she were walking a steep slope.

The sky was beginning to lighten in the east when Clayton's truck pulled in. I almost missed it. He got out, stretched and headed for a room upstairs. Suddenly, I realized that I hadn't considered whether he'd be alone or not. I paid the bill, and when I walked outside the dog was at my feet.

"Go home." I pointed somewhere toward town, and he looked in that direction but didn't move. "Go home."

He just wagged his tail and followed me over to the truck.

"You can't come, you know."

The truck was unlocked. I figured it would be. I looked around before I got in to make sure nobody just happened to be standing at their window watching me. The rear seat was covered with clothes, tack and some muddy boots. I moved them neatly onto the floor. It felt strange to mess with someone else's stuff. There was a flannel shirt that made a good pillow, and I lay down to get out of view. The truck smelled of diesel and sweat and manure. As I drifted off, I thought about my last visit to Granddad's rest home, something I had done, I think, because it was what Mom would have done.

HE HAD BEEN ASLEEP when I got there. I sat quietly by his bed, thinking how much like a child he looked that way. Defenseless and dependent. He looked more sad than scary, and

I felt guilty. I knew he wouldn't like it, me staring at him while he slept.

I closed my eyes and almost fell asleep myself. I heard him move, and when I looked up he was staring at me. I tried to smile. Granddad pushed the button that raised his bed, and the electric motor hummed and levitated him until his eyes were level with mine.

He didn't speak right away so I felt compelled to start a conversation to fill the awkward silence. He always got me to say something that ended up sounding lame, something I specifically did not want to say. "You look just like that picture, that old picture of your great-uncle, Major Brennan."

His voice was rough and thin. "Captain," he coughed. "He was a captain."

I guess I knew this already, a captain not a major. I smiled as neutrally as I could manage. For a moment he seemed to forget that I was there.

"He's your great-uncle, too. Your blood. An Indian fighter with General Crook and Mackenzie. Fought the Apache in the south and he fought Crazy Horse in Wyoming and Montana."

"Not the Bighorn, though, right?" I offered.

"Crook fought at Rosebud."

"Rosebud?" It sounded familiar; maybe Uncle Leonard had mentioned it.

"Yep." He waved with his hand to the East, out the narrow frame of his window. "That was a real battle. Not women and children running buck naked in the snow, either. Crazy Horse retreated, and the army buried the dead and rode the whole column over the mass grave so the damn Indians wouldn't find it and dig up the bodies." Granddad sounded like he might choke on the story. "People forget what those Indians were like."

He glared at me, as if he knew I were especially guilty of forgetting.

"They just flat-out forget. They were wild men and they loved to fight. Hell, the whole plains was at war from before Lewis and Clark showed up. It made them men to steal horses, take scalps and kidnap women—a bunch of bandits. People just forget about it. It's not politically correct, or whatever damn thing they call it." He was getting red in the face. "They'd be making war today, if it weren't for Indian fighters like your great-uncle. The whole West would be a wilderness."

The room darkened with a passing cloud. A nurse knocked on the door and came in. "Fightin' Injuns again, eh Pops?" The nurse laughed. He was an Indian himself. Somehow Granddad didn't make the connection. "Time for dinner." He pushed a wheelchair over to the bed. "Come on Pops, sit up. Even old General Crook had to eat his spinach."

▲ ▲ ▲

MO'É'HA'E WAS NOT there to witness it herself—the killing of the horses. Another child told her who'd heard the story from her father, one of the warriors hidden in the dark trees only a couple hundred yards away listening to what General Crook's men were doing with ax handles and knives to the horses they'd stolen from the Cheyenne and the Lakota. The group of children was gathered around a smoldering fire, which glowed in their faces as they listened. The cold night pressed at their backs, encouraging them to inch closer to the flames for comfort. The girl told her father's story almost in a whisper, as if she were afraid to repeat it. Her audience was silent and the fire crackled in the gaps of her telling. The children waited for her to resume with wide, white eyes.

When the girl finished her breathless tale, Mo'é'ha'e put her hands over her ears, trying not to imagine it, that terrible sound, all those horses screaming their last breath through severed windpipes. She tried not to see the blood, sticky on the white men's hands, making a foul warm mud in the dirt. It didn't make sense to her. Why kill horses? It could only be for the sake of the blood itself, an inhuman lust for killing. For the children who retold the story over and over, each time more fantastic, with more horses and more blood, it was a tale of monsters.

They did not yet know that those same hundreds of cavalry were on their way back, headed north, their own horses and mules shod with iron, crossing the plain as the sun arced through the sky through its highest point to set in the West. If Mo'é'ha'e had been there laying in the grass she could have seen the soldiers coming, the men following Crook, chewing and spitting, cursing and laughing, or staring mutely into the ass of the horse ahead. Most of their faces were grimy from the dust that rose in a cloud —these veterans of the bloody Civil War, who were used to soldiering and knew nothing else, and these recently joined immigrants who had been starving in the overcrowded ports of the East, who did not yet speak English but came to fight because they had nothing else.

If she understood their many languages she might have heard them talking loudly as they passed, about the gold that lay waiting in the Black Hills for pick and shovel. Once this military chore was done, this bit of thuggery, they fantasized being rich men.

Far out ahead of them all, ahead of Crook, was the Captain. Mo'é'ha'e did not know about him yet, had not yet seen him bear down on her tribe with his saber high in the air, leading the charge. With Crow scouts he was still searching for the enemy. His eyes cut through the folds and rolls of the prairie ocean that might conceal a camp or an ambush. He rode his bay horse with a precise grip on the reins, keeping his mount as taut and rigid as a parade horse. He chewed an empty pipe, holding it habitually in his teeth. His hair was long and dark and dusted with gray, though he didn't look that old, maybe forty. His uniform was a bit wrinkled and well worn, but his face was clean shaven. He wore a Colt Army Officer's–model revolver on his hip and a belt of cartridges. Occasionally he stopped his horse and his gaze settled on the horizon, as though he saw already the battles and blood, life falling before him.

The Captain and the two Crow had been out for many days without new rations. He had a little tobacco left, but that was his only luxury. Otherwise it was molding hardtack, some dried meat that was supposed to be beef though it tasted suspiciously like mule, and water where they found it. For two days they'd been following the tracks of a large herd of horses along the foothills of the Bighorns. Late in the afternoon they found a camp in the cool shade of a rock outcropping. The ground was beaten down and wet. Moss grew heavily on the north face of the rock over a shallow pool. The Captain got down from his horse. As he walked around the remains of a small camp, his horse followed him with its ears pressed flat against its head. He must have smelled something that the Captain could not, something of what had happened there.

The Captain kicked apart a small fire ring, one fire deep, and when he rolled a piece of charcoal in his fist, it was cold. It seemed an unusual place to camp, more like a place to hide, cold and wet, even on a warm day. He wandered some more, and the horse plodded behind. He found some ground that was torn up where a small herd of horses must have been startled, and then, resting against a tree like something forgetfully left behind, a human arm. The Captain picked it up by the elbow, turned to the Crow scouts who were still on their horses and raised it for them to see.

One of them laughed and the Captain tossed it to him for a closer look. The scout's horse spooked and started to buck while the man fumbled trying to keep hold of the arm. Like an act from a circus, the Crow danced wildly around with the dismembered

arm circling crazily about his head. The other scout nearly fell off
his horse laughing.

"What do you think?" the Captain asked impatiently in English, then in Crow, "Whose is it?"

The Crow looked it over and then tossed it back.

"Cheyenne."

"Why?"

The other scout nodded, "Cheyenne."

"How in the hell do you know?" the Captain burst out in English again. Something about this made him angry. "Is there a
goddamn tag on it that says Cheyenne in your Crow language,
and I just can't see it?"

Neither man responded. After all, he'd asked them what they
thought and they'd answered.

"Do you think I'm stupid?" The Captain stormed over and
grabbed the arm again, studying it more closely. There were no
markings, other than some buckshot wounds near the elbow, no
rings. It was damp and cold and looked untouched. Nothing had
been chewing on it. He tossed it away again. It thudded heavily on
the compacted wet ground, rolled end over end and came to rest
at the base of the big mossy rock.

"I say it's a Crow arm, or Shoshone," the Captain spit. "Where's
the rest of him?"

They looked around but found nothing more to prove or dis-
prove the arm's identity. Whatever had happened to the man who
used to own that arm, the rest was gone. From there, the trail of
the horses scattered in a stampede, deep hoof marks tore black
holes in the sod in all directions. It took them the last two hours
of daylight to sort out where the tracks were headed because they
had to circle back on the camp several times, and by then it was
too late to follow. The trio camped by the rock, as there was no

other flat spot around and no water other than the still, dark pool at its base.

They built a big fire, bigger than they normally would have, to chase the chill from that place. The Captain sat with the arm in his hands again, flexing the elbow, which at first was tight with rigor mortis, but finally began to give. He stared across the bonfire at his two companions. With every bend of the arm, he felt surer that it did not belong to a Cheyenne. He took a bite of dried meat from his other hand and chewed it for a moment. He made a bizarre site, this grim man with three arms, gnawing jerky.

"*I say Cheyenne caught this man stealing horses, killed him and cut off his arm.*" He waved the arm as he made his point. "This is Cheyenne territory. Makes more sense for Christ's sake."

The scouts shrugged, and then nodded. They seemed to find the Captain's obsession with the arm and its fate a little strange, and the Captain found their easy agreement even more irksome than their earlier proclamations. He knew that the scouts had said that the arm was Cheyenne only because those were the Indians he was looking for; not seeing the difference an arm might make to him, they were just trying to please him. He threw the arm into the fire. It sizzled and popped in the flames; the skin blistered until finally it was charred completely black.

"*I don't want the arm of dead Shoshone. I want a camp.*"

The oldest scout nodded and pointed to the north, then he looked at the charred arm in the fire and covered his nose with his hand as the wind twisted the sickening smoke his way.

SOMETIME IN THE NIGHT while they slept, a bear wandered near camp. The horses smelled it and stomped and pulled at their tethers, nickering and blowing air. The Captain rolled over onto his side and slid his rifle a bit closer and listened for the animal. But it was impossible to discern its movement because of the racket the horses were making. It was so dark under the trees with the fire died down, that he could not see even as far as the mossy rock. He was going to have to rely on being able to smell the beast to know how close it came. When a faint eddy in the still air finally brought the bear smell to him, he knew that it was only a few feet away, but behind him, near the dead fire. Now he could hear it pawing the coals, and he raised the rifle as slowly and quietly as he could manage, rolling over silently. Then as he heard the clicking sound of the bear's teeth picking the charred bone out of the fire pit, he fired.

For a brief second the light of the blast from the barrel showed the black bear where he thought it would be, by the fire, the bone in its teeth like a dog, and the two scouts also sitting up with their rifles ready. Blackness returned with the sound of the bear bawling and thundering off, hit, but not mortally wounded. It crashed and moaned, and the Captain could hear it for several minutes even above the frantic noises of the terrified horses. The younger scout calmed them down, and after that, it was completely quiet and dark again.

In the morning they ate without mentioning the bear, then saddled up. The Captain sat on his horse, looking off into the darkest part of the trees while the two Crow spent an hour sorting out the mix of horses' tracks. They headed north and after a few hours of easy riding, they found the main Cheyenne camp. The Captain turned to the two scouts.

"See, fools, it was a Shoshone who lost his arm and his horses." He looked down the slope to the camp bustling by the river. Smoke twisted up from the cooking fires and then flattened into a haze.

CHAPTER THIRTEEN

CLAYTON YELLED AT the dog and managed to chase it off a few yards, but there the stray held its ground. As soon as he turned his back, the dog drifted in closer again. He didn't see me right away, and I kept my head down, unsure of how I wished to reveal myself, a little afraid of being chased off like the dog. The sun was up and it was already getting warm. I struggled with the thick-headed feeling of waking up after having slept for less than an hour.

Clayton threw his saddle into the back with a loud bang and opened the door, and as he pushed away some of the things I had moved onto his seat, I sat up, and he jumped.

"Holy Jesus, you scared me."

"Sorry," I said sleepily.

He yawned, and rubbed his face, which needed a shave. I tried to look comfortable, normal.

"Looking for a ride, or just a place to sleep?"

"Kinda both."

He climbed in with a funny smile, and then the dog tried to follow him in, too.

"Hey, get the hell outta here." He chased it with his boot. "Looks like everybody wants a ride this morning."

"Thanks."

"No comparison." He grinned. "I'm leaving right now . . . for good, you know."

I nodded.

"Not comin' back."

"That's the idea," I said.

He started the truck and backed up as if he was in a hurry, but it was probably just the way he always drove; either that or it was meant to impress me. I lay back down, and the last I saw of Billings was the motel sign, glowing unsteadily against the pale sky. I pulled Clayton's coat over my shoulders. He sipped coffee from a thermos that was hot enough to give off steam. It felt good to lay there as we made long, slow turns along the river. I slipped into a strange sleep in the backseat of that extended cab pickup, dreaming to the smells of a stranger's life and the loud hum of mud tires on the highway taking me away from home.

When I woke, it was hot. I pushed the coat off and struggled to sit up, looking down the road. Clayton was slowing down to take an exit. Nothing much had changed in the scenery, despite the miles. This little town clinging to the highway could have been any little town. We rolled slowly down the business loop. Even though it was late for breakfast, Clayton wanted pancakes—pancakes and some coffee. I used the rearview mirror to straighten up a bit, trying to look a little less like I'd been hit by a truck. My hair rioted, and eventually I gave up. Clayton stopped at a café that advertised home-cooked food, which was sort of true, since at least they did heat the frozen stuff up on the premises.

We didn't say much, except to order. He needed to eat first, that was the main thing. I watched him take huge, teenager-sized bites. I wondered what he was thinking. His pretty face looked distant and unreal, but he seemed to feel that our arrangement was just fine. When he was done eating, he talked about the rodeos that were coming up, Wyoming, South Dakota, North Dakota, and what he was going to do with the money as if he'd already won it. He didn't care to know much about me at all, at least he didn't ask, and that was fine. I was trying not to think about me either. I just cared that Clayton picked the rodeos farthest down the road.

"You know, I asked Jennifer if she wanted to come with me." He said it with a bit too much sincerity. I wasn't sure who he was trying to convince, me or a guilty conscience. He shifted in his chair, unconsciously preparing to squirm when I gave him a hard time, but I let him off the hook.

"Her dad wouldn't have let her go anywhere, and she's not the type to run away." I guess that meant I was. I hadn't thought about that.

The waitress took our plates and filled the coffee cups one more time, and she laid the check down next to Clayton. He ignored it at first. I think he was giving me time to respond, to decide what I was going to do. But I couldn't spare the money. So it sat, and I took another drink of the milky coffee. Finally, I thought I'd better say something.

"How much is it?"

He took the check. "I can't have a girl paying for her own breakfast."

And that's how it was, how I thought it was going to be. For this ride at least, he was taking care of me, and I was with him. He smiled and dug out his wallet.

"Let's just hope I keep winnin'."

As the miles burned away, I looked out at the horizon, slipping in and out of sleep, dreaming and daydreaming. It was surprising what a relief simply moving could be. We didn't have much, and yet we had a radio and air conditioning, leg room and gasoline, and someone like my father had paved the way, leaving not a single pothole to jar the smooth whisper of our traveling. I tried to imagine riding across this expanse, with only a horse to carry me, and nowhere to stop where the coffee was already brewed and the food just a few seconds in the microwave away from being hot.

We quit driving just a little after dark. It was quiet except for the sound of the motel keys jingling and slipping into the lock and far off, the steady buzz of cars on the freeway and occasionally the rumble of air brakes as trucks slowed down to take the exit.

I walked into the room behind Clayton and left the door open. It was still warm out. He threw himself onto the stiff, fire-retardant covers, and lay there looking up at the ceiling.

"Another fleabag motel on the interstate! Does that air conditioning work?"

I gave it a kick, and it rattled a bit and then died. "Guess not."

He sat up. "Should I get some ice or somethin'?"

I shrugged.

"Or I could go out and get us a couple of beers."

He seemed to be hoping that would not be necessary. But there was also something in him that was hesitating, too. So I walked over and took a pillow from beside him on the bed and went out to sleep in the truck, saying good-night as I shut the paper-thin door, which had a big, patched-up hole in the middle about the height of a man's shoulder.

I barely had time to find an uncomfortable position in the back, my legs tucked up behind the driver's seat, before the door opened and Clayton got in. He started the truck.

"What's up?"

He didn't answer. He jerked the truck back, throwing me off-balance. He spun around, went about a hundred feet, then slammed on the brakes and left me in the car as he went into the office, the motel keys jangling in his hand. I saw him shouting at the manager and the manager shouting back, and it looked like he might just walk around the counter and hit the guy. Finally, the manager threw some money at Clayton, and Clayton threw the keys back at him. And he stormed out to the truck, slamming the door as he got in.

He didn't say a thing as we headed off down the bare street to the freeway again. A few miles down, he pulled off at a ranch exit, drove down the dirt road a ways and turned off into the ditch. He climbed into the bed of the truck and pulled a saddle blanket over himself.

The truck leaned too much for me to sleep. All night long, I lay awake thinking about Charlie, wondering if he knew why I left, why I had to, at least part of why. But I knew he didn't. He couldn't. There was no good way for him to take it. I tried to concentrate on the image of his sleeping eyes and calm face, and eventually I fell asleep.

▲ ▲ ▲

THE WHITE BOY was getting thin, his eyes losing their color. White Bird thought he should be put to work, but Mo'é'ha'e's mother wouldn't allow it. She treated him as she would a sick child. She put food in front of him at mealtimes, wrapped him in blankets at night and spoke quietly to him even though he only stared away. But when she wasn't looking, Mo'é'ha'e took his food, and the dog began to get fat.

They brought him along when they went out to hunt for spring mushrooms, though Mo'é'ha'e thought he should be left lying mute in his sleeping robes. Her mother put the boy on a rock to sit in the sun, and Mo'é'ha'e helped with the gathering. They hunted the banks of the stream for morels. It was a perfect day, warm after some rain. In places the grass was still wet, but the mushrooms weren't turning out to be easy to find, and it looked as if a herd of elk might have gotten there ahead of them. There were little bite marks in the dirt here and there with just the white stem of the mushroom left in the indentation.

Mo'é'ha'e stayed close to her mother. She had something to talk about, and she was looking for the right moment when she wouldn't be hushed. Finally her mother paused. She stood up and breathed in deeply. The trees stirred as a spring breeze moved through the boughs.

"*Mother?*"

Sweet Rose Woman looked at her daughter of a million questions.

"*Mother, will we stay here?*"

"*Who knows. It's a hard time.*"

"*But, Mother, they found the buffalo. We have to stay.*" Mo'é'ha'e sat by a spring where the air felt damp and cool. "*I don't like the Kit Fox Soldiers,*" she said, thinking of one of the warrior societies that acted as a sort of police force for the tribe, helping settle disputes and organizing the moves. "*They never let us rest.*"

"*They are only looking out for us,*" she said, but she didn't like them much either. Last Bull had too much influence over them.

"*Mother?*"

"*Yes,*" she said patiently, recognizing the slightly formal introduction of something that Mo'é'ha'e had rehearsed.

"*Mother. Porcupine said this is our last summer, that we will have to move to the Agency and live with the Loaf-Around-the-Forts.*"

Her mother sat down with her. Porcupine was a mean little kid.

"*He's a liar,*" Mo'é'ha'e said confidently.

Her mother looked at the child's feet, her new moccasins, a first attempt at beading. She wanted to be able to say something that left room for hope. She probably wanted to believe herself that it was not hopeless, that the beautiful spring day was not a lie.

"Nobody knows what will happen."

"He says the white soldiers will come and kill me while I am sleeping, cut my throat and take my scalp."

She would have picked her daughter up, but she thought it would only scare her. *"Your uncle is a strong man, he is a shirt wearer for the tribe, and his medicine is very powerful against the enemy. He'll protect us if the white soldiers come."* She stood up to leave, but Mo'é'ha'e wasn't done.

"If we go to the forts, then there will be no horses for the tribe, then how will my uncle ask a bride price? Will I never be married?"

Her mother had to laugh. *"Not if you don't learn to sew."*

Mo'é'ha'e looked down at her hands.

"I have a surprise for you."

Mo'é'ha'e brightened, *"What?"*

Her mother unwrapped a small deerskin bundle and laid it in front of her daughter.

"What are they?"

"They are made by the white man. Your uncle found them in the raid. They're for sewing, to help you push the needle through the hide. You need just one." Her mother put one of the thimbles on Mo'é'ha'e's finger. It shone brightly in the sun. *"You must take care of it. Always wrap it up in the deerskin when you are done working with it. It's not for play."*

Mo'é'ha'e nodded, and the light from the thimble danced in her eyes.

"Okay. Go on now. Watch the boy for me, and finish your sewing."

Mo'é'ha'e left her mother and sat down in the shade a few

yards away from the boy. Her spot wasn't nearly as comfortable as his in the sun, though he seemed indifferent to the beautiful day. She tried to ignore him and enjoy her new present. She worked hard for a while, but she couldn't get the boy, who was sitting in a lump on the rock, out of her peripheral vision.

Mo'é'ha'e picked up a small rock. The boy was sitting perfectly still. *He has nothing to worry about,* she thought. *If the white soldiers come, they will rescue him. If he stays, he has all my mother's protection. He doesn't have to worry about anything.* She weighed the rock in her hand, warm from the sun. If her mother saw her, if she knew what she was contemplating, she would be in terrible trouble. She started to feel guilty. She shouldn't do it. But then she thought about moving to the forts, or the soldiers sneaking into her tent while she slept. She threw the rock hard and fast, hitting him in the shoulder. Though it bounced off of him with some force and must have hurt, he didn't turn; so she threw another rock.

"You stupid boy," she shouted. *"You're going to starve to death."*

Then she threw a big rock, almost big enough to knock him over, and it hit him hard in the back. She looked for her mother but she was still out of sight. She looked at the bright day, which seemed dimmed by her anger, as if a thin cloud had passed over the sun. She looked at the boy who was hurt, and she cried. The world blurred. She looked down at her sewing. It was a bad job, careless. Her tears made big, wet drops on the elk hide.

Mo'é'ha'e didn't see the boy through her tears as he got up painfully and slowly because he had not eaten for so long and he was weak. He stood in front of her, looking at her with those colorless eyes, and that pale, sickened white face.

"Don't cry," he said in English.

She heard the words, and though she didn't know what they

meant, she stopped crying. She watched the boy walk back to his rock to sit in the sun. After a minute, she found the lunch of dried meat and chokecherries her mother brought for them. She sat next to him, put it into his hands, and held them tightly so that he could not let the food go.

"*Meséestse*," she said. *You must eat.*

Chapter Fourteen

IT TOOK DAD a day to figure out I was gone. The first day, Friday, he headed off to work as usual. He didn't look up and see my window yawning open. And when he came home, though his coffee cup was still sitting by the back door, and the house must have felt subtly different, undisturbed, he didn't put it together. By evening, though, he came upstairs looking for me. He stood for a long time with his big hands resting on the frame of my door, looking at my unmade bed and then out the half-open window at the tree shifting in the fresh breeze. Finally, he walked to the window and looked down at the yard. I believe he could almost see me, the child me, running across the lawn with Sadie when she was a pup, or swinging high and slow in the tire-swing. He moved a step closer to the window to gaze at the empty yard, and his breath lingered there for a moment after he left my room.

THE NEXT MORNING he was out in the garage looking for the box. The thought must have come to him in the middle of the night. I know he never believed my answers about the Indian girl. Still it took him a while to decide that the box was actually gone, to believe that I had taken it. He went through the pile twice. Then he went outside and looked up at the hills, as if I might have left that way, just run off into the sagebrush with the box in my arms.

"Damn it!" he yelled, not caring what neighbor might hear.

He looked around as if he half expected to see some sign somewhere, some indication of which way I had gone. But he didn't know enough about me to have any idea where to begin looking. There were no tracks to follow. The rest of the day he told himself he was overreacting, that I would show up. He worked in the garage with the door open and an eye down the street, expecting me to come home at any moment.

After eating dinner alone, he went out onto the deck and sat on the steps and watched Mrs. Gibbs trim roses in the last of the summer light. Dad never seemed to consider what his face looked like when he was thinking hard about something. I don't think he had a clue how scary he could be. She quit in the middle of the job, as if she just remembered a phone call or something, and hurried back to her house. She must have thought it odd when Dad waved to her, the anger in his face so out of his control, wrecked like a derailed train.

He sat there until it got dark, and I imagine Mom's ghost walking out on to the deck to sit with him, wrapping a sweater around her shoulders as though she couldn't seem to keep warm enough. I don't even know if he would have noticed her, when she sat down next to him and took his cold hand with her cold hand and watched him worry. They'd always seemed paralyzed to me. Was there ever a time when they thought about running away together, found themselves doing something they had never planned? Not Dad. He always knew his next move. His arms were always so warm, but maybe that was only the symptom of good circulation that hid his true nature. And I don't get it, really, how you could go around with no idea at all of what you feel, no emotion, like some kind of experimental android.

I think he would say that he tried with Mom and with me, too. My running away was a mystery to him. Or maybe it wasn't. It's what he half expected, because I just couldn't get over it like he did. Move on. His hands lay uselessly on his knees, unable to help him. Mom was humming something, a song she made up, just pretty notes, disconnected. And maybe Dad could actually hear it, even though he would never admit to something like that.

CLAYTON AND I pulled into town, late in the afternoon. It was quiet, an honest-to-goodness cow town. The smell of the feedlot nearby was sweet and thick in the air. Clayton headed for the bar, and for a while I just sat in the truck. A group of girls passed on their way to some hangout, just like my friends at home, the same age, on the same mission, just a different town.

Eventually, I got tired of sitting in the pickup where I'd already spent most of the day. I wandered down the street and ended up going into an arts-and-crafts shop, the kind of place that sells needlepoint supplies and perfumed pillows with long-eared puppies to be embroidered on them and scented votive candles. The proprietor sat by her cash register tatting little white knots that would be doilies for somebody's wedding.

I guess there was something in the way I wandered around that gave me away. She watched me closely, and I caught little glimpses of her between the rows of Hallmark cards. The perfume in the store was heavy, like in JCPenney's, and it made me feel a little sick, hungry and nauseated at the same time. I started to walk out. But she stopped me.

"Can I help you find something in particular?"

I wished I wasn't the only person in the place. "Nah, I guess not."

"Needlepoint?"

"No. Thanks."

"Knitting?"

I could see her thinking, trying to figure out what I could be doing there, washed up in this little town. "No hobbies?"

"I guess not."

"You ought to take up sewing, young lady."

"Sewing?"

"It's practical. It's something useful. Make your own fashions. It could even be a career. Quick cash!" she chirped. "Your mother must have a machine."

"Sure." I said a little too brightly, and I could see that she sensed something wrong with my answer, that there was no mother.

She was watching me turn white. "Are you okay?"

"I need a bathroom."

She leaned her heavy bosom over the counter and pointed to the far back of her store.

"That way. Turn the light off when you're done, please."

I found the bathroom between the bolts of printed cloth and made a mad dash for the toilet, barely making it. All I wanted to do now was sneak out without a grilling from Mrs. Arts and Crafts. But today was not the day.

"Feeling better, sweetheart?"

I nodded weakly, and decided stupidly that buying something was the only way to escape. I picked out a couple of the Lion's Club mints by the register, and gave her two quarters. She gave me one of those grandmotherly looks that writes off a whole generation. And the irritating thing was that if she did know the truth, it would only have confirmed her judgments.

She reached for some colored index cards that she sold by the counter. You were supposed to use them to organize your craft projects somehow. God forbid, you have a messy hobby. I tried to take my mints and leave.

"Hold on honey, I want to give you something."

She wrote her name and the name of her pastor on a bright orange card with a purple pen. She handed it to me with a sincere smile. Now I felt like a jerk. She just wanted to help.

"Thanks."

"You don't have your mother around anymore?"

I took a breath. She'd guessed. "She passed away, Ma'am."

"I'm sorry, dear." She looked at me as I struggled to think of something else to say and came up empty.

"Your poor old dad doesn't know quite what to do with you, does he?"

"I don't know." My breath felt short again. "I really should go." I turned to leave.

"If you keep getting sick, you go see a doctor, okay?"

I turned at the door. "I'm alright."

She didn't say anything, just gave me that look Mom always gave when she knew I was lying about something, but she was going to let me get away with it. I nearly walked into a woman and her daughter as I stepped out onto the sidewalk. It was one of those awkward moves that makes you remember you don't belong.

▲ ▲ ▲

Mo'é'ha'e's uncle carried her on his shoulders through the new camp, talking to her about the confrontation with the white man that was coming, trying to prepare her for something that was beyond his own reckoning. No one knew what was going to happen, how it would end.

"*The buffalo are being killed off,*" he said quietly. At first the slaughter had seemed no more wasteful than a buffalo jump, but now some began to see it for what it was, a military strategy. Their survival depended on the buffalo.

"But the hunters found a great herd across the river; everyone is talking about it." Mo'é'ha'e frowned. It seemed as if every time the news was good, it was actually bad.

"Yes, but they're fooling themselves, making themselves blind, because no one knows what will happen when the buffalo are gone."

Mo'é'ha'e didn't answer. She was surprised by her uncle's sudden seriousness.

"Tomorrow we will go find the soldiers and steal some of their horses if we can."

"I want a black one."

He put her down and knelt in front of her, brushing her hair away from her eyes, and laughed.

Mo'é'ha'e smiled. *"How many horses will you ask for when it comes time for me to marry?"*

He looked away from her, hiding his smile, and she thought he was considering the question seriously, trying to come up with an answer. Would it be five, or ten, fifteen?

"How many do you think?" he asked.

She shrugged, frustrated that he was going to leave it up to her. But before she could respond, he took her shoulders in his strong hands and held her firmly.

"Sooner or later, soldiers will attack our camp. It will be before dawn and you will still be sleeping in your bed robes. It may seem like a dream at first. Everyone will run for the big trees by the river, and the warriors will get their guns and try to keep the horses from being run off. The soldiers will charge through camp, shooting at the people who are running away." He looked at her with fiery eyes now, dark and serious. *"You must not run. Stay in the tepee no matter what you hear, and cover yourself with buffalo robes, as many as you can."*

"But won't they catch me?"

He looked down at her feet. *"Did you make those moccasins?"*

She looked down, too, puzzled by her uncle, who seemed so preoccupied.

"Yes."

"The bead work is good."

He stood up, and looked off in the direction of the sun faintly coloring the sky. *"Soon, I will find for you a black horse."*

He turned to her again. He seemed almost angry. *"Remember what I said. You must hide."*

"But they'll find me, Uncle."

"Little one, you must do what I say." He turned to leave his niece, thinking of her extra burden, to have come into a world like this, where even the adults could make no sense of it. He turned back to her and looked her in the eyes. *"Hehnovetanoste, Mo'é'ha'e."* Be brave. *"I will ask twenty horses for you, and they must all be black horses. Now go home to eat."*

CHAPTER FIFTEEN

HUNGER WOKE ME. Clayton was sleeping in the bed of the truck in the clothes he was wearing yesterday, and the sun was already hot, turning his face red but not waking him. He was still drunk. I could smell it. I dressed behind the door of the pickup. I liked having only a few clothes to choose from. I put on what I had, and went to sit at a small picnic table in the community park where we'd stopped for the night.

When the automatic sprinklers came on, they woke Clayton. His eyes were puffy from the alcohol and the dust in the bed of the truck. He got up and headed for the bathroom. When he came out, he'd shaved and his hair was wet. It wasn't hard to see why Jennifer and a lot of girls would fall for a guy like him. I could tell he had already decided that I was a bit weird, and I could sense he was trying to come up with a plan to get rid of me. If he had been a different kind of guy he might have left me someplace already, taken off when I was out. At least he was not like that.

After breakfast we headed down to the rodeo grounds. By the afternoon it was so hot you could feel the sun firing the ground like clay in a furnace, and the boots of the crowds churned the dust into a haze that smelled of livestock, beer and popcorn. I found a place to lean on the fence near the chutes. Clayton was stretching in preparation for the bareback event which was up next. The cowboys were sitting in the dirt in back, taping their hands, spitting chew and laughing. The audience waited, a bit stunned by the heat, for the next bareback rider to come out of the chute.

Clayton was up. He had one foot on the gate, one leg already on the horse, and he was tying his hand into the front rigging. The horse kept dropping down in the chute and the cowboys had to harass it to get it back to his feet, then it made a wild attempt to climb right up out of the top of the gate. When it got a hoof caught in the rail, Clayton was obliged to get off until the animal calmed down enough to get unhooked. He slipped back on once it had stopped lunging and was reduced to a wild trembling. He'd drawn a crazy horse.

The bronc came out of the gate hunkered down, as if it wasn't going to do much bucking. Clayton was perched on top, his spurs up where they were supposed to be, by the bronc's shoulders, waiting for something to happen. The moment seemed longer than the actual time it filled; the horse, like Clayton, tensed with anticipation, its muscles drawn up tight. Then it jumped with such violence that Clayton was nearly ejected before he'd even started.

He held on as the horse began to spin, but gravity and the bronc's momentum were working against him. He raked his spurs at the horse's shoulders and bounced like a rag doll tied to the horse's back. When the bronc abruptly changed direction, Clayton's right arm jerked so hard it looked like it might come right off. The crowd cheered when he managed to stay on, but he was only half a second away from losing his grip. I could see it. He made it to the buzzer, almost limp, as if he might pass out, right there on the horse. The pick-up men rode in, and he let go of the horse and fell to the ground. It looked like a sure win, but he wasn't getting up. He was on his knees holding his right arm. I could tell before the crowd stopped applauding that he had separated his shoulder; it just didn't look right, and his face was white.

The medics came out. I watched them struggle with his arm, and for a few horrifying seconds I thought they were going to try to reset the arm right there in the arena. But I guess they thought better of it and got him up on his feet, supporting him by his good arm. Clayton got another cheer from the crowd, and I could tell he had already decided despite the pain that this was a glorious moment. The judges gave him a seventy-eight and I could see him thinking he was going to lift that right arm for a victory salute, but the arm wouldn't move. When I got to him at the medic's wagon waiting for the doctor to show up, he'd already declared victory, though there was still another section of riders and his seventy-eight wasn't invincible.

"Did you see that horse?"

"Yeah, how's your arm?"

"It's alright."

"It doesn't look alright."

"It's just numb. Did you hear any higher score yet?"

"Nah, the next guy didn't make it very long."

He smiled. He figured he had it nailed. But then the crowd was cheering again, and it was hard to tell. Had they already forgotten him? He listened intently, trying to decipher if his score had just been beat.

"I think the judges docked me for getting hurt. I should have just got up and walked off on my own."

When the doctor came in, he seemed put out. He hardly glanced at Clayton's arm, which was hanging unnaturally low. Clayton smiled with a wince, but the doctor ignored him. Instead he looked at me. It was a small trailer, and I was in the way.

"Who are you?"

"Nobody. Just a friend."

The doctor looked over at Clayton and then back at me again. "Well, nobody, just a friend, you need to leave so I can jerk this kid's arm back where it belongs. Okay?"

I walked around the rodeo for a while, bought some popcorn, a waste of money I didn't have, and by the time I got back to the stands everyone was leaving, getting in their trucks and turning on their radios. I wandered out around the back to the chutes. The cowboys looked as if they'd been through a battle, wrapping wounds, sitting exhausted in the dust. Among all the cowboy hats and crew cuts an Indian lay on his back breathing hard.

When I got back to the medic's wagon, Clayton was sitting outside on the wood step. His arm was in a sling, and he was drinking a beer with his good hand. The bareback was won by eighty. He didn't look in a lot of pain, but he looked mad. He glared at me as if I were the one who had yanked his arm out of its socket.

"Four weeks. Four son-of-a-bitchin' weeks," he said and took a big gulp of beer. "I guarantee I'm not waiting four weeks. I'll be back in two. You watch."

The sun was just about down. The thick breeze blowing off the arena was finally beginning to cool. I didn't ask Clayton what he was planning to do, if he had enough money to last even two weeks. The purse he'd won for second was paltry. He stood up after a while, and we went down to the main street of town to celebrate by blowing a bunch of the cash on a steak. He ate the meat, twenty ounces, and I ate the potato and the dried-up little carrots and rusted lettuce from the salad bar. Next to us was a couple who looked dressed up like they might have come from a prom. They were sitting on the same side of the table sharing a Diet Coke and a dessert that was mostly whipped cream.

Clayton paid for his meal and I followed him outside. It was a special night because of the rodeo. They'd closed off Main Street and three bands had set up along its length, one every couple of blocks. We wandered for a while through the swarms of mostly high-school-age kids or older folks. The cowboys and their girls were crowded into the bars, since they were not allowing drinks out on the street. Clayton wanted me to come in with him, but they seemed to be pretty serious about carding, and the bars were so crowded anyway it looked like you'd have to fight your way in. I sat down on the sidewalk to wait, leaning against the old brick building, watching the heavy traffic of boots on the pavement, or the grinning faces against the last glow of the evening sky.

There were no Indians out on the street that night. I guess they went somewhere else to celebrate. I thought about Charlie, what he might be doing, and I guess I didn't even know enough about him, really, to imagine. Still my chest felt tight and I could only make the feeling go away by tightening the rest of me, my fists and my jaw until my fingers were numb and I couldn't breathe.

I felt weak and afraid. I wanted to curl up on the sidewalk, hold my knees to my face and protect this child inside from the darkening sky.

▲ ▲ ▲

MO'É'HA'E LEARNED THE white boy's name, Henry, a difficult and strange word for her to pronounce. They lay on their backs on a bluff above camp, looking up at the night sky. Below them, fires lit the cottonwoods and cast long, distorted shadows. Henry named the stars he knew and drew their constellations. He knew Ursa Major, the great bear changed by Zeus from the nymph Callisto, and Polaris, the star that kept him company across the wide curve of the plains, always on the right, and he remembered being shown the white warrior, Hercules, though that constellation was faint and hard to see.

Henry had learned a few words of Cheyenne. He knew words

that were important to Mo'é'ha'e—*náhko'éehe,* "my mother," and *naxãne,* "my uncle." He knew "meat" and "buffalo," and "dog," *oeškeso.* He'd learned "quiet," *he'kotóo'estse!* And he knew the words, or the general sound of them, for the moving of camp.

Mo'é'ha'e pointed to the stars, *hotóhkeo'o.* She swept her hand across the glowing cloud of the Milky Way, *Améó'o,* the path across the sky that led her people to the afterlife.

"My father," Henry said, thinking of heaven.

She pointed to the sky and tried the English. "My father."

CHAPTER SIXTEEN

DAD FOUND THE kids by the Circle K by accident. He'd spent the day looking for me in all the places he could think of. He'd even gone to Jennifer's house, but she wasn't there, and when it came to admitting to her mother that he hadn't seen me for two nights, he decided to skip it. He acted as if he must have just had the name wrong and that I was sleeping over at someone else's house. It was late in the evening when he drove by some kids hanging out in the bed of an old pickup by a Circle K.

They probably thought he was going to offer to buy for them. What else would motivate an adult to walk over? Unless maybe he was out to bum a cigarette. He approached them as though he was expecting a problem, and he must have looked scary, as big as he is. One of the boys hopped off the tailgate to intercept him, took a long drag on the end of his smoke and threw it at his feet.

"Buy us a six-pack?"

"That all?"

The boy laughed. "That's all the money we got, old man."

"My name is Jack."

"Yeah?"

One of the girls shouted from behind, "So what about the six-pack, Jack?"

Somebody mumbled it. "Six-pack, Jack."

Dad's arms rested calmly at his sides as he scanned the group, looking for me. The boy who approached him sat back down on the tailgate.

"Hey, we don't want any hassle, man."

A car pulled in behind Dad, a rumbling Trans-Am. The driver got out, glanced over at the proceedings as he headed in. His girlfriend sat up, half watching Dad and the kids, half playing with the fur dice that hung from the rearview mirror.

"My daughter's name is Erin, Erin Douglass."

The kids were silent.

"I guess we don't know her, old man. So why don't you shove off?"

Dad should have had a boy, or maybe he shouldn't have, but he sure didn't like back talk, not from some kid, not some cigarette-smoking, weird-haired kid. In two quick steps he was standing almost on top of him. "You need to learn some better manners."

The kid looked up at him; for a second he was afraid, and then he wasn't. He'd been hit before. Dad sat next to him and put an arm around him, as though he was the boy's father. The Trans-Am guy came back out, noticing Dad sitting with the kid. He gave them a puzzled look as he started up his car and pulled away.

"That's no way to talk." He held his shoulders tightly in his arm. I'm sure the boy would rather have been hit. It would have been less humiliating. "Who here knows my daughter?"

Nobody answered again. And Dad just sat with them. He wasn't going anywhere. Finally, one of the girls spoke up.

"She didn't hang with us."

Dad looked at her. He picked up on the past tense. The boy was getting impatient.

"Get your fucking arm off me, man," he tried.

Dad ignored him, holding tighter. "But you know she's gone, right?"

"Yeah, maybe."

"Where?"

The kids decided talking was the only way to get rid of him.

"We don't know."

"Ah, come on. Sure you do."

"She didn't hang with us, really. Swear to God."

"You oughta ask her boyfriend. Maybe he knows." One of the boys shouted from inside the cab. Dad hadn't noticed him before. The girl next to the boy put her hand over his mouth.

Dad stood up, letting go of the boy on the tailgate.

"He didn't know about the boyfriend," laughed one of the girls near Dad.

"Shit, everybody knows," another said.

"Daddy never knows," the girl giggled.

Dad started to leave.

"For a six-pack, we'll tell you who he is."

"Six-pack, Jack!"

The boy he'd been holding was still angry. His face was red. "Ah, fuck it. Your goddamn Indian-loving daughter ran off with him like a fucking squaw." The boy's voice was hoarse and dry from cigarettes.

Dad stopped.

"Uh-oh, shouldn't have told him that. Daddy doesn't like Indians," one of the girls said.

The boy looked defiantly at Dad. "She ran away with a reservation kid, Pop. Hear me?"

"You just blew our free six-pack all to hell."

Dad walked back to his truck, thinking hard.

"Fuck you, old man," the kid shouted after him, spite thickening his voice.

One of the kids hit him on the shoulder. "I bet he has a gun in that truck. He's gonna come back over here and blow your fuckin' head off. He looks pretty psycho to me."

"Shut up, okay?"

"Hey, Pop!" the boy in front shouted.

Dad didn't respond; he opened his truck door. The kids scrambled into the back of their truck in case a quick getaway became necessary.

"Hey Pop, don't you want to know his name?" He shouted, "For a six-pack!"

Dad ignored them. He didn't want to know a name. He put the truck in gear. He noticed the guy behind the counter in the Circle K watching him, as though he'd been keeping an eye on the situation. As Dad drove back to the house, I think there was a sick feeling in his gut and the empty house was a slap in the face. Its dark windows stared back at him, making the point; he didn't know what to do.

FOR A COUPLE of autumns, when I was eleven or twelve, Dad and I used to get up early in the mornings together, when it was still dark. He would knock softly on the door of my room, but I would be awake already. We'd eat a quiet bowl of corn-flakes, and whisper while he sipped his coffee. Then we'd sneak out the back door. You could feel the dew settling. I remember the sound and feeling of sitting in the cab of the truck, while the diesel rattled and warmed up, the smell of our dog, Sadie, who we let ride in front with us.

Hardly saying anything, we'd drive out of town, way out. Finally, we'd come to this spot where a brushy creek crossed the road. And we'd almost always be there too early and have to wait for the light to come up. We'd listen to the doves anticipating it. There ought to be a word for the sound they make. It isn't cooing, like pigeons. Not at all. It's one of those untame sounds that belong only to places that are wide open.

Then Dad would take the shotguns from the rack in the rear window. He had a 16 gauge, and I had a .410, an old one which was his when he was a kid. And he'd fill a couple pockets in his jacket with shells from the glove box, and we'd start walking.

Sadie was suddenly alive. She'd take off ahead of us until Dad called her back in. And we would hike until lunch. We were hunting for sharptails, pheasant, prairie grouse or doves. Most of the time, I never got anything. Dad would get the one sharptail we did see. I usually didn't even shoot. I knew he'd get it; he wouldn't want to take the chance I might miss. Mom hated grouse. She refused to cook it because she didn't like the smell. Dad would put it in the freezer, and one day he'd barbecue it when friends were over and end up eating it by himself.

But this one time we got into a mess of doves. They were everywhere. And even with my .410, I hit a few. I remember the first one Dad took from Sadie's mouth and put in the back of my hunting vest. I could feel its warm weight against the small of my back. And Dad and I felt like great hunters who had gone out into the wilderness and provided.

He piled the cleaned birds by the sink in the kitchen. There were a lot, and I remember the birds in Mom's hands as she prepared them. She held each dove one at a time lying on its back, its wings falling to either side of her wet hand.

We never went again. Maybe it was because I was getting older, wearing dresses and he assumed I didn't want to go anymore. Or maybe we just didn't have time. I don't remember. But it was quiet around the house, because more and more we were all so busy, and Dad and Mom weren't talking much. Dad got home so late most of the time, anyway.

• • •

THAT NIGHT, THE night he was looking for me, Dad sat in front of the house, and I know any memory, any thought of Mom or me was like an ache in his bones. He was afraid to go find me, afraid to move at all. Finally, he got out of the truck and walked into the house without turning the lights on. He grabbed a coat and a shirt and a couple pairs of socks and threw them into a bag. He grabbed some Fig Newtons and an apple from the refrigerator and took all the stuff back out to the truck.

He was digging around in the toolbox looking for a thermos to fill with black coffee when several kids from the gas station drove by. Jennifer climbed out when the car stopped and leaned back on the hood waiting for Dad to come around the truck. He'd found his thermos and was walking back toward the house. He almost missed seeing the car, but when he did, he stopped. Jennifer didn't move. She was as cool as a teenager can be, waiting for Dad to come to her. The boys in the car turned the music up so that all Dad could hear was the boom of the bass. They were laughing about something. There was fire in Jennifer's eyes.

Dad was puzzled; he didn't remember seeing her among the kids at the Circle K. But she must have been the girl he couldn't see in the cab of the truck. There was a hard, sexual look to her. He didn't walk over too close but stood in the driveway with nowhere to put his hands.

"Hey, Jack."

"Jennifer." He answered warily. This was not the girl he knew. I guess she felt different, too, after Clayton—stronger and weaker.

She looked away down the street. Dad looked too. There was nothing there, just an empty suburban block. It was quiet. Riverview was asleep.

"I'm not going to tell you his name."

Dad looked at her. "Is that what you drove all the way over here to say?" He started to walk back to the truck.

"No."

The song stopped. The boys came back to the realization that they were waiting on some sleepy subdivision street far away from the action.

"Hey, Jennifer. Get back in the car. We're outta here."

"Cool it, assholes." Her face changed as she turned back to Dad, for a moment unable to completely hide the emotion that was shaking her. She looked hurt, like a little girl who would like to cry and be held.

"That Indian boy . . . "

"Yeah."

She stopped for a long pause.

"Yeah?"

"He got her pregnant."

Dad's hands knotted in fists, suddenly clammy and cold. He stared at Jennifer with a face that scared her. She jumped off the hood to get back into the car.

"About time. Let's get the hell out of here," one of the boys said, then leaned out of the window, and shouted as if he was at a football game taunting the opposition. "You owe us some beer, Jack." The engine of the car revved loudly. The boy driving had forgotten to put it in gear. The other guys forgot about Dad as they jumped on the opportunity to make fun of the driver. The boy popped it into first and the car lurched forward.

Jennifer leaned out the window. "Charlie White Bird. That's the father's name!"

I've tried but I've never been able to imagine how Dad reacted. I can see his face, that's easy, but not what was inside.

CLAYTON REEMERGED FROM the bar no doubt feeling better, or at least numb, as he leaned in the doorway with his arm in the sling. "Wanna dance?"

"Yeah sure," I said, wishing that there could be another response. "Do you think you can?"

He grinned a lazy, drunken smirk.

So we danced with the rodeo crowds in the warm summer air.
It was mostly kids dancing, and it was unexpectedly fun. Clayton
was a good dancer; the rhythm was right, the steps were right,
even with his bad arm. The whole time he watched me with a wild
eye. He wouldn't let go of me, and we danced for an hour until the
band took a break, and then we danced to the canned music they
left on in between.

He held onto me when I tried to slow down, and people started
watching us, wondering what was up. Clayton's drinking had
begun to hit him, and he started staggering as much dancing. I
leaned closely to his ear to speak.

"Clayton, I have to stop."

He spun me one more time and dipped me dramatically, acting as if he was going to kiss me, but he didn't. He loomed over
me and said, "Let's go."

It was almost a mile to the edge of town and the park, and as
we walked, I listened to our footsteps. Though mine scraped and
clicked unevenly, his fell rhythmically, each step heavy and determined. The closer we got to the park, the more afraid I became,
and the more I thought I knew what Clayton had in mind.

His hand held mine too tightly. I wasn't sure how to react, because part of me expected and assumed this, too. But part of me
could not understand how you could owe something like that,
and what that was, if it was owed, or given, or taken, as some
kind of payment. I know that Clayton never thought of it exactly
like that. But when we got there he pushed me against the truck
and kissed me. I kept my mouth tightly closed but his breath was
so strong with alcohol, it made my gut wretch. And when it seemed

there had been enough of that, his hands began to move on. They felt angry, his bad luck I guess.

"Clayton, no." I tried to say it gently first. I guess I didn't want him to be too embarrassed later. Also I think I was paralyzed by the guilty feeling that I had brought this on myself, that the conventions that were meant to protect me, the things that I had been taught, had been left behind the moment I thought of this possibility back at the Broken Spur Motel and came with him anyway. I tried to get out from between him and the truck, but he grabbed my arm, and it hurt.

"Knock it off! Stop it!" I said much louder. The pain of his grip made me angry enough to react. I hit him as hard as I could on his injured shoulder. And it must have hurt, too. He moaned and dropped to his knees.

I moved away quickly, and he didn't come after me. He stayed kneeling on the ground with his head against the truck. He was silent. He was so drunk I wondered if he would even remember this happened. I waited to see if he would get up but he didn't. So I left him alone. I climbed into the cab of the truck and locked the doors. After a while I heard him get up and crawl into the truck bed. I fell asleep in the cab under his coat that smelled sickeningly of him.

IN THE MORNING Clayton banged on the hood of the truck to wake me up. He didn't say a word, not about last night, not about the truck being locked. Either he was embarrassed or, more likely, he told himself that I'd led him on and then changed my mind. It was *my* problem.

We headed north this time, back in a loop to a rodeo up in South Dakota, right on the border of Montana. Puffs of white clouds stretched in uncanny, quilted evenness across the wide horizon. He laid his foot on the gas and the truck surged ahead even faster. The fence along the side of the road sped to a blur, and the wind blasted through the window. A butterfly caught in the hood ornament, its vivid purple wings trembling in the gale. I wondered at the sensation, to be caught like that and suddenly hurled at this terrific speed, racing through the blue-and-white sky.

He had a shortcut in mind. We pulled off the highway and took a dirt road for some miles northwest. The washboard was heavy, but Clayton took it at such speed that we hardly noticed the vibration unless we tried to talk. He talked about girls. I think he figured out that I wouldn't let him touch me again. We both knew it. So he was punishing me, or not that, he was scolding me. He just wanted to make sure I knew that all the other girls had wanted it, wanted him. He even talked about Jennifer, as though he had forgotten that we were friends. And I was glad to know that he would never talk about me that way.

The sky was simmering and the beaten gravel of the road looked hot. Cattle wound slowly through the sagebrush and grass looking for water, and when we passed a stock tank in the distance, it looked like an oasis. I could easily imagine these rolling grass hills covered with buffalo and antelope.

I felt free on this ribbon of county road, on this empty dirt track, and I felt captive. Captured. I couldn't help looking at the pine ridges and imagining them lined with hostile Indians, the way everyone thinks of Indians, lining a mesa, ready to descend like wilderness devils on the poorly protected, God-fearing settlers. But it was just me I saw, alone, walking, my horse left some miles back, still standing with its head down waiting for the inevitable. And when they rush down the hill whooping and coming to kill me for being a white invader foolish enough to run out of horse in this open plain, they begin by beating me with clubs. Killing comes after. I picture it the way children playing Cowboys and Indians would, as torture—stinging ants, the blinding sun, and finally death, scalping and my body left, ruined, in a plain so empty that even the coyotes would only find me by chance. And these warriors, whose hands and arms and faces are covered with my blood, race their horses to the north as free men.

▲ ▲ ▲

JUST AFTER DAWN, half a sun hovering at the horizon, White Bird and the warriors charged into camp, racing from one end to the other, raising the alarm. Mo'é'ha'e scrambled out of her tepee behind her mother. Everyone was rushing out of their lodges, and there was a lot of confusion. They all expected to see the U.S. cavalry charging into one end of the camp, the attack already under way. Some yelled for the men to get their horses and their guns. Some picked up the youngest children, ready to run for the cover of thick cottonwoods by the river. But as the warriors doubled back, Mo'é'ha'e could hear her uncle shouting that there were no soldiers yet.

Eventually the tribe's warrior societies were able to calm the people down, and everyone gathered in a group in the middle of camp around White Bird and the seven warriors who had made the warning with him. Mo'é'ha'e stood as close to her uncle as she could. He was covered with sweat and dirt, and she could feel the heat coming off his body.

The men had been hunting buffalo about a day's ride to the southwest when they saw some riders which they took to be their allies the Lakota. They planned an ambush as a joke, but when they charged over the hill they saw that the riders were Crow scouts and right behind them there was Crook's cavalry moving steadily downriver, over a thousand men and horses. White Bird and the other hunters raced back down the hill as fast as their horses could carry them. There was very little cover anywhere except in the river bottom, and if the scouts cleared the hill, they would easily spot them. White Bird hugged his horse's neck and hissed in its ears to encourage it to run even faster.

The Cheyenne reached the trees in the nick of time, but they didn't stop. They crashed through the thick brush that tore at their bare arms and legs, like a mad swarm of bees, making them bloody. Flies-High-Above lost his pair of binoculars, a prized trophy taken from a dead soldier many summers ago, but he did not stop. They ran for two or three miles before they paused to catch their breath. They stood in the middle of the river letting the water cool the horses, while their hearts pounded. No one spoke, and then a flock of crows flew overhead, cawing a warning and spurring them back into flight.

Soon the horses could no longer run, but kept at a steady trot, staying with the river to keep out of the open plain. And when night came without a moon, the horses were tired, stumbling over the slick riverbed, shaking and frightened, and the warriors were covered with dried blood, exhausted. But they rode the rest of the night without stopping again. By the time the moon finally did come up, some of the horses could only manage a walk. White Bird's horse stumbled and they fell together into a deep black hole of the cold river. The horse swam wide-eyed to the shore. White Bird held a knot of mane in his fist and came up out of the water with the horse without ever losing his seat.

Mo'é'ha'e looked up at the faces around her. The people seemed excited, not afraid; they wanted a good fight with the white soldiers. There were more Cheyenne warriors gathered already than had ever been in one place, and they felt strong and ready. They sent a young man to tell Crazy Horse, who was camped with several hundred Lakota warriors only two miles farther downriver.

Mo'é'ha'e followed on her uncle's heels, and she asked about the number of white soldiers and where the battle would be and who could win it, but got no answers from him. She and Henry stopped outside his tepee as he went in, and they sat by the fire with White Bird's oldest son and watched in awe and fear as the warriors in their camp prepared for the fight. They had killed a badger and put the animal's blood in a wide bowl. As each warrior filed past its slick surface, he looked for his reflection. If he saw himself as an old man, he knew he would survive the battle.

THE ARMY HAD camped less than fifteen miles away. At dawn, orders came that they would march in two hours, which seemed ponderously slow to the Captain. His Crow were already prepared to leave. They vented their impatience by racing through camp, getting their horses into a second wind and shouting war songs. The Captain checked his supply of ammunition. It seemed ample. He checked the action of his revolver which was well oiled and showed no rust despite the constant exposure to weather. The hammer clicked back with precision and released smoothly and easily with pressure on the trigger. His horse stamped its feet and pawed the ground, anxious to be with the other horses which were still grazing nearby, but the Captain knew to pull his animal off the grass before a fight. It was something he'd learned from the Indians. His horse would run longer on an empty stomach. He would let him drink his fill of water, though, when they crossed the river.

The Captain gave orders to his sergeant to be ready to ride in half an hour; he intended to be waiting for the generals. "At this rate, Sergeant, the enemy will find us in *our* camp."

The Captain looked over to the Crow, wildly painted and

adorned with dried scalps and ragged feathers. This is what they were fighting, this savageness, this possession of the wild, to bring some sort of dignity and order to the conduct of men, some progress out of the wilderness. The Captain had a word—civilization.

MO'É'HA'E COULD ONLY imagine the fight. The soldiers never made it as far as the camp, not even close enough for her to be able to hear the shouts, or the guns, or even the dull thud of the cavalry's cannon. She sat by the river with her sewing. It was unseasonably hot, and cicadas buzzed in the trees overhead. Henry looked afraid, his face like that of a ghost, but she didn't speak to him. She could not calm the angry feeling in her chest, the dryness in her throat. She looked away from him at the water for a long time and half expected to see it turn red with blood from the fight upstream. But the water was clear, the gravel bed merely golden.

By the end of the day, she could not stand it anymore, not knowing what was happening, wondering who might have been killed. She left Henry with her dog and went to climb the bluff above camp.

Instead of taking the long way around the back where the slope was gentler, she climbed the outcropping directly. She picked her way through the tumble of rocks below the bluff until she came to a wide cliff. It was twenty feet or so up to a ledge, but after that it looked like it would be only a short distance to the top. She scrambled up the first third without much difficulty, but then she came to a place where the next good handhold was just out of reach. She looked down and because of the steep slope at the foot of the bluff, the drop looked even worse than it was. Getting down was going to be almost as risky as trying for that handhold. She shouted out loud as she strained, digging her nails into the rock and finding places to grab where there were none.

When she made it to the ledge she lay down with her heart pounding. Her fingertips were bloody. She felt like crying, but she did not know if it was from the fear of nearly falling, or because she was so worried that her uncle would not return from the fighting. She stood and walked the rest of the way to the top of the bluff. It was late in the afternoon and heavy thunderclouds obscured the sun. She'd known she might not be able to see anything, even from that height, and there was nothing more than a small herd of elk grazing in the middle distance. She sat in the grass and laid her head back against a rock.

She woke to the sound of thunder, which for a second of panic sounded like the army cannon, until it faded and rumbled out across the hills. It began to rain, and she rose with the heavy feeling that she must have been sleeping for some time. To the southwest she could see the groups of riders coming back to camp. They walked their horses slowly, not retreating, but not clearly victorious, either. There seemed to be many, but there was no way to count and guess how many might have been killed. The rain fell in fat, summer-sized drops, soaking her hair and pouring down her face. Drums beat in the camp, signaling a victory dance, and that made her hopeful as she ran down the shallow slope at the back of the cliff to see if her uncle had come home.

She got there as he was riding in, and she picked him easily out of the group. To her he looked a little bigger than the rest. The dancing began, and she darted through the wild and joyous legs trying to get close to her uncle. The celebration in the camp was big, almost bigger than the battle, wilder than Mo'é'ha'e had ever seen. The Cheyenne and Lakota had met the column of soldiers on the field and turned them back. It was not the massacre of a village, like Sand Creek or Washita, not the murder of women and children and old people. The strength of the warriors had stopped a thousand U.S. troops and more than two hundred of their Indian allies. A great fire was built and it cast their shadows up into the trees as if their spirits might just dance away, up into the night sky. It would have been a good time, too, to leave, early in the summer of 1876, before the end of June.

CHAPTER SEVENTEEN

I WAS SICK. At every stop my face turned a new shade of green. I was hungry, but the thought of food made me feel worse. Clayton still hadn't figured out anything. Boys can be pretty stupid. I guess he thought I was just like that—sick all the time, not wanting to eat, starving myself, anorexic or bulimic.

Clayton still planned to follow the rodeos so he'd be ready to compete the moment he decided his arm was up to it. He was now sure he'd be ready in two weeks, though I could see it still hurt him a lot. We arrived in a small town at the foot of the Black Hills of South Dakota at dusk. It was like every other we had passed, a historic Main Street ringed by chain restaurants, motels and Quick Marts. Nearby was a famous mine called the "Open Cut." Billions in gold had been dug out of the mountains, but you couldn't see that from town; from there the hills looked wild and untouched.

We stopped at the grocery store that had a twenty-four-hour pharmacy. Clayton came back with Advil and some mega-vitamins, and handed them to me as though they were flowers.

He reached them across the center console with his injured arm, twisting his body awkwardly to manage it. It was sweet.

"Thanks."

He got back into the truck. "Let's hit the motel tonight. A regular shower."

I nodded. It was up to him anyway, but he wanted me to appreciate the offer, and I tried to smile through my nausea.

We got the room, and I lay in one of the two beds facedown in the pillow, which smelled of stale cigarette smoke. Just a few months ago, I could never have imagined this future. I'd always planned to leave home as soon as I could, but I was going to finish high school first then maybe go to Bozeman to MSU, or at the farthest Missoula to U.M. I never thought of going east, and going nowhere. I buried my face deeper in the pillow and fell asleep listening to the muffled sound of Clayton whistling in the shower.

Sometime in the middle of the night, I woke up. Clayton had put a blanket over me, though he was gone. A streetlight cast weak shadows of the window frame onto the threadbare carpet. In my stomach I felt something like bubbles, which I thought had to be the baby. She probably didn't have hands yet, really, but I imagined them anyway, laying softly against my tummy on the inside, reassuring me.

The night was a safe place to think these kinds of things, no faces of people who didn't know me, who would tell me that I could not do it alone. I had no money, no job, no place to live. A chill washed over me and the blankets were not enough to keep me warm. What would Mom have said, what would she have told me to do? I looked into the moonlight glowing on the dull carpet. She might have held me and shaken her head. She would have wanted to know who the father was. And I think it would have surprised her. No. It would have shaken her up pretty good. She might have had to look away, to think about it, but there would be no question about keeping the baby. I don't think there would be. Maybe she would even take care of her for me after she was born, for a while at least, so I could do the things I still needed to do, like finish high school.

I could hear Mom saying the practical things. "Honey, you have to find a place to have this child. Nine months is not forever, and soon you'll start to show, and people will know you are pregnant. Strangers. Everyone."

And Dad? How could I explain it to him? I used to sit in his lap, begging to be teased, knowing that he would do anything for his little girl. I guess I didn't really know how it felt to have a father anymore. I didn't know how to explain the change in him. When I was younger, he was everything, or maybe it was that I had the power to make him everything, and when I lost that, he was what he was, and what he is—not that much of a dad and the only dad I have. I'd gotten in the habit of not needing a father. I guess he had to feel that. Would it have ever mattered if Mom hadn't died and left us all alone?

DAD WAITED UNTIL late in the morning to go find Charlie. It took him some time to decide that's what he needed to do, but once he was on his way he smashed through the gears as he climbed the windswept hills up to the pine ridges of the reservation. It was a colorless day, one of those days when the clouds drag on the hills and remind you that winter can visit almost any month in Montana.

In Lame Deer he stopped at the casino. The building was newly finished so there was no landscaping, only plain dirt on a fresh grade and a Dumpster out front full of insulation scraps and busted-up sheetrock. Inside the smell of new carpeting and paint competed with clouds of cigarette smoke. The main room was in the shape of a big circle like a traditional lodge. It was dimly lit with a fine line of blue neon that wrapped around the room and glinted off the new gaming machines. Only a few were attended by gamblers. The cash register was run by a middle-aged Cheyenne woman. She sat reading a newspaper, *Indian Country,* by the greenish-white fluorescent light of her booth. She didn't look up when Dad stopped in front of her.

"Excuse me," he said, his voice a little hoarse.

She set her paper down and reached over to open the register, assuming he wanted quarters for the poker machines.

"No, I don't need any change. I'm looking for somebody."

She looked him straight in the eye. "*Who* are you?"

"Nobody. Don't worry. I'm not the law . . . just looking for a kid who sometimes works for me."

"What for?"

"He didn't show up at work," he tried.

She almost laughed. "And you come lookin' for him?"

"Look, I just need to find him. It's not a problem. Charlie White Bird is his name."

"Lotta White Birds." She shook her head.

"You don't know him?"

"What do you think, huh? He's an Indian so I should know him?" She laughed. "No, I can't help you." She picked up her paper and started reading it without looking up at him again.

After a minute of just standing there, Dad walked away. He was mad, but there was nothing he could do. A man at one of the machines reached out and stopped him as he was about to pass. He was a big guy, and his hands looked clumsy touching the screen to draw new cards. His face was puffy as though he hadn't slept that night. He whispered, "Who ya lookin' for?"

Dad looked over his shoulder at the woman at the cash register. The man pulled on his arm to get him to move so the machine was blocking her view and said it again a little louder. "Who ya lookin' for, man?"

"White Bird. Charlie White Bird."

"Yeah, I know him. Sure." His face went blank, waiting for Dad. He rolled the few quarters he had left in his palms.

It took Dad a moment to notice. He took out a ten and gave it to the guy, who folded it quickly into his pocket. He told Dad where to go, and thanked him with a big handshake and a loud voice that made the cashier look up.

DAD PULLED OFF the highway into the town the man had told him about. It was beginning to rain, and the streets looked deserted. The wet, faded houses and shacks were scattered along the red-dirt side roads. A few horses stood with their tails to the wind, heads low. The air smelled heavy from fires burning sappy wood. A dog ran out and squared off with the truck, barking at the grille. Dad stopped, glaring back at the puny, fuming mutt. He gave the horn a blast and raced the truck forward, nearly running it over.

He drove slowly, looking down each street for Charlie. The guy at the casino had given him the description of a house, but now that he was here it seemed to apply to at least half of them. He turned down another street with deep potholes. A child ran out in front of him, hurrying to get out of the rain. She hit all of the puddles she could, splashing brown muddy water on her pale-yellow dress. Then the street was empty again. He stopped at the end and turned the truck around to watch the neighborhood, the rain falling on the scattered buildings and yards, soaking laundry and plastic red wagons and broken Big Wheels, piles of cinder blocks and barely functioning bicycles, old wrecks running and not, hairless dolls, and flat balls. He watched the dust become mud, and off in the distance, he watched the clouds boil.

The windshield wipers swiped the window with a wet squeak. He was trying to decide what to do. Or maybe he wasn't yet; maybe he was too angry to actually think. He worked his jaw, and imagined that somewhere, in one of these houses, the Cheyenne had me as a kind of captive, as if this were some old Cowboy and Indian movie, and he was meant to take that gun, that black pistol he kept hidden under his seat, storm in, gun blazing, and take me home to our town of white dresses and white churches and white clouds and white people. The pure stupidity of his rage broke over him like a wave.

He got out of the truck not sure of where he was headed, but going there anyway. He walked to the low, blue house where a dog was barking. His footprints behind him were black in the mud. He pushed through the gate, leaving it open, and up to the window, and peered into the dark interior. No one was home. He saw the blackened face of a TV set and on top of it some photographs, a well-used couch, almost bare walls, and a shelf full of tiny horses and bears, puppies with big wet eyes. It was somebody's grandparents' house, not Charlie's.

The next house was also dark. There was no gate, no landscaping, nothing added to the empty lot and simple rectangular house provided by the NCHA. The bare cement foundation was unadorned, like the graphite pencil of the bureaucrat who'd requisitioned it. A bare bulb above the door had been left on and cast a feeble warm light on his face as he peered through the uncurtained window. Inside, things were much the same. Utilitarian. A table with metal legs and four chairs, a plain brown couch, a bag of something next to it on the floor. A shelf with a few books, fat worn paperbacks. And then a TV, which was on.

He tried the door. It was unlocked. Inside, the air was stale from closed windows, as though no one had been there in a while. He looked cautiously up and down the street then walked into the house and shut the door behind him. The TV blared a daytime soap.

He went into the kitchen. There were dishes in the sink, and the room smelled of bacon. On the table, next to a plate with yellow egg dried on it was a pile of mail. He picked it up, and started to go through it looking for names. There was White Bird on every one of them. He walked back into the living room and watched the TV without registering it for half a minute.

"Damn it." His hands were shaking. He looked around the room, as if desperate to find something, anything, that could tell him what to do next, any clue that could help him solve this problem, which had gotten out of his control.

He walked over to the TV with an eerie calmness, and then he kicked in the screen with his boot. It almost exploded, smoking as the internal workings shorted out and filled the room with the smell of burnt wire. Then he ransacked the place. He pulled the bookshelves down, pulled drawers out and threw them across the room. He behaved as if he might actually be looking for something, but there was nothing to find. It wasn't Charlie's house, either. Half that town was named White Bird. He hurt his hands, cutting them and bruising the knuckles. His face sweat and gathered dust, and he kicked holes in the walls until he injured his foot and had to limp around the room.

Then there was someone standing in the front door, a very old woman. She started yelling at him immediately. She threw a broken ashtray at him, hitting him in the shoulder. She was blocking the only exit, so he ducked and dodged, looking for an escape as she screamed and threw things at him.

Finally he ran straight at her. She hit him again with something hard in the forehead, but he made it past. He slipped in the mud as he ran across the road. The old woman chased him all the way to his truck, yelling long after he slid sideways around the corner

and then raced out of town. He was breathing hard, and an awareness of what he had just done was sinking in. His hands were
slippery on the steering wheel. He didn't know to be thankful
that his license plate was covered with mud, that the old woman
didn't have a phone to call the BIA police, that she was too upset to even remember the color of his truck—and that "some
crazy white man" was too general a description to be useful to
the authorities.

I wonder if he thought about the fact that he'd committed a
crime that fell squarely under the tribal jurisdiction he so loathed.
Would he complain about their sovereignty if they'd caught up
with him, suggest that it was unfair to be prosecuted under a sys-
tem that didn't guarantee him a bill of rights? I wonder if he even
thought of it as a crime. I'm sure he was aware it was something
more than merely bad manners. He was always so levelheaded.
He came from a long line of men who *always* did what had to be
done, men who buried their women and children in prairie dirt so
unyielding that it could break a metal plow. How good it must
have felt to kick in a TV set just because he was angry at all the
things that weren't working, all the things out of his control, to
watch it hiss and explode around his boot.

He spent the afternoon stopping at gas stations and convenience stores, but he wasn't having any luck. Near the end of the
day he stopped at a bar that was open at the border of the reservation. It was probably clean when it was new; now the dust had
sealed it. The proprietor was white. She leaned against her bar as
she watched Dad walk in. There were half a dozen people in the
whole place. Two men sat at the bar, one missing teeth and so
filthy that he looked as if he'd been propped there. The man next
to him, a little younger, but headed down the same path, turned
with him to stare. At the end of the bar was an Indian woman
who looked at him as if she might walk across the room to spit on

him. A middle-aged Indian man leaned on the broken-down pool table and watched Dad walk over to the bar.

"I'm looking for a Cheyenne boy, Charlie White Bird," he blurted out before a hello or anything, and the owner responded with a twisted grin.

"That so?"

He looked around the bar, aware that he was the center of attention.

"What for?" the Cheyenne woman asked.

"Long story." He looked over at the two drunks and addressed them even though they were not Indian. "I'm looking for a boy named Charlie White Bird."

They just glared at him. The bartender shrugged, and Dad stood there getting angry again. Then an older Indian man he hadn't noticed leaned forward and smiled with an empty mouth, sucking in air where his teeth used to be.

"Charlie's not around here, captain," the man cackled. "Must have known you were comin'."

"You know him?"

The man spit.

"He ran off?"

"No." The old man laughed. "I saw him yesterday. He was drivin' around."

"Where?"

"Around."

"Was he alone?"

The man looked around the nearly empty bar.

Dad didn't wait for him. "What kind of car was he driving?"

"Blue. An old car, you know, one of those with an Indian name." The man lifted his beer as a kind of salute.

Chapter Eighteen

"You're getting fat."

Clayton snatched a bag of barbecue potato chips from my hands, and took a great handful for himself. I hadn't moved from the bed all day, but I hadn't really been eating *that* much either. I didn't feel hungry any more than I felt like moving. He walked to the window and raised his good arm high over his head. He was always stretching. It was like hanging out with some kind of cat. I laid my hand on my stomach. I could feel the bubbling and gurgling. I wanted the potato chips back.

He looked at me in a hard way. "You have to get out of bed."

I did have to get out of bed, but I could hardly lift my head. I don't think it was the pregnancy as much as the weight of the future pushing back on me, or the past running me over. God, I felt sick.

"If you're going to lie on my damn bed, anyway . . . ," he started, but even he could hear how bizarre that sounded. I couldn't imagine that I looked any sexier than a sock.

"I feel sick, Clayton."

He seethed and stretched again. "Well, you're getting fat."

I closed my eyes. He stood there for a while looking at me, this girl with uncombed hair, lying in a motel bed, sick and afraid to move. I heard him dressing and then felt his weight on the bed, and tensed up involuntarily. But he was just pulling his boots on. He stood by the door with his hat in his hands. "I'm going out."

I didn't move.

"You better be out of that damn bed when I get back."

The door shut with a slam.

For hours the only thing I thought about were the sounds I could hear outside the room. I heard the cars going by at first, and then I began to distinguish sounds beyond that, the dinging of a bell on the door of the convenience store next door, someone talking on the street. A dog pacing in his run behind the motel, rhythmically jumping against the chain-link fence at each lap. A muffled argument, a man and a woman next door. Silence and then the hints of sex. An unmuffled engine revving somewhere, almost unbearably loud, and an odd, syncopated banging that I couldn't decipher. Then there was music, distantly, a car stereo no doubt. Someone parked with a door open or a window down. It sounded like opera.

I was asleep when Clayton came back. It wasn't the sound of the door opening, or him sitting on his bed and kicking off his boots that woke me. It was the strong smell of perfume on him. Its sweetness hurt my stomach, and I buried my face in the pillow.

DAD SLEPT IN the bed of his truck, in a canvas bedroll he'd had since he was a kid. He was parked in a gravel pullout. There was no traffic, and it was quiet enough that he could hear cattle grazing over the fence. He dozed more than he slept. A pain in his hip kept waking him up, and finally he rolled over on his back looking up at the starry night sky, the occasional white scratch of a meteorite, trying to drift off again.

Eventually, he gave up. He pulled his half-frozen boots on and a jacket. A heavy dew had gathered on the metal of the truck bed, making it slick. A clear dawn was not far off. There had been no moon all night, but there was still enough light from the stars to see the black road, the pasture stretching away, and the faint shadows of grazing cattle. He shivered, shoving his hands into his pockets as he walked off down the shoulder of the road, navigating mainly by the sound of the gravel popping under his boots.

He was getting used to walking on that dark road when he stubbed his foot on a big rock lurking at the edge. It hurt. He limped in a circle, walking off the pain, hurling insults at the rock with irrational, painful anger. Then he got down on his knees to find the rock and punish it, crawling like a furious child until he found it. He picked it up, the stupid heavy stone, and hurled it into the ditch. He didn't get up right away but knelt there with his head down, breathing and clenching his jaw rhythmically. Then he looked up to where the sky was beginning to pale in the East and he began to pray.

He prayed to Mom. He prayed that he could find me, and that he would have some idea of what to do when he did. Or maybe he prayed simply that I could take care of myself. He prayed for Mom's return, and the reversal of time, for all of the impossible undoings that would make things easy and right, to the time when things *were* right, when I was little and Mom wanted another child, and he put it off.

His praying found him still there, as the light came up, and dawn began to fill in the low hills and flat bottom pasture. Around the distant corner a motor home approached like a large white Conestoga wagon, a prairie schooner without oxen. He got up quickly, before the driver saw him out in that empty road on his knees. He brushed the dirt off, and began walking back toward his truck as the motor home caught up with him. Instead of passing, it slowed down, and the driver, whose soft, heavy shape seemed molded to his seat, rolled down his window.

"Is this the road to Custer's Last Stand?"

Dad looked around, getting his bearings. It wasn't the normal approach to the monument. "I guess it is."

"Do you know when they open?"

"No, sorry."

I imagine the retired man's face as soft and happy, his body made of what he had always eaten, mostly deep-fried potatoes and fat steaks. I doubt he'd ever had a real fight with anyone in his life, not even a serious argument beyond bickering with his neighbor over trimming an apple tree along the fence. His wife looked harder and even bigger, her eyes more angry, though it may just have been the pain of her arthritis.

"Is it far?"

"I don't think so."

"Have you ever been?"

"A couple times."

"It's pretty interesting I'll bet."

"Sure." Dad was still walking and the motor home rolled slowly along beside him, a big American flag pasted in the window.

"Hard to imagine, huh?"

Dad looked up at the man. "What?"

"All those Indians, painted up, ready to ambush the soldiers." Dad nodded. The man gazed at the long horizon. "Where do you think they hid out?"

"I don't think it was that planned out."

"Really? It wasn't an ambush?"

"That's what I've heard."

"They have an exhibit at the battlefield, right?"

"Yeah."

"Maybe they know how the trap was set."

"I'm pretty sure they have it all worked out."

"We're making coffee when we get there. We zap water in the microwave. Got a big box left of those sticky cinnamon rolls from Costco, too. You want to join us?" The man smiled.

I guess the coffee sounded too good to pass up, or Dad just didn't know how to say "no thanks." He followed the motor home up the hill to the gate of the visitor's center. Nobody else was there yet, and the sign said they opened at eight, still more than an hour away. For a moment there was only the sound of the ropes slapping in the wind on the flagpole by the cemetery before the couple kicked on their generator to run the microwave. The coffee was ready quickly, and Dad sat with them and looked out across the bottomland below the monument, waiting as the yellow sun came up and began to warm his face. The woman came out of the motor home with some powdered creamer. She was so big that the vehicle leaned and groaned to let her down. She sat in the folding chair and looked up at the white marker on Custer Hill. "Do you suppose it happened at dawn, like this?"

"I think it was sometime in the afternoon," Dad offered, though they hardly seemed to credit him with any expertise.

"What do ya suppose they're building over there?" the man asked, pointing to a temporary chain-link fence surrounding a pile of dirt and rock.

"It's an Indian memorial."

The man nodded. "Took 'em a while to get around to that, eh?"

"You can just imagine the politics. You know, the tribes trying to decide what to put up. What to say." Dad shook his head.

The man thumbed through a pamphlet, something he found outside the gatehouse for just such folks who showed up early ahead of the rangers. On its cover was a painting entitled *Here Fell Custer*. It depicted a soldier struggling to hold up an American flag amid the last few survivors at the peak of Custer Hill. His face was turned away, his long hair falling over his shoulders. The man held it up, so they could see it, and read from the caption: "*Here Fell Custer* is considered by Custer historians to be the most accurate portrayal on canvas of the battle. . . . "

Dad took a sip of coffee. "Except the guy holding up the flag, right?"

The man flipped it over and looked again at the painting. "You mean Custer?"

"Or whoever it is." It wasn't that Dad was unpatriotic, he was just ruthlessly pragmatic. "There's at least one theory that he died pretty early on. Some Indians say he was killed by a woman fighter, trying to run away."

"Of course it's Custer," the woman said, adjusting herself somewhat indignantly in her folding chair.

Dad cleared his throat, aware that his questioning of the official position bothered them, but he kept going anyway. "It doesn't seem likely he'd be trying to put up a flag in the middle of a massacre, though. Not much point in that." Dad tried a laugh, but they did not join him. Apparently they felt that there was a point.

"Says here there were 263 men killed from the Seventh Cavalry." The man shook his head. The woman tightened her lips into a fine line of disgust.

▲ ▲ ▲

A GRASSHOPPER CLUNG to the blade of grass a few inches from Mo'é'ha'e, its fat thorax pulsing. She moved as slowly as she could, watching the insect intently. It must have escaped three times already, and even though she had two smaller grasshoppers in her pouch, she wanted this fat one. She wanted the praise from her uncle who was fishing and needed the grasshoppers for bait. He had an old rusted hook and some gut leader bartered from a fur trader last summer. She knew that this big grasshopper would catch the biggest fish.

She moved closer and then stopped as the insect shifted its grip, preparing to spring. The heat of the sun stung the back of her neck, but it didn't weaken her concentration. She inched her hands a notch closer and still the grasshopper did not move.

As she reached for it, the grasshopper seemed frozen, victory seemed certain, but when she opened her empty hands and looked up, it was flying, yellow-and-black wings against a blue sky, headed over the top of the hill. She ran after it hoping to mark the spot where it would land, but when she got to the top, hot and out of breath, she forgot about the grasshopper. Out in the bottom on the other side of the river, a cloud of rising dust caught her attention. It took a moment to make out the tiny figures of several warriors racing on horseback toward the camp, and behind them in the distance, a large contingent of soldiers. She tore off down the hill, yelling for her uncle.

"Ea'eotse'tovovo!" They're attacking the camp! She ran so fast down the steep hill that her speed got away from her and she fell, tumbling through the tall grasses, but as soon as she got to her feet she was running again.

White Bird dropped his fishing pole and caught her with his strong hands. *"Stay in the timber. I will find you there after the fight."*

She looked into his fire-black eyes. She could not ask what she should do if he did not come for her. He simply must. Henry was sitting near the river, and he could tell from the tone of her words and the fear in her face what it must be. He looked down at his feet, avoiding her eyes.

"Drink some water now and hurry to the trees and hide there." Her uncle instructed.

"I saw a great cloud of dust and smoke," she said.

He kissed her forehead. *"Then we shall make an even greater cloud."*

He ran off. When he was gone, it was as peaceful as it had been when they came to fish a few hours earlier, as though nothing was happening, the charge of the white soldiers on the camps, the killing. Her life itself was as carefree and safe as the white cumulus building in the hot afternoon sky. The soft warm breeze lied, too. It whispered that all this violence, just across the river, must be impossible.

She took Henry's hand and they crossed the river into the trees where her uncle had disappeared. She ran hard until her throat burned, and Henry kept up, his face like stone. Soon they could hear the gunfire faintly popping a mile away like dried maize cast in a fire, and then the muted screaming of men and horses. They ran to the edge of the trees where they could see some of the fighting at the end of the lodges. The crisscrossed peaks stood in silent witness above the chaos.

Beyond the tepees she saw black smoke rising from the guns. This, the greatest gathering of Lakota and Cheyenne, was being attacked in broad daylight. The sun beat down relentlessly. She began to hear bullets, a whistling, ballistic sound, creasing the air near them. More warriors on horses raced to join the fight. She glanced up at the hills only to see more soldiers pouring down from there.

"We have to hide," Henry said in English.

But Mo'é'ha'e did not want to be too far from the lodges in case the soldiers overwhelmed them. She was afraid to be left behind, and worried that her mother might be caught up in the fighting. She pulled him with her, and they made their way to the timber between the camp and the river then ducked behind an old fallen cottonwood. Close to the fighting now, they covered themselves with branches as a group of soldiers retreated in their direction. Several dozen dropped back not forty yards in front of them, and for a few long minutes, they made a stand there. Mo'é'ha'e and Henry hid like fawns, watching bits of the battle through gaps in the branches and leaves.

Without warning, the soldiers broke and ran. Those that still had horses thundered by. A young soldier on foot jumped over a fallen tree only a few feet away and stopped. His hands shook as he tried to reload his weapon. Mo'é'ha'e held Henry's hand tightly as they watched the man jump up and fire three wild deafening shots, which made their ears ring. The shooting and yelling from the warriors was getting closer. The man jumped up to run, just as one of the mounted warriors cleared the log. Mo'é'ha'e strained to see what happened to him, but couldn't through the dense brush. The sulfurous scent of black powder was heavy and sweet in the hot air.

Now they were trapped between the lines. The warriors advanced steadily as the soldiers on the other side of them stopped their retreat and fired back as fast as their guns could be emptied and reloaded. Mo'é'ha'e and Henry clung to the ground, digging their fingers into the rotten leaves, listening to the terrifying sounds of the bullets ripping murderously back and forth overhead. On both sides of them were the screams of panicked horses, war cries of warriors, death cries of soldiers, the thick thud of lead hitting the dry ground or the high whistle of lead shot hopelessly and desperately into the sky. Then the soldiers turned to run again and the warriors raced by, the horses' hooves falling closely as the children huddled, waiting for a blow from somewhere in the whoops and thunder and choking dust. The remaining soldiers fell back in panic, terribly overwhelmed.

Many of them were cut off by the swarm of warriors, and one by one they were killed in the timber. Mo'é'ha'e watched two soldiers aim their pistols at each other and then fire. One fell like a rag doll, but the other dropped to his knees as if pausing for a moment. A warrior helped him down with a running blow to his head with a tomahawk that took his hat and a piece of his skull with it.

One soldier broke away, but his horse would not go the way he wanted. In desperation, he beat on its head with the butt of his pistol, sending the animal careening wildly and then bucking, causing him to lose his grip and fall to the ground. Before he could run off, one of the Cheyenne quickly shot two arrows, and their black obsidian points found the man's soft flesh.

The warrior dropped from his horse, and for a moment they faced off. The soldier seemed to have forgotten his pistol, and the warrior seemed frozen by the image of the wounded man before him who was spitting blood but who should have been dead. Finally, the soldier raised his gun with his left hand and emptied it, shooting at the warrior at close range. The last round grazed the Cheyenne near his groin, causing him to stumble. And then in fury, he charged the white man and stabbed his knife so deeply into his enemy that he almost could not pull it back out.

Henry shook, his eyes closed, his hand tight in Mo'é'ha'e's.

The warrior grabbed the white man's long hair, set the knife to his forehead and used the weight of the dead man's body to rip his scalp off, letting him drop, finally, to the ground. He limped back to his horse, his leg covered with his own blood, and his face and arms covered with the white man's blood. In an amazing feat of strength, he jumped up onto the bare back of his horse and rode back toward the battle, with the bloody scalp over his head, screaming a scream that would not be recognized by anyone as human.

Mo'é'ha'e was crying. Out of fear. Out of shame. Out of triumph and victory. The soldiers retreated away from them up into the hills where she had been hunting grasshoppers. And then suddenly from the opposite direction down by the river there came a furious din of rifle fire, which built to a crescendo and then died out.

THE HOT AFTERNOON ebbed slowly into evening. Mo'é'ha'e and Henry stayed hidden under the fallen tree, and eventually they fell asleep, their arms wrapped around each other like babes. When Mo'é'ha'e woke, a coyote was standing a few feet away, testing the air. It shied when it saw her move, and she stared into its wet eyes until it ran off to look for someone dead. Then she began to hear the wailing of women moving out of camp looking for fallen loved ones. She woke Henry and they walked silently back toward the camp. Up on the battlefield they could see them moving among the bodies, taking clothes and boots and weapons or stooping over the soldiers with knives, working some horror of vengeance. They stripped them all, leaving naked bodies, which were white as snow.

Mo'é'ha'e found her mother sitting silently in front of their tepee. When she asked about her uncle, her mother nodded and quietly told her that he was not hurt. The children sat with her, but she seemed deep in thought, and after a while Mo'é'ha'e touched her shoulder to say she was leaving and took Henry's hand.

They fell in with a group of children who were headed up to the main battlefield. They had sharpened sticks, like spears, for poking at the fallen soldiers. As they approached the first of the dead, they stopped speaking and hesitated. But then curiosity and their own fear drew them in, and though they prodded tentatively at first, they slowly became bolder with the corpses. They jabbed sticks into the bellies until they broke, or gouged out eyes.

Henry turned and ran away, back toward the lodges. Mo'é'ha'e yelled for him to stay, but he didn't stop running. She started to chase after him, but one of the older girls chided her. *"Nēšenet-*

se'oreha." Let the white boy run. "Or maybe today we will kill him, too."

And so she stayed, poking with her stick, and digging through the blue army clothes of the white men, who smelled strong from the adrenaline of the massacre. In the soldiers' pockets the kids found pretty paper. The troops had all just been paid. They kept it for decorating their toys.

Together they rolled a body over, which the sun had not yet let cool and stiffen, and the joints were loose, and alive. Under him the ground was muddy with his blood. With sticks they stirred the mud and painted his face. None of them would touch the white man with their hands. He still had his hair, pulled back in a pony-tail; he had not yet been scalped. Slowly the horror of the afternoon was dulled by their physical exploration, though it did not calm their terrible and justifiable anger. These men had come to kill them. And they would have. General Sherman had famously said it: "Nits make lice."

Mo'é'ha'e felt suddenly sick. The smell was overwhelming, and without being able to turn or prepare, she vomited. When she finally was able to look up, the other children were gone, having run away, and she was alone with the dead soldier.

AT NIGHT THE women's wailing was joined by the distant squabbling of coyotes and wolves and camp dogs over the marvelous battlefield spoils. In the dark, Mo'é'ha'e made her way back to the camp. Some had built a victory fire, but there was little celebration because even though the white man had been wiped out except for the few soldiers still holding out on a hill across the river, too many warriors had also been killed, and the mourners would not allow a dance. Besides everyone knew what revenge they could expect because of that day. They could sense it in the silence, which settled too quickly over the battleground.

Mo'é'ha'e found her uncle sitting by his tepee, eating. His sons hovered near him staring at the fifteen scalps, laying at his feet like dead rats. Mo'é'ha'e, too, looked at them in wonder.

"More white men will come now, more than we have ever seen."

She nodded, though it didn't mean much to her. She'd just seen more white men than ever before, more than she ever imagined there could be, and the warriors had killed them all. Her cousins responded to their father's words by running off through the tepees, shouting in mock battle.

She sat down beside White Bird, and he smiled. *"I have a horse for you, a black one."*

She rested her head on his chest, and he held her in his warm and war-tired arms, which smelled of sweat and gun smoke and dirt and blood.

All night the wailing haunted Mo'é'ha'e's dreams. This should have been a great victory, but there was a sense of doom hovering over the camp. They would leave in the morning, and soon enough the soldiers would be after them. That was what she dreamed about. All night the soldiers chased her, and all of them had the face and strange red hair of the body she had found in the dirty spring snow.

Henry cried, too, that night, mumbling English in his dreams. She woke and watched him in the near darkness, tossing, his face beaded with sweat, and she could feel a little of the hate that they all felt, like a little black stone squeezed in the sticky palm of her fist.

THE CAPTAIN HAD SHAVED, and his face was still pink from the bracing cold water. He walked out of his tent loading a pinch of tobacco into his pipe then folded the bag and slipped it into his pocket. General Crook had been away all morning fishing, and a messenger sat at the Captain's fire waiting courteously, trying to hide the impression that it was unfitting, even embarrassing, for the general to be out fishing while such important news waited for him. What was worse, of course, is that he was probably fishing the day the Seventh Cavalry had been massacred.

A journalist from the *Rocky Mountain News* had been coming by all day trying to pry the details from the young messenger, who said he would report only to General Crook. But the rumor was already out. General Custer and the Seventh Cavalry wiped out at the Little Bighorn—by the same army of Cheyenne and Lakota that battled Crook to a standstill on the Rosebud.

Wiped out.

The newsman sat with the Captain and lit his cigar from the Captain's pipe. It was a blustery day. The thunderheads had been building for the last few hours as the whole camp anticipated the general's return, thinking that it might be hastened by the weather. But the fishing had been good. The general had been out almost every day catching basketfuls of fat cutthroats. And who knows, he may have run into a grizzly, or elk, or buffalo, something really big to shoot. That could add hours to his expedition.

The newsman frowned at the messenger and shook his head. Salt had dried on the young soldier's forehead below his matted hair, and he held his hat piously in his lap. The boy's enthusiasm for protocol was infuriating. The word was out anyway. All he wanted was some confirmation, a few details to send home to Denver. He had a man waiting to make the ride. "Come on, boy, you can tell us your news. How many were killed? Was anyone left alive? When did the battle happen? Was it after the twentieth of June, or much before?"

The boy sat quietly, nervously.

"Ah . . . " The newsman looked away disgusted. "What do you think, Captain? Is it possible?"

The Captain smiled. "Seems it must be. This boy wouldn't have ruined a horse getting here just to send us Fourth of July salutations, even with the centennial coming up."

"Wiped out, though?"

"There were a lot of warriors there Mr. Newspaper." The Captain knocked the tobacco from his pipe.

"Well it's the beginning of the end, then."

The Captain nodded.

"The wilds will be purged of the savages now. Even the bleeding hearts in the East will not be able to make a case against it."

"No doubt." The Captain put the pipe back in his pocket. "I hope you're prepared for a winter campaign."

"It won't take that long."

The Captain shrugged.

The newsman looked up from his notes. "You know something?"

"Just supposing."

The newsman nodded, taking his own rhetoric seriously. "The public will demand an overwhelming and immediate response to this outrage."

"Yes, your public will be quite happy, once they realize the good news."

"Good news?"

"We shall kill them in the white snow and paint it red."

The boy shifted uncomfortably.

"What do you think, boy? We *must* avenge Custer."

The boy turned white. He looked at his hands. "I don't know, sir."

▲ ▲ ▲

THE SUNBURNED VALLEY lay perfectly still, silent and unmoving except for the vague sparkle of the river hidden in the trees and the nearly imperceptible drift of clouds across the hills beyond. Not a single tepee stood where hundreds had once been gathered. Not a person was moving where hundreds had fought and died.

Dad pulled off onto the gravel shoulder to look at the battle-field alone and rolled his truck window down to get a better view. Slowly his mind erased the freeway and the farms and convenience stores at the off ramp. The lay of the hills made it easy to see where the camp had been, white-painted tepees dotting the valley as far as the ground was flat. He could see the hills where Captain Reno and the men who had first charged the camp had been forced to retreat, the steep bare gullies above the river, and just to the north of that the monument, standing alone, as popular history imagined Custer, where Crazy Horse and a thousand warriors had come like a storm upon the United States Seventh Cavalry.

The sounds of the fighting were easiest to imagine, the dust gathering and climbing in the afternoon thermals. Dad could almost see the Indian girl running out there, running hard, her small legs reaching through the grass almost as high as her head. All the rest of the ghosts were gone, only this one young girl running for her life in this wide, empty, suddenly silent place. Or maybe that's me. That's what I see. Dad isn't like that. He thinks differently; he would have known that, whatever happened here, the Cheyenne girl got away this time. He knew his history pretty well. But at least he was thinking about her, wondering how it went. It had to have happened sometime during that summer. Was she finally caught by a stray bullet, or one deliberately fired? Or did she die of fever? Just sickness?

In his heart, I think, he wanted her to get away, too.

Chapter Nineteen

CHARLIE WAS SORE for a while. His side and back hurt most. When he woke up in his car at Uncle Leonard's, he knew I was gone for good. Some days he could convince himself that I might come back, but I don't think he was really that surprised I was gone. He killed time fixing fence at his uncle's place, cutting his hands on the rusted wire. At night he slept out by the buttes, his head pillowed on the soft sandstone, watching the clouds race across a field of stars and wondering where I might have gone.

It was easy to figure out that getting me back would only lead to losing me again. It was the same fight that stirred inside him when he thought about going to college, taking the scholarship, leaving Teddy and the rest of them, and leaving his home, too. He was afraid to find out later in life, too far down the road, that he had betrayed someone—his mother, his friend, his uncle, himself.

One Sunday his dad came back from Seattle. He had two weeks off from his construction job. Despite his parents' being divorced, the whole family gathered at his mother's house for dinner. The air was moist with body heat and stew cooking on the electric stove in the kitchen; the smells of her house and the wet boots by the door all muddied together with the competing voices of his family and Uncle Leonard's coughing.

"Plenty Crow's gonna have a Give-away—big Give-away," said Charlie's aunt, his mother's sister. She had the kind of voice that carried in a group. Whatever she said sounded like an announcement.

"Yeah, I heard that, too," said Charlie's older sister, Mary. "At the Labor Day powwow. The old man died a year ago."

"Won't be nothin' like the Little Wolf's." Charlie's dad shook his head, remembering. "They had nothin' left after that. Even gave away their car."

"They lost their son. That's why they gave away so much."

Charlie's mother nodded her head; her sister was right. They still didn't have even a couch left to sit on.

"Well, something happens to Charlie, I'm keeping *my* car," his dad said, and this got a laugh. "Maybe I'll give away that sorry old horse you used to ride when you were in diapers."

"That horse has been dead for years, *né-ho'e*," Charlie pointed out. His dad just shrugged and everybody laughed again.

"Charlie, you and Mary come peel potatoes for me, okay?" his mother called from the kitchen. He'd been avoiding Mary the whole night. He knew she'd want to talk about college, what he was planning to do about it. In some sweet but vaguely condescending way she would be looking out for him. Now she had him cornered. One of these days she was going to figure out that he let the application deadline pass for Chief Dull Knife College.

"Somebody says you have a new girlfriend."

Charlie frowned. That wasn't the subject he was expecting.

"Do you?"

"None of your business." Charlie's face clouded and she laughed.

"Teddy says . . . "

"Teddy . . . " Charlie rolled his eyes.

"He told me about those bones you found, too. He thinks maybe you're protecting your new girlfriend's dad."

"I should never have dug her up, that's all."

"You have lots of secrets, little brother."

Charlie looked around for an escape, but he was surrounded. His dad had already turned to listen to Mary's interrogation.

"What are you doing about college?" she asked. "Gotta do somethin'."

Charlie didn't know what to say. She'd got her AA at Dull Knife, went two years at MSU, Bozeman, now she had a job at the BIA. She was always winning at the powwows, royalty at the grand entrance. She thought she had the perfect formula.

"I should ask Mom. Maybe she knows what you're up to."

His dad joined in. "What do you think? Somebody's gonna walk up and just hand you a job?"

Suddenly the whole room was quiet. His mother was listening, too. "Maybe Charlie wants to stay home," she said. "Everybody doesn't have to run off. Being a big success ain't everything."

"Maybe Charlie will win the lottery. Maybe Charlie wants to work down at the new casino." His dad laughed.

"Charlie's going to college, Dad," said Mary.

Charlie's dad seemed to take it personally. "That's the solution to everything, eh? Go to college, get a bigger degree, come back take somebody's dumb-ass agency job away from them." He lifted his hands and imitated typing at a computer.

Charlie's mom walked out of the kitchen. "Why do you want to go bad-mouthin' college? Learnin' something. You think being a steel worker, living off in Seattle or Portland or wherever is so great?"

Charlie stepped between his parents. "Everybody doesn't need to be figuring out what Charlie is going to do. I can handle it, okay?" It sounded twice as ridiculous out loud as he expected, but whether he could handle it or not he wished they'd drop it.

His dad shrugged and shook his head. "I can still get you in the steel workers' union, 'til you're twenty-one." He raised his hands as if to say, it's your life, mess it up however you please. "Don't say I never tried to help you out."

Charlie waved him off and picked a potato to peel. His mom was laying pre-made dinner rolls out on a cookie sheet. Whatever she was thinking, and he thought he knew, she wasn't saying. Sure thing she had an opinion, an idea of what he should do. It wouldn't involve falling for some white girl either. That's not what she hoped for. Though, at least with her, he knew she'd back him whatever he did. She'd adapt. He peeled a few more potatoes until he couldn't stand to be in the room anymore.

"I'm takin' a walk, Mom."

"Not too long, okay? We'll be eatin' soon."

His first breath of air outside felt good, cool in his lungs. As he walked he tried to remember how the neighborhood had looked when he was a kid. He thought he remembered the bright colors of the houses that were now faded, but maybe they'd always been that way. Where there had been toys everywhere now there was junk. Maybe he *should* just go with his dad to Seattle. Give himself some time to make up his mind. At least his father had no other agenda.

A few houses down he saw Bad Face sitting on his porch, the same old man who'd always sat out in front of his house with a lap full of cats, scaring kids who passed by. He braced out of habit, then laughed at himself for reacting like a child. Bad Face hissed at Charlie as he walked by, and he jumped despite himself. He shook his head and kept walking, and the old man spit and hissed again. "Where you going, boy? Show some respect."

Charlie slowed and turned enough to say politely, "Afternoon, Mr. Bad Face."

The old man smiled. He liked to be called Mr. Bad Face; he liked his Lakota warrior's heritage. Most people only used his first name.

"Hear about that crazy white man?" he asked.

Reluctantly Charlie stopped. "Yeah?"

Mr. Bad Face glared at him. His eyes were wet. He leaned forward. "He was looking for you, boy."

"Huh?"

"The crazy white man was looking for you."

"How do you know?"

Bad Face laughed, and the cats in his lap jumped away. He got up and limped over to the fence close enough that Charlie could smell the alcohol on him.

"Watch out!"

To the old man's delight, Charlie stepped back quickly, and hurried away, trying to get back the feeling of calm he'd almost found. He headed up into the hills above the town, and found a place to sit where he could see the mountains, just the faint white peaks of the Bighorns, miles to the south. He thought about what it would be like to walk all the way there, to hike across so much empty space. He thought about the possibility that I might have gone to do something like that.

When he got back to his mom's trailer, Charlie scraped the red mud off his feet on the steps. Through the steamed windows he could see his dad laughing. They were getting ready to eat, but Charlie's stomach didn't want food. He almost turned to leave, but then Uncle Leonard spotted him. Even dimly through the glass, his eyes looked bright. Charlie pulled back the sliding door.

Nobody paid much attention to his return. They were having a lively discussion about that old mare Charlie's dad said he'd give away.

"Hey, Dad," Charlie said almost too softly and waited for him to break away from the story.

"Yeah?" he said finally, in the pause in the laughter that anticipated the next tale.

"I gotta get out of here."

"We're about to eat," his mother said.

"I'm not really hungry."

The family was suddenly quiet.

"Why don't you wait until after dinner?" his dad asked, as though Charlie must be crazy.

Charlie shrugged. They all took it as a sign that he'd decided to do the sensible thing and started talking again. Soon it was so loud in the tiny trailer he found he could not focus on any one conversation. Eventually he noticed his Uncle Leonard waving him over to the couch. He seemed to need some help getting up. Charlie went over and gave him a hand. His arms felt as frail and brittle as dry butterfly wings. Instead of letting go of Charlie's hand when he stood, his uncle held on tightly.

"Charlie's taking me home," he said.

"Uncle Leonard, the food's almost ready," said Charlie's mom again, clearly frustrated.

Uncle Leonard patted his stomach as if he weren't feeling well, and pulled Charlie with him, holding onto his hand for support as they crossed the trailer past Charlie's father.

"Dad, I need some money for gas."

His father scowled.

"A loan," Charlie added quickly. "I don't have any cash on me." He didn't like lying to his father, but he needed as much gas money as he could get.

As his father handed him a twenty, he seemed to suspect that something was going on. Charlie was already out on the porch helping Uncle Leonard down the steps, when his mother yelled, "We'll keep something warm for you, Charlie!"

They drove back across the reservation through the pine hills and red willow bottoms. The road out to Uncle Leonard's place was slick with mud from the recent rain. They slipped and slid up the hill. Charlie helped his uncle out of the car. When Uncle Leonard got his balance, he reached into his beaded wallet, took some money out and pressed it into Charlie's hand.

"I think you're going to look for her, eh, Charlie?"

"I don't know."

"You go. Do what you need to do. "

Uncle Leonard smiled and dug for something in his jacket pocket. He pulled out an old eagle feather that was nearly worn out, wrapped with leather at the quill. "This has always been lucky for me." He handed it to Charlie, then his face seemed to get serious. "My father's grandfather fought Custer. He remembered him like I am now, a very old man. My father always wanted me to remember my language, my culture, but he also wanted me to go out into the white man's world. He wanted me to compete with the white man." He took a breath and tightened his grip on Charlie's hand. "That's the way things were supposed to be."

Charlie shook his head; he couldn't figure out why Uncle Leonard was bringing this up now.

"Don't be angry at me for saying this. Your heart is on fire. You're young."

"It's okay. Don't worry about me."

Uncle Leonard looked fiercely into his eyes. "You must not let this pretty woman change what you have to do. You are a Cheyenne warrior." He let go of Charlie's hand and started back toward the trailer.

Charlie watched him cross the yard to the porch. He struggled with each step then opened the door and slowly stepped into the trailer. Charlie waited until he could see smoke coming from the chimney pipe. When he drove back down to the asphalt road, it was almost dark.

Chapter Twenty

I could see the McDonald's across the street from the bathroom window of the motel room. I brushed my hair and put on a T-shirt and pants that almost matched and went out into the day. The brightness made my eyes hurt, but there was a coolness in the shade that hinted of fall. My thongs slapped on my bare feet as I made my way down the cement stairway and across the warm asphalt parking lot.

From the looks I got, I guess I must have seemed half dead. I wanted to turn back, but I had to eat, some french fries or maybe some Chicken McNuggets with honey mustard. Beyond the golden arches the Black Hills loomed, dark velvet hills of pine. Granddad always said that when the trees look black on the mountains, it's going to snow. And they looked black, despite the sunny day. He never liked the snow, or winter. Whenever I looked at a blank field of fresh snow, I saw something simple and beautiful, but my granddad could see it for what it was: death, even and white. He knew that the only reason at all for hope was that the grass buried underneath the snow had learned how to die each year—then somehow come back.

I dug the few worn bills and coins I had left from my pocket. This McDonald's wasn't particularly new, but the floors and tables were clean. It cheered me up. The french fries had plenty of salt, but I added more from a little white packet, and then another, until they were so salty that they burned my mouth, but it made my stomach feel better.

CLAYTON WAS AT the hotel when I got back. The door to the room was open wide, and it was dark inside. He already had most of his stuff in the truck. My suitcase was sitting by the bed. He'd been working fast to make his escape. I leaned in the open door and watched him grabbing the last few things from the bathroom. The room looked lonely with just my brown suitcase to keep it company.

"Hey, Clayton."

He turned, looking guilty. I guess he had something of a conscience when it came down to it. "What's up?"

I waved my bag of french fries and looked around the empty and anonymous room, with its ragged carpet, heavy curtains and dull walls. It still looked good to me, a cave where I could curl up until the storm blew over.

"I paid the room for a week," he said. I was quiet, so he felt the need to continue. "Since you've been sick and all. I was just giving you a ride, right? It's not like we're together. Anyway somebody might get the wrong idea with you being a minor and all." Oddly it didn't occur to him that so far he was the only one who'd gotten the wrong idea. "You can get a ride out of here easy — when you feel better."

I leaned back. His eyes moved to my stomach. I looked down too, still unsure, not really meaning to.

"You gonna be okay?" he asked.

It was the wrong thing to say to me. Tears warmed my eyes. I looked down to hide it.

"Ah shit," he said and sat on the bed. My hand moved on its own, held my stomach. I was close to telling him. I wanted to lift my T-shirt above my tummy, already softly rounded, hinting of the future.

He came over to me and touched my hair with a gentle, big hand. "I guess you can come with me, if you need to."

I nodded, still afraid to say anything out loud.

"That's okay, this is far enough." I looked around as if to convince myself that this really was where I had intended to land. And even though it wasn't, I suddenly felt like I couldn't go any farther.

His shoulders relaxed. I could tell he wanted to get the hell out of here before I changed my mind. "Maybe you should just go home."

I shook my head.

He dug around in his pocket for the room key and handed it to me and walked out to his truck. I stayed in the doorway ready to wave. He got in and started it up; a puff of blue smoke drifted up into the cold air, like it might be followed by a genie. But the genie didn't appear, I didn't get three wishes and the wind blew away the exhaust curling up from the pickup. Clayton backed up into the parking lot and drove off.

I walked back into the room. The woman had cleaned with a vengeance while I was gone. The floor in the bathroom squeaked under my sandals. I turned on the fluorescent light and sat on the toilet listening to the lights hum. When I washed my face, I was careful not to catch a glimpse of myself in the mirror. I didn't want to see me.

▲ ▲ ▲

THE FUGITIVE SUMMER PASSED. The wind shed the leaves from the aspens in quiet storms, and the stony peaks were glazed again in white. The Cheyenne had grown weary from months of pursuit across the labyrinths of hills and plains, and they were on the move again, walking and riding, stretched out in a long line. Mo'é'ha'e was near the end. Ten families had split off from the main group to meet up with Dull Knife, a chief who was not at the Little Bighorn. They expected to find him high up in the mountains. Each horse followed the travois before it, head down. Though the shimmering sun and wide blue sky seemed vividly alive, Mo'é'ha'e's tribe was too hungry, too pressed for survival, to see it that way. The end of summer came as a final threat. No one believed that the soldiers would leave them alone to winter unmolested.

They entered the forests of ponderosa pine, Engelmann spruce and Douglas fir on the shoulders of the Bighorns where it was cool and dim and deep green. Here the wind seemed to whisper strange secrets, and the ground felt cold in places where the frost had stopped melting during the day. The great trees bent over and tickled Mo'é'ha'e's neck as she rode by and told her unbelievable stories about Cheyenne maidens marrying tree spirits disguised as warriors, who bring with them strange, beautiful horses that, when the magic fades, turn out to be only saplings and twigs. They laughed at the solemn procession of people.

They asked her, "Why are the people so quiet?"

She said, or thought, "Because of the war with the white man. Everyone says the end is coming."

A great spruce laughed so hard he shook, and pinecones dropped from his shoulders, spooking the horses and nearly causing a wreck with one of the travois. "We have been at war with the prairie for millions of years. Sometimes we win and the grasses recede and the forests spread and sometimes the grasses begin to win and the prairies stretch far and wide."

"Ahhh," another tree bent in the wind as if waking and stretching. "But it never, never ends."

And she thought, "But the white man has killed many of the people. More and more go to the forts to live."

Several trees answered, "The prairie has terrible fire and burns hundreds of thousands of trees. You have seen it."

And she thought of the great prairie fires that outran animals, or the forest fires that lit up the night for a week or a month, and choked the sky with smoke and ash.

"Did the people lose? Where are the wounded?"

"In the summer we won a great battle. The warriors killed many white soldiers," she told them.

And a great mossy old Douglas fir, almost ten feet through the middle, spoke in a booming voice from the tops of its great boughs. "In three or four hundred years, then we shall know who won."

"I can't live four hundred years," said Mo'é'ha'e, now dizzy from looking up.

"The only way to beat fire is to outlast it."

"But I'm just a girl."

Then all of the trees seemed to laugh. And Mo'é'ha'e who'd felt so strong riding on her new black pony, felt cast down. Who could fight the white man's fire for four hundred years? She patted the neck of her horse and whispered to it, "When the time comes, you must run fast. As fast as the wind."

She kicked it in the flank, and they loped alongside the slow procession. She tried not to hear the trees' laughter as her horse stumbled over branches and logs and stumps. Then suddenly the trail narrowed and she tried to cut back into the line, but her excited stallion didn't want to slow down. It hopped and threatened to buck and nearly collided with one of the warriors. She was inches from him when she at last managed to stop.

He rode a paint, and his head was wrapped in dirty old rags, one eye covered and the other scarred. There were burns all over his face from the white man's gunpowder. Though he was blind, he heard her nearly run into him and turned toward her, expecting her to identify herself. But her throat was too tight to speak. She didn't know him, or if she did, she didn't recognize him with his wounds. She held her horse tightly as he turned away from her, understanding the fear in her silence and the line moved ahead and slowly disappeared into the forest.

That night they camped near a bright, clear creek. Mo'é'ha'e tied up her horse, wanting to keep it close to her, rather than let it loose with the others, and she lay down by it in the deep bed of pine needles and stared up through the sleeping conifers at the darkening sky. The scent of pine was rich in the dusky air as it mixed with the sweet smell of cooking fires.

A flock of crows flew low over the trees, and Mo'é'ha'e sat up on her elbows. A few fires away she watched the blind warrior sitting at his fire eating dried meat while his wife tended to him. He was listening to the crows cawing, too, trying to hear what they were saying to him, a blind warrior, who was young still but who would not be able to hunt or fight, who still had teeth to eat with, but took food from the men who hunted, with nothing, not even years or wisdom to offer in repayment.

Henry sat a few feet from the fire with his back to her. She couldn't see his face but she could see his hands, which were red with the cold, as he drew his knife along a pine stick, curling off white shavings that fell onto the damp pine needles.

Mo'é'ha'e's mother left the fire and came and sat by her while it burned itself down to coals that could be cooked over. Mo'é'ha'e turned to her and responded to the air of defeat in the gloomy camp. *"But we won, Mother. And my uncle gave me a black horse."*

"Héehe'e, e'nèhševa." Yes, he did.

Mo'é'ha'e thought for a while. *"I never thought I would have my own horse. Not until I was grown."*

"I think your uncle did not want you to have to wait."

"He takes good care of me. He said he will ask for many horses as a bride price when the time comes."

Mo'é'ha'e seemed proud, and Sweet Rose Woman let her dream. She closed her eyes and tried to feel what her daughter felt. Some fear, but mostly boldness and hope for a future unchanged. The creek bubbled musically and made that hope seem almost real, almost possible.

"You will have to let that horse eat something, little one."

In the morning Mo'é'ha'e took the horse out and let it graze among the thin lodgepole as she watched over it. She tried to ignore the unusual silence of camp. She closed her eyes and tried to imagine this morning as the beginning of a normal day, any day out of the thousands of winters that had come before this one, but her heart was not in it. Even the squirrels seemed to chide her from the branches. By the time she was back with her horse, camp was ready to move. There was little talk as they filed through the trees up the narrow canyon.

THE CAPTAIN FROWNED darkly at the black coals in his hand. They were cold, and the gray ash had been rained on, which meant it was at least three days old. He looked off through the trees, imagining the backs of his quarry disappearing into the forest. He dropped the coals and brushed his hand on his blue woolen pants, then looked over at his scouts who sat on their horses, sullen, almost sleeping. This small camp hardly seemed worth pursuing. They expected to go back and return to the main trail.

"They can't hide forever," the Captain said. But it sounded hollow, pointless, even if it was true, because the words were English and there was no one to hear them. The Crow scouts regarded him mutely. The Captain wandered around the old campsite looking at the ground and stopped where the soft bed of rotting pine needles had been torn up in a circle around the base of a young Douglas fir.

Someone kept this horse tied up when the other horses were loose grazing, he thought, then looked closer at the hoofprints. Iron shoes. *This horse belonged to Custer's Seventh.*

He stood up, breathing in the rich pine air. *But why keep the animal tied up?* He looked around for more clues. There was the circle of a small tepee where he counted only three people sleeping, two of them small. At least one adult was missing. There was also a small cooking fire, some stones set aside for heating water.

Then he found the shavings of a whittled stick, a boy playing near the fire. *A Cheyenne boy whittling?* It didn't seem right. These were not the shavings from making arrows, the wood was wrong. The Captain picked up the shavings to confirm it. He smelled them. Pine. He walked twenty yards to the creek and looked for tracks. In the sand, by the cool water was a set of prints, small, and delicate where the child walked into the water, not for a chore, perhaps, but just to feel the cold water and listen to the creek sing. A girl definitely, maybe eight or nine years old, and that must be her horse, tied to the tree away from the others, a new present. She wanted to keep it where she could see it. So much pride for a stolen horse. Nits make lice. And this nit had a cavalry horse, the horse of a murdered soldier.

Then he saw the prints of small shoes with heels in the mud, a child who had stood and watched the girl wading. Shoes! It had to be a white child, the boy who was whittling. He looked over at the Crow who were still waiting on their horses, having hardly moved. He spit. *These Cheyenne have kidnapped a white boy.* Originally he had thought of leaving this trail, going back to find the larger band, since there were only few fires here, just a small group that had splintered off. But now he felt it was his duty to find and rescue the white child. He got up on his horse.

The Crow had already turned their horses around to go back to pursue the main body of Cheyenne. They were puzzled when the Captain signaled that they would follow the faint trail that lead out of the camp up a steep slope, farther into the mountains.

Chapter Twenty-One

CHARLIE DIDN'T HAVE extra gas to burn. He couldn't just drive around until he picked up my trail, and he also couldn't ask around for some white girl and expect to get an answer. He had to find Dad to find me, but he'd been to the house and Dad was obviously not there. He started with Jennifer. They'd never met, but I'd pointed out where she lived when we drove past one time. I can just imagine the look on her face when he pulled up next to her as she walked away from her house down the sidewalk of our neat little subdivision.

"I'm not telling you anything," she said and started walking faster.

Charlie cruised along next to her.

"Her dad's in big trouble, you know. Broke into a house on the reservation. Maybe the sheriff wants to know."

She shook her head. She didn't believe him. "Go tell him, then."

"Where'd he go?"

"How the hell do I know?"

Charlie drove his car a little closer.

"How come she left her car?"

"Maybe she thought nobody'd find her that way. *I* thought she ran off with *you*."

Charlie watched her walk; there was something about her. She seemed pissed, and not just because he was following her. "Where's your rodeo boyfriend?"

She didn't answer.

"He left town too, huh?"

She stopped and glared at him. She didn't think of it, but Charlie did. We disappeared around the same time.

"If you don't stop following me, I'm going to call the fucking sheriff myself."

He rolled up his window. He knew the rodeo schedule well enough; he had ridden a few events. He headed east. It was just a hunch, but at least he had another person to look for.

DAD FIGURED IT OUT, too, at almost the same time. He'd been checking with people at gas stations and cafés along I-90. He'd ask about me first, then add the part about Charlie only if he had to. No one had seen a white girl—not traveling with an Indian boy. They were sure they'd remember that. At one gas station the cashier remembered seeing a rodeo cowboy come through with a young girl who could have been me. But no Indian.

"Sorry, I can't be more help." The woman looked genuinely concerned. She was trying.

Dad shrugged it off. He went back to the truck and started to pull away. He stopped at the road and dug my picture out from under his coat. He looked at my image for a moment, then he put the truck in reverse, backed up and brought it into the Mini-Mart. He let someone go ahead of him in the line so they wouldn't be looking over his shoulder when he showed her the picture.

"Yeah, I think so. That could be her. I mean she looks different in the picture. But I think so." She looked at it closely again then gave it back to him. "She was with a good-lookin' rodeo boy. I think they headed east. I don't remember the color of his truck."

"Thanks," Dad said. He waved from the door without looking back. He tried not to be too hopeful, but he couldn't help wanting to believe that maybe Jennifer had made up the story about Charlie. Maybe I wasn't even pregnant, just run off with this bronc rider.

After that he started trying the rodeos and found another person who thought he might have seen me. He tore a schedule off a phone pole, folded it into his pocket and headed for the next town, just one rodeo ahead of Charlie.

By chance he drove right by the park down by the river where we'd camped out one night. It was empty by then, just a squirrel making a mad dash for a tree as his truck bumped by on the rutted dirt road out to the rodeo grounds. The arena was deserted except for the local man who maintained the place. Dad showed him my picture.

"I've seen her," he said as if he'd just won something. "She's with one of the cowboys. A kid named Clayton."

"Are you sure? Not with an Indian kid?"

The man raised an eyebrow. "I told you I saw her, and she was with that kid. He busted up his shoulder last Saturday."

Dad studied him, trying to decide whether to believe him. I know he wanted to. It sounded better.

"Do you know where they've gone?"

"Nah."

Dad started to leave. But the man stopped him. "I know a guy who might know. He knows all the rodeo cowboys."

THE BAR THE MAN sent him to was a big place, dimly lit, mostly empty in the middle of the day. But there was an older guy with a dark beard who had a calculator and some papers spread out across the counter. He had tattoos all over, the kind men used to get overseas in the navy. It was his place.

"What do you want?" he said to Dad as soon as the door had shut behind him. He could tell Dad wasn't there for a beer.

"Lookin' for a guy. Maybe you've seen him."

He'd heard of Clayton, but didn't know about any particular girl. "He was here with lots of girls, always a different one, but he's gone anyway, hurt his arm and must have gone home to Momma."

Dad nodded and turned to leave. It didn't sound right; he thought maybe it was the wrong guy after all. About halfway to the door, the man shouted.

"You lookin' for him or the girl, man?"

Dad didn't answer, but the man guessed and laughed. Dad opened the door and cold air blew in. He caught the last thing the man said as the door banged shut.

"Better try the motels!"

I WATCHED FAITHFULLY through the open window of the room as the light dimmed and the rain began to turn to snow. The big flakes did not fall for long, but soon it looked like winter had come, even though it was only the end of August.

There was always snow for my birthday in February. I thought about my mother in the kitchen, years ago, her hair pulled up, her hands wet and a little raw from doing dishes. A chocolate cake cooled near her on the counter, filling the room with a wonderful smell. Nine candles lay, already counted, in a neat pile, and I stood on a stool as close to the cake as I could be. Something slipped from her hands in the soapy water and broke, a glass. The clear sharp edges cut the flesh of her finger so cleanly she didn't even notice it at first, until big warm, red drops of blood began falling on the counter. She wrapped it in a dishcloth without saying a word, and the blood soaked into the white cotton.

"It won't stop," she said and wrapped her wound in a Mickey Mouse Band-Aid, and then another because it was too small. And I had to have one, too. I watched Mom's hands, as she spread the dark chocolate frosting on the cake and saw the blood already soaking through the Band-Aids. She was telling me a story, one she made up, as always about a prince who comes to rescue a princess. The kitchen was bright and warm, but still I could feel the chill of the forest in her story, and smell the dirty hands of the tree trolls tying the princess to the gnarled roots.

"Mom," I remember saying, "you should go to the doctor. It's still bleeding."

She looked at her finger and frowned as it began dripping blood again. "No," she said, "it's only a small cut. It hurts a little, but it's not that bad." And she wrapped it in a fresh bandage so the blood wouldn't drip on my cake. I handed her the candles, red and blue and yellow. She continued with the story. "They kill the prince and drag him to an icy pond, tie wet stones to his neck and let him disappear into its bottomless depths. And the princess remains a prisoner forever." Mom laughed. You'd never think there would be something that warped in her. She would almost always do that to a story.

"Mom!"

"What?"

"You can't do that."

"Sometimes the prince has to lose."

"No he doesn't."

She just smiled, and brushed her hair away from her forehead. "Princes are highly overrated, honey."

"Change it."

She put the last candle in, ignoring my pouting.

"Okay. The prince doesn't get killed by the trolls; he rescues the princess and they live happily ever after." She took a big lick of frosting from the mixing spoon and handed it to me. "That better?"

"No."

Mom was like that, though she never let anyone see that cynical side of her personality. She had been raised not to. To most people she seemed poised, generous, maybe a little quiet, but she seemed happy. I guess that's what we want to think about everyone, that they're happy, that we don't need to worry about them.

I stared out at the street for a while without really thinking. It was night, and the snow had stopped. Cars and trucks drove by in a steady but syncopated rhythm. I think Mom *was* happy, in the beginning. Toward the end, probably not. She seemed disappointed. Usually she was quiet at dinner. I remember the sound of forks on plates, and knives cutting meat and serving plates clunking on the table, without words at all.

▲ ▲ ▲

WHEN THE SCOUTS found the blind warrior in a small, mossy cave, he was barely alive, weak from trying to starve himself to death. As the cold rain had turned to snow he'd had visions of his death, and so he was not surprised, nor even afraid of the Crow scouts or the Captain behind them who sat watching sternly from his bay horse.

The scouts killed the blind warrior. He was going to die anyway. He meant to. They pulled him apart by the joints, and tore at him and his pieces long after he was dead. And when they finally quit they never thought again about the badly spoiled man they had ruined. They built a fire, pissed, ate and slept for a while and then moved on. The Captain wrote in his official report that one of the savages had been found, wounded from his fight with Custer, yet still alive, and he had been killed without much of a fight. He wrote that he thought they were now perhaps two days behind the

Indians. He set his notebook down and looked up at the trees, black above and lit from underneath by the orange fire, and he could see the snow accumulating on the branches.

Heavy snow, he wrote, *The winter will begin to do our work for us. We see very little game each day. We need only wait for the true cold of this cruel country, which must come soon.*

MO'É'HA'E WATCHED THE snow more with delight than apprehension. Warm in a robe made by her father long ago from a black bear, she stared through the slightly open door of the te-pee. It was night, and at first she heard the snow rather than saw it. The heavy flakes made a sound so nearly silent she thought she might be imagining it. The smell was good. Not like rain. The crisp iciness did not draw out the scent of the earth as rain would, but covered and cleansed it.

Mo'é'ha'e yawned and stretched her arms out of the robes over her head, feeling the chill, and then she threw the robes off altogether to feel the tingling prick at her skin. She felt goose bumps forming, and then after that, her fingers and toes began to lose feeling. She didn't pull the robe up but let the cold sink into her stomach and seep into her shoulders. She was not afraid of it, and she left the robes off until the gray light began to gather in the camp and her skin was almost blue.

Chapter Twenty-Two

THE WOMAN WHO cleaned the room was getting impatient with me. She came around eight and pounded on the door until I answered. I asked her to come back later, said I was sleeping, but she came in anyway. I sat on the bed, while she vacuumed and scoured the sink. The strong smell of cleaning agents invaded the room, and when she came out of the bathroom, her hands were wet and pink. She plugged in the vacuum cleaner and began sucking the dust and air from the room. I could feel my breath coming with more difficulty. I tried to catch her eye, to see what she was thinking, but she wouldn't look at me. She must have been sixty, her hair was deep reddish-brown, but I could see the gray roots through the thin hair on her scalp. Her lipstick was brilliant red, almost like a lacquer. And though her makeup was fierce, her eyes looked tired. She wasn't thin or overweight. She was like a balloon that had begun to lose its air and shape. My mother would never get to this age. I hadn't ever thought of her that way, growing older.

I put my hand to my stomach and burped one of those horrible burps which normally sent me reeling to the bathroom. But I couldn't with her there, so I floated on the bed in a swamp of nausea, my stomach hot and burning, praying for her to finish her tedious work. Mom was never this methodical in her cleaning. It seemed like she never had a plan or a process. She'd do the job she had thought of, often not finishing it, and then she would be outside on the deck with a book.

The woman finished cleaning, carefully removed the trash bag from the bathroom and tied it in a knot. She walked past the bed and stopped, scowling at my feet hidden under the stiff covers. "Tomorrow I will change the sheets."

I nodded. I must have looked green. Her wrinkled angry face hovered before me.

"You can't stay here forever, you know. This is a motel, not an apartment building. There are regulations."

I nodded again, and choked.

"I've seen that boy of yours." Her red lips smacked thickly. My stomach turned threateningly. She didn't know that he was gone. "You two aren't married."

I shook my head. If I didn't empty my stomach soon, it would be too late.

"I've seen him out, you know." Her eyes were black. "*Out.*" She seemed furious, as if this represented somehow a betrayal of her hospitality. "With other girls," she enunciated. "Do I have to spell it out?"

I thought about telling her he wasn't around anymore, but then I thought better of it. "He's not a boyfriend, he's my brother."

She didn't believe me or almost didn't; for a moment, at least, she was unsure. Then she decided that I was lying. Perhaps some wave of sickness washing over my body made me look particularly guilty. She moved closer to the bed, right by my side. I could smell her sharp breath though I couldn't see beyond the hard, icy surface of her eyes. "I don't approve," she hissed and waited like a snake for my response.

And I couldn't help it; the strong smell of her perfume mixed with her hissing breath. I didn't even hear the words, though I felt their meaning in the pit of my stomach like an acid. The vomit came out of my mouth through my clenched teeth in a slow river. I could see it reflected in her face, the grossness pouring down my T-shirt and onto her precious sheets. When my stomach was empty, neither of us knew what to do. What to say. I took a burning breath, aware mostly of feeling a lot better for the moment. "Sorry. I'm sorry."

She said nothing. And after a moment of stunned shock, she turned and walked away, shutting the door carefully behind her. I got up and did my best to clean up the mess with the new towels she'd brought. When I was done, the bed was soaked, and the room hardly smelled better. I pulled off the T-shirt and put it in the sink to soak. I stood in profile to the mirror studying my body for changes. But it seemed unchanged. It would take the tiniest mental shift to deny the whole thing, to say I had dreamed it up, it wasn't real. I wasn't pregnant. There was nothing to insist on it except that sick feeling in my gut, and that could be so many things.

I sat at the table by the window to calm my stomach with some crackers. Outside the wind had begun to blow in earnest, rolling plastic grocery bags out into the traffic, which caught under the cars as they passed. The little bit of snow from last night had melted away.

DAD PULLED OFF the highway, came down the exit ramp and turned into a Denny's. He stood in line to get a table behind a whole troop of Boy Scouts, uniformed kids who had come for the all-you-can-eat specials. He sat down where he could see the street, and out beyond that, the curve of the highway. The Muzak drowned out the low rumble of motor homes and tractor-trailer rigs. He opened his menu to the faded pictures of cheap steaks and twice-baked potatoes.

He had just been to the sheriff, shown the picture, got the usual response, "I haven't seen her. I'll pick her up if I come across her, but it's not like we're going to be able to launch some kind of manhunt. She's just one of hundreds of runaway teenagers out there."

"This is my daughter!" He slammed a fist on the sheriff's desk next to my picture.

"I understand, sir. I do." The man cleared his throat, feeling uncomfortable, working himself up to a question. "Is she traveling alone?"

"Of course."

"You're sure?"

The sheriff dug through his drawer, found four pens that didn't work before he got one that could write and grabbed a scrap of paper to scribble his notes on. Dad stared at him with his jaw set, his shoulders stiff.

"Sir, it's my job to ask."

Dad looked around the cluttered office which smelled of overheated coffee. There were a half-dozen Styrofoam cups scattered around the room plus one steaming in front of the sheriff.

Dad shifted uneasily in his chair. "She might be with a rodeo cowboy. A kid named Clayton."

"How old?"

"I don't know."

"Sounds like he's not a kid. At least eighteen, then?"

Dad nodded.

The sheriff tried the pen but it ran out almost immediately, so he threw it at the basket but missed. "Kids can get pretty crazy at this age."

Dad was getting impatient.

The sheriff rubbed the back of his neck. "When's she turn eighteen?"

"Next February."

The sheriff shrugged as if to point out that it would make no difference soon enough. I don't think Dad had ever had that thought before, let alone heard the idea from a stranger. The world would soon treat me as a legal adult no matter what he thought. He stood up to leave. The sheriff walked over to the coffeepot to fill his cup.

"Watch yourself."

Dad turned at the door.

"Look I'm just saying, I understand. It'd be easy to lose your temper over something like this."

IT WAS COLD OUT. Long clouds stretched across the sky like mud smeared by a child's hand. From his seat at the Denny's, Dad watched the steady flow on the interstate, the trash blown into the barbed-wire fence, tattered and trembling in the wind. In the booths near him, groups of tourists also stared outside as if trying to comprehend how the weather could do this to them when it was supposed to be summer.

He laid his menu down and ordered without looking at the waitress. With all the reservations out in eastern Montana and South Dakota, you'd think you'd see plenty of Indians out on the highway, going places like everybody else, and one Indian boy in a Pontiac wouldn't really stand out. But when Charlie's car pulled off of the interstate, coasting down the ramp to the stop at the end, Dad spotted it immediately. He knew it was Charlie. He left his fork on his plate, paid the bill as fast as he could, and was waiting with his truck idling across the street when Charlie came back from the rest room and then pulled out onto the interstate heading east. Dad kept back as much as he could, letting a few cars pass, trying to remain inconspicuous. Charlie was driving way under the speed limit, which made it hard to follow him.

A gust of wind pushed at the side of the truck. Dad leaned forward to look up through the windshield at the sky. High up, a crow drifted by, unable to hold his own against the growing storm. The clouds were building, and despite being midday, it was getting darker. When he looked back to the highway, Charlie was turning off on to a county dirt road, headed south. When he turned to follow, the Pontiac sped up.

Dad gripped the steering wheel more intently, but it was a silly chase. That road was straight as an arrow, and the dust cloud could be seen for miles. There was no place to hide. The truck banged and rattled over the potholes and washboard. It was a desolate stretch of road, dry and treeless. The bunch grass was sparse, cured and yellow, fighting for space in the hard ground with the gray-green sagebrush. Charlie turned again and careened off to the west, into the wind. Dad stomped on the accelerator.

Soon it began to rain, a fine, cold, stinging rain. Over the mountains it was already snowing. Dad's pickup sped down the dirt road behind Charlie—the only two things moving out there, the beat-up old Pontiac and behind it a blue Ford pickup, going as fast as each engine could burn fuel. The rain put the dust down and quickly turned the road to gumbo. But the heavy, nearly shockless two-wheel-drive Pontiac seemed almost unaffected, as if it carried so much momentum that no amount of wet, gooey clay could slow it down.

Then they rounded a corner. Charlie slid toward the ditch, fishtailing, trying to stay on the road. Dad's pickup was empty in the back, and he nearly spun into the ditch, too. His hands whipped over the steering wheel as he whipsawed in the opposite direction. The heavy rain came down in sheets and the clouds dropped so low that the plain was almost swallowed up in them. Dad's windshield wipers swung madly, screeching like a strangled bird. By the time he was able to make out Charlie's car off the road stuck in the ditch, it was too late. He slammed on his brakes, locking them up on the mud slick, and started spinning. The desert streaked by before him, uniform in its plainness, except for Charlie who was jumping from the Pontiac and running to get away before the spinning truck collided with it. One more revolution and Dad could see that he was going to hit the car with the tail of the truck. It slammed into it with a jarring crunch of metal that stopped him. The Pontiac slipped a little further into the ditch and the trunk popped open.

Dad relaxed his pressure on the brake pedal and turned off the shrieking wipers, and for a moment the only sound was the intense hush of rain. He could just make out Charlie with a pipe wrench gripped tightly in his right hand standing in the downpour a few yards away from his smashed car. Dad took his .357 out from under the seat, shoved it into his pocket and jumped out. As he walked toward Charlie he noticed the empty box open in the trunk.

Charlie started to back away from him. "What do you want from me?" he yelled through the biting wind and rain.

Dad gripped the pistol in his pocket. Charlie used to be just some kid who'd worked for him. He looked scrawny, even for his age. His hair was matted to his face. His jeans were covered with specks of different colored paints, and his jacket was patched. He looked to Dad like a bum, unworthy of me, something I'd found in the gutter. Suddenly, all of the things my father had ever been mad at were directed at Charlie, this skinny, rained-on, adolescent Indian kid who'd knocked up his daughter. He took another step toward him.

"Back off." Charlie's voice broke. He raised the wrench.

"Listen you son of a bitch . . . " Dad started.

There was a moment of hesitation, perhaps that vague, instinctive inhibition that's supposed to keep human beings from attacking each other. It stopped Dad for a few seconds, but then the anticipation of violence encouraged him. He *felt* like it. *Goddamn kid, waving a fucking wrench at me.*

Charlie crouched, getting ready.

Dad took another step closer to him, his hand tightened on the wet pistol, enjoying the threat. He must have felt strong, bigger than this boy. He didn't notice the rain or the wind anymore.

"Where is she?" His voice was loud, a big booming voice, like someone too used to being listened to.

"I don't know where she is," said Charlie.

Dad charged him, knocking him down before he could raise the wrench to swing. The air rushed out of his lungs as Dad's heavy body hit him. He sprawled backward in the mud. Dad got to his feet ready to tackle him again, but Charlie scrambled up and threw the wrench, hitting him hard in the right shoulder. The wrench was heavy, and the blow knocked him off-balance. Charlie turned to run, but Dad got a leg and they both went down in the mud again.

Charlie twisted free and made it to the door of the car just as Dad caught him again. He held onto the steering wheel while Dad tried to pull him out of the car. Then he managed to kick a foot loose and boot Dad in the face. Charlie took advantage of the free second to grab for the glove box and the gun—the gun he hadn't looked at or thought about since he took it from me and put it there. He rolled on his back across the big bench seat of the Pontiac and pointed the pistol maybe a foot and a half away from Dad's face.

"You aren't going to beat me up."

Dad moved back, and Charlie got out of the car.

"Put that away."

"Fuck you!" His voice shattered.

Dad backed up some more. Charlie looked around. He couldn't just drive off, the Pontiac was stuck. He stared at Dad's face.

"I told you I don't know where she is."

"Bullshit," Dad spat.

They stood there, caught, letting time eddy around them.

"Where is she?" Dad thought he might be able to pull the gun out of his pocket before the kid could do anything about it, as long as he didn't move too fast. But Charlie looked shaky, and there was no one else around.

This fucking kid got my daughter pregnant. The thought of it enraged him on a level that was completely out of his control. The trespass, the violation of it.

"You keep your filthy hands off my daughter," Dad shouted, real emotion stealing the usual strength from his voice. "You're in serious trouble. She's a minor. Taking her is kidnapping, and getting her pregnant . . . " He lost his words.

Charlie slowly lowered the gun.

He didn't know. Stupid kid.

Charlie dropped the gun, and he turned and ran. He made it fifty yards before Dad reacted. And then it was as if none of what was happening was real. Dad pulled his gun out with his hurt arm, which was already getting stiff. He aimed it at Charlie.

He was running away as fast as he could. His legs burned, but the space did not seem to give way. It must have felt like his heart could explode in his chest with effort that would not dent the limitlessness of that plain.

The wind blew the rain directly into Dad's face. He fired the gun. It made a dull pop, but Charlie kept running, and there was nothing to say a moment later that the gun had even fired, except that the metal was warm in Dad's hand. And again he fired.

Charlie kept running. He had nearly cleared a shallow hill almost a hundred and fifty yards away when Dad fired again.

This time Charlie fell. Dad lowered the gun.

For a long, strange and scary moment he could feel the whole world change. The gun was hot enough to burn him, and all of his anger evaporated in the rain and the wind. The clouds dropped again as a fog, and he couldn't see Charlie anymore.

It took him a while, standing there stunned, soaking in the rain, but finally, he went to look for him. And somehow moving jogged his mind and brought him to some sense of reality. He threw the gun off into the sagebrush, far enough that he didn't hear it land in the mud. He was shaking. He was thinking that he'd never meant to hurt anybody. That all he wanted was to find me, without conditions. To make sure I was safe. And my dad's eyes clouded with tears. He fell to his knees, and with every breath some of the poison poured out of his lungs and heart. Then he let his head fall into his hands and the rain soaked into his broad shoulders.

When he looked up again, the clouds had lifted enough that he could see where Charlie had fallen at the top of the rise. But he wasn't there. Dad got up and ran to the place. Far off in the distance, at least a mile away, Charlie was still running. And then the clouds descended again, and he disappeared like a stone falling into a dark pool.

Dad trudged back through the mud to the vehicles. He hooked up a tow rope to the Pontiac and made a mess of the road, digging ruts in the muck with his spinning tires, but finally he got the car out of the ditch. He laid the wet keys on the seat, even rolled up the window on the driver's side. Then he got into his truck and turned back to town.

Chapter Twenty-Three

A FINE SNOW FILTERED through the trees and hid the earth of red pine needles. Mo'é'ha'e looked at her footprints, watching them fill up, soften and fade. Without the sun it was not easy to tell direction. And the slope of the hill was confusing; it lay in a jumble of ridges that ran parallel and then contrary to the general fall of the mountain. When she and the boy had left Dull Knife's camp several hours before, she never dreamed they would have any trouble finding the big camp again. That many lodges made a lot of smoke and noise. But she hadn't heard the creek bubbling for hours, no distant barking of camp dogs, no smell of smoke mixing with the snow and pine. Henry sat every time they stopped. His lips were blue. He wasn't used to the cold. Mo'é'ha'e tried to use the wind to find her way, but the clouds were too diffuse to perceive movement, and the gusts in the trees swirled and changed direction constantly. Her dog whined.

"Hush."

She walked confidently forward, looking over her shoulder just to see that Henry was following her. Gripped in his pink hand was the stiff body of a squirrel they'd caught together. His steps matched hers, and his toes were red where they peeked out of his worn shoes. If they could keep walking, they would keep warm and they might cut tracks that would lead to camp, though the falling snow made that less likely by the moment.

Mo'é'ha'e quartered down the slope figuring that they must have climbed too much. She marched through the dark, wet lodgepole, keeping a straight line even when they had to scramble over the logjams of deadfall crisscrossing their path. Moss hung from the tree trunks on all sides, and the visibility gradually diminished to less than thirty yards. Nonetheless, Mo'é'ha'e was encouraged; the ground seemed wetter, and the rich growth indicated a spring, and a spring might find the stream. She stopped to listen. At first all she heard was the dog panting and Henry's heavy breath.

Then instead of the stream, Mo'é'ha'e heard something that chilled her blood in a way the storm had not. She turned suddenly to Henry, warning him with a wave of her hand. Her eyes frantically searched the forest. Then she could smell it and turned to look upwind. The trees were thick and dim and the snow blew through in a blur. It was there somewhere. She could feel it now. The trees around them were all lodgepole and bare of limbs. Impossible to climb. Her dog began to growl, his hair stood up on his neck. She grabbed his muzzle and whispered desperately in his ear.

"He'kotóo'estse!"

A shadow appeared and disappeared, about eighty yards uphill. Then it came back, in full view. Tawny, silver, arched at the shoulders, lumbering down the ridge — a boar grizzly, maybe nine hundred pounds. The dog barked and the bear stopped for a moment, standing up on its hind legs, testing the air. Then the whining dog tore loose of Mo'é'ha'e's arms and ran at the bear, yammering furiously.

"*Amáxéste!*" Mo'é'ha'e shouted. *Run!*

The bear charged. Henry tried to keep up with Mo'é'ha'e as they scrambled through the forest downhill. The howls of her dog stopped her. Thirty yards away or less, the bear had stopped because of the dog. It was already mortally wounded, and its desperate barks sent shivers through her. It charged the bear again, ducking a sweeping claw and biting into a wad of fur, only to be shaken off like a rag doll.

Henry stopped, too. Both of them stood transfixed. The bear connected with the dog again and sent it sprawling. He roared furiously, and Mo'é'ha'e and Henry started to run again. The dog charged in for a last time, foaming and spitting blood, and then after a sudden blow, it hung limply in the great bear's mouth. The beast stood up on his hind legs and shook the dog violently, its thundering voice ripping across the mountain. Mo'é'ha'e and Henry ran desperately, and eventually the roaring subsided.

Mo'é'ha'e stopped. She thought she could hear the stream, at first only between gusts of the wind, and then steadily as they moved in the right direction. They climbed down a steep slope, slipping nearly every other step, but they found the creek and followed the tumbling water down.

The water was black and bitterly cold, rushing and foaming as it carved its gorge with scarcely a pause to make a clear pool. The green moss covering the rocks was wet under the new snow, but it offered a grip as they struggled along the steep bank of the creek, banging their ankles and shins raw on the slick black rocks. Mo'é'ha'e prayed that she had chosen the right way, that camp was not upstream, because if it was, it might be a fatal mistake for Henry. He was in bad shape already.

Finally, they passed through a narrow gap in the rocks. It required them to walk up to their knees in the seething water, but on the other side, the slope eased, and the banks of the stream spread and they were again walking on a soft bed of pine needles. Mo'é'ha'e was still worried about the bear. Normally, a grizzly would not follow them, but the forest and the cold inspired a foreboding that made her watch carefully. She motioned for Henry to follow behind her as they moved through the trees.

And then her caution was rewarded. Her heart pounded. She had been anticipating the bear, and now she wished it was, for what she saw was a hobbled horse with a U.S. cavalry saddle on it. A man stood with his back to the children looking ahead through the trees. Then she smelled what he smelled, the cooking fires of camp. They slipped back quietly toward the stream to a thick stand of willows. She pulled Henry with her under them and peered out through a small opening to watch the army scout. The smell of the smoke was clear now and it sent pangs to her stomach. She wrapped her arms around Henry to stop him from shaking.

"Shhh," she whispered. His cold skin made her cold, too. The man was joined by two more, two Crow, and she could just hear the low murmur of their talking. They stayed for a long time, and her feet went numb. Henry began to tremble and cry.

"*He'kotóo'estse,*" Mo'é'ha'e hissed.

But he could not stay quiet. The men stopped, as if they might be hearing something, and Mo'é'ha'e covered Henry's mouth and nose, smothering the sound; she let go for a moment to allow him to breathe. It occurred to her, as she watched her enemy's faces searching the bushes, trying to confirm that there had been a sound, that Henry might *want* to be discovered, that he, too, was her enemy. She covered his mouth and nose again with both hands, turning his head so that he could see her eyes, so that he could see that she would not allow him to give them away. And what she showed him was terrifying, and he stopped struggling. She offered him little bits of air between her icy fingers.

The men returned to their horses. They unhobbled them, tightened the cinches on the saddles and mounted. They did not gallop off but walked the horses slowly and quietly away through the trees. When they were well gone, Mo'é'ha'e released Henry, who was blue with cold, and silent.

THE CAPTAIN FOLLOWED the progress of two coyotes skirting the perimeter of the huge army camp until they disappeared beyond General Mackenzie's tent. The general was sitting out front with a great bearskin wrapped around his shoulders, smoking a pipe. To the Captain he had always seemed weak, an officer who lacked the visceral commitment to battle, to the violence of it. The Captain approached with his two scouts and began speaking before he had come to a stop. "The enemy is camped in a cul-de-sac, higher up in the mountains. We have been following them for a month, sir. Game is scarce, and they are in a weakened, demoralized condition."

"Good morning, Captain."

The Captain smiled slightly, ignoring the civility. The two Crow stopped a few feet away from the council, watching. One had his hand resting on the shoulder of the other; both were stone-faced and unreadable. The general found his attention drawn to them.

The Captain gestured to the sky. "It should be very cold for the next few days."

"You seem anxious, Captain. I have not even finished my smoke."

The Captain didn't respond.

The general emptied his pipe into the snow; the black coals burned down to a patch of yet green earth. "In that case I should expect the savages to be all the more easily subdued, Captain."

"Possibly, sir."

The general did not miss the slight impatience and derision in his tone. "Possibly, except for what detail, Captain?"

"Except for the detail that they are as unpredictable as animals, sir."

"Yes."

"And a raiding party was spotted. They're undoubtedly attacking a nearby camp of Shoshone, right now."

The general patiently considered the Crow again, their copper skin, their black hair and hairless faces, their ragged, wild clothes and the red-and-yellow mud in their hair. *Such strange allies,* he thought. What had they been promised, beyond a few Cheyenne and Lakota scalps, a strike against an old enemy, a better deal in the coming order? They seemed calm, not at all violent.

"So you believe them to be of a fighting temperament, Captain?"

"I would fight." The Captain said it willfully.

"Then let us bring these heathen in." The general yawned and refilled his pipe with tobacco.

MO'É'HA'E WAS HAPPY to be back at Dull Knife's camp by a fire. She felt safer among the bustling lodges. She sat cross-legged as she ate some boiled root and a berry cake that had been pounded into a loaf and dried in the fall. There was no meat for women or children. Henry sat across the fire from her, holding his cake as though he expected it to be taken away, as though he sensed that soon things would get so bad that to feed him, a white boy, the enemy, would become unaffordable. He poked his foot in the fire until it started to steam and burn through his shoe, and then he pulled it out a few inches. Mo'é'ha'e's uncle stood nearby watching the fire. He seemed troubled by her news, though it was already suspected by the camp that the soldiers were following them. He wrapped his robes tighter. Mo'é'ha'e looked up at her uncle and shivered.

"You should not go so far for a few nuts and a squirrel, little one. It isn't safe," said her uncle.

Mo'é'ha'e looked down at her muddied moccasins, feeling chastised. She had expected to be useful, a hero, warning the camp of the danger. She put her bread down and turned away from her uncle.

He looked down at the disappointed little girl. She always seemed brightly lit from within, even in her frustration.

"Ne've'éstse méstse." His words came out more sternly than he intended. *Come with me.*

She regarded him apprehensively. *"To sa'a?"*

White Bird did not answer but took her cold hand and led her away from the fire. His hands felt good, strong and warm. They walked silently through the camp together toward the main lodge. Outside, an older man was splitting wood. He left the bigger pieces, taking the smaller ones to split into kindling. His arms looked weak, but his hatchet fell precisely, and the wood splintered neatly. He stopped his work as they approached.

"Dull Knife?" her uncle asked.

"Hotoma'e." Inside.

Mo'é'ha'e expected to wait outside, but her uncle did not release his grip on her arm, taking her in with him. She had never been inside the great lodge before, and it was only because she was still a child that she was getting this opportunity now. It took a moment for her eyes to adjust to the dim light. Seated on the floor were several older men. The air was thick with the sweet smell of smoke and sweat. Someone coughed, and the silent faces all turned to the little girl. She felt weak, but her uncle's hand held her tightly.

"My niece has something to say."

Dull Knife nodded. He was known mainly as a peace chief but he looked strong and frightening to Mo'é'ha'e, as if all the men he had ever confronted in battle had left some mark on his face. Her uncle released her hand and gently pushed her into the circle. One of the chiefs passed a pipe by her to White Bird, and the smoke burned her throat.

"*Now,*" said Dull Knife, "*Tell us your story.*"

His face was strong and frightening this close, and she felt his hot, smoky breath pushing at the soft skin of her face. The other men turned their sharp gaze upon her. She could smell them more than see them in the close, humid gloom of the lodge.

"*I saw white soldiers, and Crow.*" At first there was no reaction. And she felt as if maybe she did not say it loudly enough. She tried again, "*I saw . . .* "

Her uncle cut her off with a firm hand on her shoulder. "*To sa'a?*"

She described the spot, and the men nodded, as if they'd already heard about it. They left her standing in the middle of their circle as they went back to a discussion about what should be done. It wasn't surprising to them that she might have seen the scouts. Box Elder, the blind medicine man, had already had a vision about it. He and others wanted to move to a more defensible position. Also Sits-in-the-Night's ponies had been run off. The other men nodded and began to get up, stiff from having sat there too long.

"*I don't want to go up to hide in the rocks,*" Mo'é'ha'e announced. "*I will fight too.*" And the men all laughed.

When the laughter died down, Box Elder touched her forehead lightly with his creased hands. "*You are very brave, little one,*" he said.

As she walked with her uncle back to their lodge she felt the cold wicking back into her moccasins. It was foolish, even dangerous, to have waded in the stream. Her moccasins had dried some by the fire, but not enough, and the walk from one end of the encampment to the other made her toes begin to hurt. Moccasins weren't much to wear in this kind of cold anyway, but at least they needed to be dry. And there would be no other pair this winter, no buffalo hide to make them from.

THE CAPTAIN SAT DOWN by the fire next to the Denver newspaperman. The sun was making a weak last stand on the mountains and on the tops of the trees at the eastern end of the meadow. The journalist leaned over to tie up the bearskin over the boots he had just acquired. Across the fire a man coughed and then swore. The Captain looked up through the yellow flames of the fire, which seemed almost hungry as they distorted the face of a bearded man. His name was Hoke, an army sergeant, and next to him was Lucius, a soldier who always seemed to accompany him. Lucius had a knife out in his dirty hands, sharpening it. The steel blade scraped along the whetstone with a rhythmic ringing sound that mixed like music with the fluttering flames and the light wind in the conifers.

"You should have your notebook out, newsboy," Hoke roared. Lucius glanced up from his work.

The newsman did not respond. The Captain was fascinated by the apparition created by the heat of the fire. Hoke did not look human, but not animal either. It was probably natural to see these regular soldiers as aliens, different; but he wondered if he could really count on his own clean-shaven face and more refined vocabulary to distinguish himself from these men.

"You could write something pretty and poetic about us preparing to bring in the last of those stinkin' animals." Hoke's eyes danced as he laughed.

The newsman sat back while the big man stuffed a great wad of chew into his yawning maw. "An epitaph," he offered.

"A what?" said Lucius.

"And what would it say?" the newsman asked. The fire flared up instantly as if to answer, and for a moment he couldn't see either man through the flames.

"I'd tell those folks back in Denver that we skinned those savages alive."

"They wouldn't understand it literally, you know," the Captain said quietly.

Lucius frowned at the Captain and then, turning to the newsman, waved his knife in the smoke of the fire. "You tell those folks what they want to hear, that we caught one of those pretty painted warriors and took his skin off with this knife while he could still sing his death song."

Chapter Twenty-Four

THE MOTEL WAS at the end of a strip, a bunch of fast-food places and gas stations, highway services. There would be practically nothing to this town if not for the tourists, and every one of them was probably thinking the same thing. *What happened? It's too cold. Can it really get this cold in August? There's supposed to be a few weeks of summer left.* I took a walk, despite the weather. I had packed quickly with nothing but summer in mind, but at least I had Clayton's jacket, which he'd left for me.

At the edge of town there was a church, very plain, just a one-story brick building with a shallow pitch to the roof, some stained glass at one end in the shape of a cross. I sat for a while at the base of the church sign with notices for Sunday Bible study and some community information. A cloud passed over the sun and stuck there, and then it was really cold. I pulled the jacket tighter around my shoulders and thought about getting up to walk back to my room.

I looked up when a man coughed. All I saw at first was his ashen face. He was cold, too. Suddenly it occurred to me that he must be the minister, and I was sitting on his sign. I stood up quickly.

"Sorry." I started to walk away, but he stopped me.

"It's okay, you can sit." He wanted to smile, but because of the cold he couldn't quite manage it. His voice sounded friendly, though.

"I gotta go, anyway."

"Why don't you come inside? Get warm."

I didn't really want to, but he offered again, and I followed him. It was quiet as he stopped to open the big double doors, just the scrape of his shoes coming to a stop. Inside it was warm, too warm, as if the heat were left on high all the time. But it felt good. There was a lobby area, small, with a well-used linoleum floor and then two more doors to the right that opened into the church hall where there was a deep red carpet.

"Make yourself at home." The minister gestured to the church then walked down a short hallway and disappeared into his office. It felt strange to be so unconditionally welcome.

I walked into the big, open room. The lights were low, and my eyes took a moment to adjust. Behind the podium was a simple, modern-looking cross of laminated wood. I sat in one of the pews and picked up the hymnal that was laying there, a simple, worn black book. I flipped though the pages and the smell was distinct; only a hymnal smelled just like that. I thought of the hands, farmers and carpenters who had held it, and their voices, deep or wavering, strong or off-key. When I was younger, maybe as tall as the back of this wooden pew, and the congregation stood to sing a selection, I didn't know the words so I just listened. It was all so muffled in that forest of legs that all I heard was the sound, not the words themselves. My dad's deep voice. The chords. Then the rustling of pages turning for the next hymn. And all around me was an ocean of fabric that smelled freshly ironed, dresses and suits, perfume and after-shave. I couldn't see the minister when he spoke, but the rhythms and solemn tone were a kind of salve, warm and scented, too.

Next to the hymnal was a Bible, the Revised Standard Version, the one they gave me in Bible school. It had the same illustrations, the same old paintings. I remembered them because after I got my Bible, I used to lie on the floor of my room and stare at the images. I flipped a couple pages until I found one of the pictures. In the Roman arena, an old man with a long gray beard stands with his arms raised to heaven. Around him, the faithful cower, a shirtless man with a long burgundy skirt, a woman in green holding the old man's hem and a mother with a child, maybe seven. The little girl has her head buried in her mother's arms. The emperor sits with his hands together, his red robes flowing down in front of him like blood, and his audience is dressed mostly in white. Circling the faithful are the lions. And I thought, *They will take the girl first.*

I looked up. The minister was at the podium looking for something. He'd slipped in so quietly that I hadn't heard him. I felt like I should say something. I cleared my throat and said, "Thanks."

He set the papers down, looking at me as if he'd thought I'd left already. Then he surprised me by walking over and sitting in the pew in front of me.

"You're a long way from home." He tried to smile again. It looked awkward and incomplete on his face.

"Yep." My voice trembled, sounding like somebody else.

He looked down at his hands as if trying to think of what to say, or maybe he instinctively knew better than to look me directly in the eyes. "Do you have a place to stay?"

"I have a room at the motel. I was just walking. I'm alright, really."

"You're a bit young to be living at a motel, aren't you?"

My throat felt tight. I wished he hadn't said it.

"If you need a better place to stay, or a job for a while. Or a phone to call home . . . "

"No."

He was quiet. He was letting me think about it.

I stood up. "No." Now I tried to smile. Suddenly I wondered, *Does he know? How could he?* My eyes burned.

"Maybe it's time to forgive?" he said softly.

"Who?"

"That's the trick, isn't it? I don't know." He looked me in the eye. "Do you?"

He was doing it to make me cry. The red carpet by my feet looked soaked with blood. I couldn't help thinking of Mo'é'ha'e running for help—then Mom lying with her face away from me. My dad struggling to stand up from the kitchen table. Forgive? Forgive us? Forgive me?

"It's not that simple." I turned to leave, almost forgetting the Bible in my hand. I laid it down awkwardly next to him on the pew and grabbed Clayton's coat. When I got to the door, I stopped as if I felt my mother wishing me to be polite. "Thanks, anyway."

Then I ran out of the warm church. The cold air wrapped its familiar arms around my weak shoulders, and I slipped and nearly fell on the wet sidewalk.

THE MOTEL OWNER stood by the door of her office, smoking. Over her shoulder, behind the desk, was a painting of Jesus. An electric cord dangled from it down the pale-blue wall. It worked like a heater, giving off warmth from the Teflon surface of the image. I think she expected me to stop, to say something, explain myself. I had to walk by her to get to the room. Her face became more twisted with emotion as I approached. But she waited until my back was to her. "You can't stay here."

I knew that. Of course I couldn't.

"I called the sheriff about you."

▲ ▲ ▲

MO'É'HA'E HAD GONE off without Henry, dragging her empty travois by herself through the sprawling camp. It bounced and skipped over the rough frozen ground. Among the trees beyond the lodges, the phantom shapes of horses pawed at the snow for anything green, eating pine needles, in the end, out of desperation, stretching their necks like stunted giraffes into the scant limbs of the lodgepole. A hard winter was coming. Mo'é'ha'e could taste the cold and feel its dryness in her lungs. As she walked through camp, she tried to think of summer, of the hot dry grasses filled with buzzing, snapping grasshoppers.

Already women were loading horses with robes and food, leaving the best for the warriors who would need them in case of a fight. They took the old nags who stood dully with their heads drooping as though they had a sense of the impending battle and a knowledge, somehow, that at least as many horses as people die in such fights. Mo'é'ha'e's mother worked with White Bird's wife, packing their horses with bundles of dried fruit and meat. Racing back and forth through the camp, a mob of children yelled and screamed with delight, disturbing the horses with their chaos but drawing no correction from the elders who were happy for them to play, giving them no chores on this day. Their laughter was infectious, and as they played more came, until all the children in the camp had joined, except Henry.

He sat only a few feet away from a small fire whittling again, peeling long white shavings of pinewood into the flames, which hissed and began to smoke. The fire had melted away the snow in a black, muddy ring, though its heat could hardly have warmed him beyond his knees. His small hands were stiff with the cold, his shoulders wrapped in a ragged deerskin that had begun to collect a fine layer of snow.

White Bird's youngest son ran over to tease him to come play with them. He circled Henry, shouting in Cheyenne for him to get up and play the game, and then some of the other children began to join this new game, laughing and taunting the white boy. At first he tried to ignore them, but the children began to grow frustrated, and their chiding became shrill and lost its fun. Mo'é'ha'e saw the group surrounding Henry just as one of the bigger boys picked up a stick. Before she could do anything to protect Henry, the older kid struck him with the stick, hitting him between the shoulders, then whooping *"Ah haih,"* as if he were counting coup. Henry turned on him wildly, his knife gripped tightly in his hand. Two of the other boys found sticks and began to circle. The rest stopped to watch.

"E'nana!" Mo'é'ha'e shouted. *Leave him alone.*

The bigger boy rushed Henry who swung his knife in a wide arc. He was already several levels of rage ahead of the children who surrounded him, and it startled them. The adults of the camp still hadn't noticed that the play had stopped. Mo'é'ha'e's mother had gone off to catch another horse, and White Bird's wife was too busy packing. The children moved in closer, and they laughed when another boy charged in with his stick and hit Henry in the leg, knocking him to one knee. Sensing weakness, two others ran in immediately to count coup, too, and one of the boys was paid for it with a knife cut to his leg. Just a scratch, but he yelled and pulled back holding the wounded limb.

"Stop it!" Mo'é'ha'e yelled again.

The children laughed, and the wounded boy realized he had won their approval. He stopped crying and raised his stick with a yell that brought them all in on Henry again.

He was struck several times before he was able to drive them off. Then one of the boys tripped, and Henry grabbed his leg and bit his calf above his moccasin. He held on despite the boy's kicking and not until the other boys beat him with their sticks did he finally let go. He scrambled away and ended up almost in the middle of the fire ring. The bitten child tried to stand up, holding his leg. The rest of the children stood silently in a loose circle around Henry.

Mo'é'ha'e saw her chance and ran in, facing Henry's tormentors. The smoke from the fire twisted and curled around her. The boys picked up their sticks, as if considering whether to continue the fight, but a shout from the end of the camp stopped them. The children turned, always alert to any news, and ran to see what it could be.

A group of warriors, the Kit Fox Soldiers, descended the low hill beyond the camp. Their faces were painted black, and the leading horseman bore a long pole with twisted scalps hanging from it. They moved in a procession, holding their horses in line, and stopped at the first of the lodges. They were waiting for a proper reception, which was slow to come. Many were still preoccupied with packing and had just begun to notice the arrivals. The first to respond were the men's wives who ran to them, trilling a victory song, which sounded weak and feeble without the support of the whole camp.

The leader of the group, Last Bull, speared his lance into the frozen ground next to his horse's feet. The scalps on the end tossed wildly back and forth like crazed blackbirds. He held his horse with reins so tight that its frothing mouth nearly touched its chest, and as he spurred the animal forward, it danced in a crisp dressage. He rode through the camp, his anger apparent in the knotted horse, which began to jump with both front feet together and twist sideways trying to escape the bit.

He shouted. *"We have made a raid on the Shoshone. We have counted coup and taken scalps."* The horse spun in a circle, desperately trying to get its head, but Last Bull would not relent. His powerful arms, bare despite the cold, fiercely kept their grip. *"What are the people doing? Are you planning to leave when we will have a scalp dance?"*

"Last Bull!" Dull Knife walked up to him, his hands were up and open, offering to take the reins of the nearly mad horse to calm him. He stopped short. The horse stood for a moment shaking and staring at him with a wild eye. *"The women are packing the lodges because the white soldiers are near and may attack."*

The horse reared, sensing a moment of relaxation, but Last Bull pulled his head back in. He looked coldly at Dull Knife, who, like any Cheyenne leader, governed only by consensus. Last Bull turned back to the people, and then to the Kit Fox Soldiers who had ridden up behind him, and finally to Dull Knife. *"Who saw these white soldiers this time?"*

White Bird stepped up close behind the chief. He thought to say something, but it wasn't his place. He let Dull Knife speak. *"Sits in the Night had horses stolen. He saw Pawnee scouts."*

"He is a famous liar."

"His horses are gone."

"He lost them and then makes up this story to hide his own foolishness!" Last Bull laughed. *"We shall have a scalp dance!"*

"White Bird's niece also saw the scouts."

"A child!" He shouted as his horse spun again. *"You've all become children, and cowardly. If there are white soldiers, let them come, we will teach them another lesson in fighting."*

Last Bull left Dull Knife and charged past White Bird over to one of the pack horses which stood nearby. Without getting off, he leaned down with his knife and cut the cinch, and the pack fell at the horse's feet. Then the rest of the Kit Fox Soldiers went about the camp making the women unpack their horses, and turned them back in with the herd.

THAT NIGHT THEY built a great fire, which soon burned high. Mo'é'ha'e sat with Henry far enough from the bonfire to be out of the way. She'd laid in his lap a hot rock wrapped in a bit of hide to keep him warm. She talked to him quietly, and though he understood none of what she said, the calming tone of her voice eased the tight muscles of his neck. She told him the story of the creation of the world, how the people came to be—how it was at the beginning when it was only the Cheyenne and there was no *vé'ho'e,* no *white man.*

As it got dark the fire glowed brilliant orange and cast its light on their faces many yards away. Henry finally moved. He didn't stand, but crawled to their tepee and curled up in a dark corner. Mo'é'ha'e watched him go, wishing he would talk again. She went to the big fire and found her uncle sitting on a tightly woven wool blanket. The Kit Fox Soldiers had begun to dance, but he was not joining them. He was angry with the young men, and he was worried.

Mo'é'ha'e sat next to him and leaned her head against the hard muscle of his shoulder. There was too much noise from the drums and the dancing and chanting to talk, so she simply watched. Against the fire, the dancers were too dark to recognize. They danced in couples. Some mothers had tied their daughters together in groups to keep track of them during the proceedings so that some young warrior might not steal away with them. Around the periphery of the circle, two *he'émánehe,* halfmen–halfwomen, played matchmaker, finding couples for the dance. And the older people watching seemed hypnotized by the drums and stared into the burning fire, their eyes lost in the past.

At first, no one but the Kit Fox Soldiers and the young participated. The moonless sky flooded with stars, and the temperature dropped even more, and those sitting near the fire sweated from the heat on one side, while the frost bit at their backs. Soon, though, almost the whole camp was possessed with a strange recklessness. Tomorrow, the white soldiers and the bullets and guns, the smoke and misery, would never come.

Mo'é'ha'e and her mother and uncle sat far from the fire and there were so many intervening bodies that they got little warmth from it, only a bright and dizzying light. It was strange to be so cold in sight of a raging flame, and it began to put her to sleep. She drifted in and out of dreams, and every time she woke, she saw the real world of the dance in fragments of pounding feet and arched bodies. Sometime late, her uncle carried her through the mad shadows to the tepee, and he lay her in her robes. He pulled them over her and she felt the warmth of them wrap around her like a cocoon.

THE WHITE SOLDIERS listened all night to the drums. They began to hear them from a long way off, as they walked their horses through the squeaking snow and black trees. Each man rode with his hand in front of his face, palm outward to protect himself from branches that could not be seen in the darkness. It gave them the appearance of saints, as though they rode toward some great and righteous battle. They traveled for hours this way, in darkness that was so cold that even with boots and overboots, swathed in wool and fur, they lost the feeling in their limbs. Sparks danced from the iron horseshoes striking rocks in the frozen ground, and the horses, too, looked like strange ghosts; their breath froze and coated their chests in a delicate white frost.

Maybe it was the distant sound of the scalp dance, but most of the soldiers thought not of the coming fight, but of sex. They imagined the parts of women's bodies they rarely saw or touched, warm and damp. Hands caressed imagined thighs, soft stomachs, slipped off hidden clothing, kissed breasts and mouths or imagined mouths that kissed with warm tongues. They shook in their saddles trying to bring their minds back to the dark, bitterly cold march, and they stared into the trees and the nothingness ahead for something else to think of.

The column halted in the trees. The horses were too tired to make any noise. The only sound was the squeaking of snow and leather, and the crisp, pitched clinking of metal as more than a thousand men tried desperately to warm themselves. Many of them lay down in the snow and tried to sleep, scattered across the ground as if caught in a surprise attack and wiped out, as if their enemy had some magic that blew through them, stopped the white soldiers in the trees, protected their camp—the old men and women and children.

The Captain stood by his horse, holding the bridle close to the bit, keeping its head near his shoulder. His feet burned with the cold and became numb. He flexed his hands to keep them useful, slowly and rhythmically. His hair was frosted as if he were suddenly very old, his dark eyes searched for the first light that would signal the coming of dawn. In his mind there was only the trap. The fight. And not a moment after that—no provision or thought of prisoners, not the fate of those who would be caught in this bitter cold, who might run into the trees to hide, nor those whose warm blood would melt the snow and then freeze red and yellow. Only the trap. As he blinked, the moisture of his own breathing condensed in his eyelashes and froze, causing them to stick momentarily shut, as if, should the breath of the wind blow just a little harder, that cold exhale of death could take any man and freeze his eyes shut forever, freeze his chest to stone.

Chapter Twenty-Five

Sleep had glued my mouth shut. I woke to pee. Outside the sky was just beginning to pale. The snow had stopped, but I could tell it was cold. Cars drifted by in clouds of steam. The room was getting cold, too. A fine, white line of snow had blown in through the crack of the door.

It didn't take long to pack the things I had. I left the door open as I gathered them to try to get used to the cold air. By the time I was done, the streetlights were turning off and the sky was a faint blue though the sun wasn't up yet. I hoped I could get a ride quickly.

I threw the keys on the unmade bed and shut the door behind me. The suitcase was heavy, but carrying it made me warmer. A traveling businessman got into his car and started the engine, which turned over grudgingly. I walked right by him, but he didn't even notice me. I watched him drive his car a hundred feet across the street to the pancake house and leave it running while he went inside. I didn't think of it then to steal that car while he bought his coffee, though I did later. At least I might have had a better option than hitchhiking alone.

246 ▲ MARCUS STEVENS

It was almost a mile along the row of cafés, gas stations and truck stops, strip malls and tractor dealerships to the freeway on-ramp. All the way there I debated which direction to take, east or west. My feet were already numb and my fingers were falling asleep carrying the heavy suitcase that banged against my leg, but when I got there, I still had not decided. There was no obvious reason to go anywhere at all. Trucks flew by on the overpass with that whining, burning sound to their wheels. I decided against the freeway. I walked under it, past the on-ramp, which would take me back west toward home and down the old county road until I could not carry the suitcase anymore. I took out Granddad's journals, sat down and turned to face the sun, to gather from it any warmth I could. I turned to the pages on the battle of Dull Knife, but I could not reconcile what he had written there with the tale that had been unfolding in my imagination.

▲▲▲

How many times did Mo'é'ha'e wake up to check that the soldiers were not already upon them? The fire burned. The people danced. The moon rose. She opened her eyes and she could see the cold in the darkness as if it had a shape or a color. Around her face, the buffalo robes were frosted from her breathing. One side of the tepee was lit by the moon, glowing dimly blue, the other side was lit orange by the fire. It shone brightly enough on the skin of the tepee that she could discern the pattern of the veins of the once-living animal. She pulled the robes around her and then scooted all the way down under them where it was very dark and warm, and the sound of the drums and dancers was muffled. She prayed for morning to stay away as long as possible, but she knew that there was very little of the night left. Eventually, sleep returned, a weight on her body like water. She dreamed about swimming in the summer sun, the glint of yellow stones at the bottom of a green pool.

She woke dreaming an explanation of what was happening. At first it was strangely comforting. She heard songs, but distantly, and as she became oriented, she realized the voices had moved to the wrong side of the tent. Her mother was up, listening too. Her robes had fallen away, but she cared nothing about the cold. War songs! A few seconds seemed to last forever as each of them tried to shake the feeling that this could not be happening. As the first shots rang out and they heard the pounding of hooves and people running, what had been so quiet and slow became suddenly mad and confusing. They scrambled out of the tepee, halfdressed. Mo'é'ha'e had only a thin robe of elk calfskin, but she had not forgotten her moccasins. She pulled Henry with her. The gunfire came more quickly now, and she heard lead ripping through the lodges around them. Already a few Cheyenne warriors were on their horses racing toward the battle.

She and Henry had run about a hundred feet when her mother yelled, *"Stop. Stay here."*

Mo'é'ha'e stopped as a group of loose horses raced by at full gallop. Her own black horse was nowhere to be seen, already stampeded off with the herd. She could not whisper in its ear to save herself now. She thought of her uncle. He'd warned her to stay in the tepee, but it was already too late for that. People were running for the steep slope and rocks to the east of the camp. The Pawnee, who were always willing to join the white man to fight the Cheyenne, had already charged halfway through the camp, but enough of the Cheyenne warriors had joined the battle that they were beginning to slow the attackers down so that the women and children and older people could get away. Then, on the other side of the encampment, to the west and south, she saw the soldiers who were going to cut them off, and there seemed to be no end to them.

Mo'é'ha'e looked for her mother, but could see her nowhere. As she searched desperately among the bodies, she finally spotted her coming out of the tepee. She'd gone back for some robes, and now she was trying to run back to them. Mo'é'ha'e stood frozen, watching. She could not even scream. Henry pulled on her arm and yelled in English for her to run, too. But she held fast and would not let go of his hand. One of the Pawnee fired at her mother but the shot missed. Because of the heavy robes, she was running too slowly. It didn't look like she was going to make it. Mo'é'ha'e willed her to drop them, drop them and escape. Another shot slammed into the ground beyond her.

Then Mo'é'ha'e's line of sight was blocked by the dark body of a horse. Uncle White Bird. He shouted at her. *"Amaxahe! Run now. I will find you later up in the rocks."*

He didn't wait for an answer. He turned to fire his rifle at the Pawnee. Mo'é'ha'e turned to run but fell because Henry did not move with her fast enough. Through the legs of the horse she could see that her mother had tripped, and just behind her one of the Pawnee was charging. He had a whip out instead of a gun as he bear down on her. She tried to stand up with the robes, but before she could, the Pawnee struck her, knocking her back to the ground. White Bird fired again, missing, but the Pawnee veered off.

White Bird turned again. His face was fierce, *"Run, child. Run!"*

Mo'é'ha'e and Henry ran, this time without looking back. They ran toward the rocks above the camp. Her lungs hurt in the cold air, and her legs grew weak in the snow as she struggled to pull Henry after her. Cheyenne charging into the battle raced by them, horses' hooves hammering the frozen ground. She could

hear the soldiers gaining in the fight on her right side, and most of
the shooting was coming from that direction.

Finally, she had to stop, just to breathe. They were halfway up
a north-facing slope where the snow was more than a foot deep.
She found a rock for them to hide behind, and for a long time the
only thing she was aware of was her lungs burning, sucking in as
much air as they could take and her heart pounding. Henry lay
in the snow. At least he had some warm clothes on, the white
man's clothes he'd always refused to take off. She took several
deep breaths to get her wind back and then stood up to see where
they were.

Instantly, she realized that they were not yet safe. In fact, if they
stayed where they were they would be cut off by the soldiers. The
fight was still moving their way. About two hundred yards away
in a tight ravine, several Cheyenne were trapped. There were about
nine of them, and they were fighting off more than one hundred
soldiers and their Indian allies. The gunfire came so fast that it was
impossible to distinguish individual shots. There was little cover
for the warriors, and they hugged the ground and returned the fire
blindly. One by one they were being hit. Most of the time, because
they were lying down, the shots only wounded them, and a man
might curl up for a moment from the pain or might be knocked
sideways by the force of the shot, but then keep shooting back,
as if nothing had happened. Small spots of red began to appear
in the snowy ravine. Then, one by one, the warriors became weak.
They stopped shooting back and rolled over and looked up into
the sky, blue and clear, to sing their death songs before their spirits fled their bodies to begin the journey across the Milky Way.

When she finally returned her attention to her own situation, it
was too late. Twenty or so soldiers had charged up the hill. She
tried to pull Henry in behind a rock, but he would not move. And
then she saw the fierce war face of the lead soldier—the Captain.

She did not run, but with a strange calm watched as he charged straight at her. His horse sat back on its haunches as it slid to a stop, and he pulled back on the reins with hands that were already sticky with blood.

AT THE BEGINNING of the attack, the Captain had dug his spurs into the horse's side, and the horse leapt ahead of the rest. He led a contingent of Bannock and Crow up the frozen creek, through willows crusted with rime ice. They charged on through the thick trees and out into the open meadow. The Bannock and Crow shouted war songs. The Captain did not need to understand either language to understand the meaning. And while it might have been better to a white man's idea of strategy to have them quiet until they reached the lodges and shots were fired, he could feel the songs heartening the charge.

Before they reached the first lodges, a group of Pawnee had already entered the lower end of the camp, and the shooting had begun. He pulled out his pistol and quirted the horse with his reins. To his right he could see the Cheyenne warriors who had joined the army's campaign as scouts, and he was surprised to see how fiercely they charged against their own. His horse leapt up an embankment, hardly seeming to slow, rocks scattering in his wake, and when he reached the top, they were under fire. Several of the defending warriors, a few of them already on horses, were running among the lodges and firing back furiously. His horse reared as if it had been hit, but the Captain could feel his men behind him and he pushed the beast ahead toward the firing line. He returned his shots carefully, firing at point blank range as they broke the Cheyenne lines and one of the defenders fell beneath his horse.

When he stopped to catch his breath, he saw all around him the Bannock and Crow entering the fray alongside the soldiers. They were pushing the Cheyenne back rapidly, and had begun to overtake the fleeing women and children. The Captain watched a cavalryman chase down a naked woman, who seemed for some reason to be running the wrong way. She dodged him for a while. It seemed pointless, this uniformed soldier stopping and turning his horse trying to catch the obviously unarmed woman without dismounting. Finally he was able to strike her in the head with the butt of his rifle, and the woman fell and did not move again.

The Captain charged up to a knoll to assess the progress of the attack. In a few minutes, the camp had been engulfed in chaos, loose horses running wild, people only partially dressed from sleep fleeing for their lives. Most of the older people and women with children were making their way to the cover of some rocks up a steep slope to the east of the camp. The Cheyenne warriors who were able were either fighting individual battles in the camp and taking heavy casualties or beginning to regroup in the more defensible ravines at the foot of the mountains.

An odd skirmish drew his focus to the near end of the lodges. The Captain shaded his eyes from the sun so that he could see what was happening. One of the cavalrymen was spinning on his mount as two old women grabbed the reins trying to pull the horse down. Then the Captain recognized the man, mostly from his size; it had to be the bearded man, Hoke. And just as the Captain recognized him, Hoke fell from the horse. One of the old women had a club and began hitting him with it before he could get up.

At first the Captain could not understand why the women had stayed to fight; then he saw several children running uphill behind them. They were trying to get to the rocks, but it was clear that they had almost lost their strength, slipping and stumbling in the snow. Hoke eventually wrestled the club away from the old woman and beat her with it. The other woman began to run away from him, and he chased after her, but tripped, and she gained some distance. When he got up, he didn't bother pursuing her, but pulled his pistol from his belt and fired three shots at her, missing each time.

Then, behind Hoke, the Captain saw Lucius appear from one of the tepees. He seemed to be tightening his belt. He stopped and the Captain could see the smoke of his pistol firing into the tepee.

A soft light fell across the camp and onto the mountains in their robes of timber. For a moment it distracted the Captain; then he heard an intense volley of gunfire, the nine warriors making a stand in a ravine. He shouted for the men still fighting with him, and managed to gather a few for a charge, to cut off the warriors should they try to escape. The ground was rough, interrupted by gullies choked with hawthorn and willow, so that they could only make short charges before they were forced to slow down and find a better way through. As they traversed the hillside, they cut off many of the people who were fleeing toward the rocks. Although they fired on some, none were hit. The Captain tried to reload as he rode the horse, but the uneven ground made it impossible, so he returned his empty gun to its holster to be reloaded when he was able to stop.

The snow got deeper as they went on, and he looked down the slope because he could hear that the firing had become fierce, and from his new position, he could see that there was no need for them to circle back. The six or so Bannock warriors who had joined him also slowed, sensing that they were going to miss the real battle if they continued. They turned back and the Captain wheeled his horse around, and then remembered his empty pistol and stopped to reload it.

He had three cartridges loaded when he saw the young Cheyenne girl and next to her the white boy. He holstered the pistol and turned back to rescue the boy, spurring his horse to move faster.

Across the distance, as his mount loped through the snow, the steady eyes of the young girl watching him ride in held his attention. He pulled back on the reins, and the horse skidded on its haunches, tossing its head back and very nearly going over backwards as it lost its balance on the uneven slope.

"Come here, boy! Come here!" the Captain shouted.

Henry looked up as the Captain jumped off his horse. He reached into his pocket and secretly unsheathed his small knife.

Despite the battle below, it was almost quiet up on the hill. The main fight had moved some way off now, a soft crackling in the distance. The sun cleared the ridge and lit the snow. The Captain had to shade his eyes in order to see the children.

Mo'é'ha'e watched the Captain closely, prepared to run, shaking from cold and fear. The Captain was about fifteen feet away, when Henry stood up with the knife still in his pocket. Mo'é'ha'e had only a thin blanket wrapped over her shoulders and she had no weapon. She dug through the snow, searching the frozen ground for a rock, anything she might use.

The Captain ran to grab Henry, expecting him to reach up to be rescued, but instead he kicked and bit him like a wild animal then pulled the knife out and stabbed it deeply into the Captain's shoulder. The Captain yelled and dropped him, and Mo'é'ha'e made a run for it. The Captain struck Henry viciously in the head and his small body went limp. Then the Captain spun around to deal with Mo'é'ha'e who was slipping and falling on the rocks hidden under the snow as she ran. Without thinking he pulled out his pistol and fired. He was still out of breath from struggling with Henry and his shoulder was bleeding, soaking his blue uniform. The shot went over her head.

Missing surprised him. She wasn't that far away. He knelt to get a steadier rest for his shooting hand, determined not to miss this time, but just as he was about to pull the trigger, she fell. He exhaled and took aim again. She got up and he fired, but the shot disappeared in the snow just beyond her.

Mo'é'ha'e kept running after the second shot, which she heard pass over her shoulder with a loud, sucking pop and then smack into the rocks under the snow ahead of her. She ran as hard as she could, though her legs had little power left to carry her. At the third shot, she tripped as one leg suddenly lost its strength. She lay there waiting for more gunfire, but none came. She reached down to her burning calf to see where she'd been hit, but she could feel nothing except the freezing snow. She looked back at the Captain in time to see him lifting Henry onto the back of his horse, and the two of them rode off down the hill. She tried to see Henry's face, to see if he was okay, to see his eyes, to say good-bye, but he lay limp across the Captain's saddle. Though the sun was up, it was still bitterly cold, and the camp was taken.

Chapter Twenty-Six

My hands were numb from holding the journal. I looked over at the empty underpass, listening to the whine of the freeway overhead. This contemporary world and the world of these journals seemed separated by so much more than a century. But my grandfather knew his grandfather when he was ninety. Between them they had lived a hundred and seventy years, easily embracing the fate of the Cheyenne girl. It was that close.

When a van pulled over and waited with the engine idling, it took me a minute to fully register that someone had stopped, that I had a ride.

"You gettin' in or not?" A man's voice called from inside, but because of the dark windows, I couldn't see him.

I got up stiffly and walked to the door, which the driver had thrown open. I still couldn't see his face.

"Put the suitcase in back." I heard the click of the automatic door lock.

I shoved my suitcase awkwardly on top of some stuff that looked like musical equipment. I still couldn't see who was giving me a ride, but I started to climb in anyway.

"Not back there. Hop in front."

The air inside the van was warm but stuffy. I half-expected a troll when I looked up to see the man's face. But I was relieved. He looked nice enough, though he hadn't shaved for a couple of days, and his hair looked like it had been slept on and left that way. I guessed he was in his thirties, maybe forty. He wasn't very tall, not even my height.

"Where ya headed?"

I pointed down the road. "West?"

"Me too." He pulled out onto the road.

I turned away from him and leaned against the window, watching the blur of sagebrush streak monotonously by. In the side mirror the freeway got smaller and the town disappeared.

▲ ▲ ▲

THE CAPTAIN SAT at a makeshift desk, smoking from his pipe and writing in his notebook. He was frustrated with the boy who lay on a cot behind him under a pile of warm buffalo robes. So far he had refused to talk. The Captain turned from his writing, and though the boy's eyes were closed, he knew that the child was not sleeping. He rubbed his wounded shoulder and then returned to his notebook. His pen scratched delicately on the pages, and his breath came in quiet clouds of steam. His chair creaked as he reached for his leather pouch and dropped pinches of tobacco into the pipe. Next to him a punk smoldered, a thin wisp of smoke, and when he picked it up to relight, the leaf crackled and the air filled with the pungent smell of his private stash of tobacco.

"On the twenty-fifth of November, 1876, General Mackenzie's forces, reinforced with a large contingent of volunteers of Bannock, Crow, Shoshone, Pawnee, Lakota, Arapaho, and Cheyenne attacked at dawn a Cheyenne camp of 205 lodges, and wiped it from the face of this earth. The hostiles have fled, deprived of their possessions. A very few have given up, and the rest have been surrendered to the tender mercies of the bitter cold."

He stopped, set his pen down for a moment and exhaled. In October, Red Cloud's band had been surrounded and given the chance to surrender. There was no doubt that a comparison would be drawn by some, even though that may not have been possible in this situation, given the narrowness of the canyon, which was approachable from only one end, and the presumed need for surprise. He tried to convince himself that a real battle had been fought here with the same warriors who had massacred Custer and the Seventh Cavalry. But he couldn't completely calm the sense of doubt that was making him feel uneasy, nor rid himself of the nagging awareness that others in similar situations had chosen differently. He thought of the well-known case many years ago of the officer at Sand Creek, Captain Silas S. Soule, who had held his men back, refusing to participate in an obvious slaughter of women and children. From beside him on his desk he lifted a buckskin bag that had been given to him by one of his Crow scouts who claimed to have found it in one of the Cheyenne's tepees. It seemed unusually heavy. He opened the bag, though he knew the contents vividly—twelve severed hands of Shoshone babies. The sight gave him a sense of resolve, for a moment, until he remembered his own actions, the Cheyenne girl he had shot. He tried to convince himself that it had been a reflex, something he would not normally have done. His arm still throbbed from the boy's knife. He closed his eyes and saw the girl falling into the snow. How stupid and unnecessary it felt to have compromised himself in that way. And there was a witness. He looked over at the boy whose cheeks were red from the warmth of the heavy robes. No doubt he was a witness to many things.

He returned to the dimly lit paper and the black scratches of ink there. "Of course some effort will be made to follow the hostiles who will doubtless be retreating as soon as there is light. They are expected to seek out Crazy Horse who is thought to be camped somewhere in the Powder River country. Who knows what sanctuary he might offer, there always being so little in the way of extra provisions for what promises to be a hard winter, but if it increases his burden, so much the better."

He realized with relief that there was, at least, a successful military goal achieved by this fight. He concluded with a hollow sense of satisfaction, "We have won here a final victory over the Northern Cheyenne."

Mo'é'ha'e looked up at her mother who was singing softly to distract them both from the aching cold. Her hands and arms felt warm, the only source of heat. Beyond her, her uncle worked to make a small fire. His sons huddled against their mother, wrapped in a robe he'd been able to bring up from the camp as he retreated. As he'd ridden his weary horse up the steep slope below the rocks, he'd spotted his niece lying in the snow. He couldn't see any blood, but he was afraid that she must be dead and his heart fell like a bird shot in midair. Mo'é'ha'e could not remember him picking her up from the snow nor the short ride on his horse up to this bitterly cold place. She only remembered, vaguely, as a dream, his arms holding her on the saddle, the faint smell of sweat and blood, a glimmer of light on her eyelids before the mountain eclipsed the sun.

She closed her eyes and concentrated on her mother's song. It took her mind away from her throbbing leg. She couldn't feel beyond the wound in her calf. When she tried to move, it hurt.

"Ovanôhóoéste," her mother whispered, looking down at her. But Mo'é'ha'e could not be still; she wiggled until she was able to sit up.

"Where are we?"

"In the rocks above the camp."

Below them fires burned. Mo'é'ha'e saw it first in a glow, subtly lighting her mother's face. Then she looked down the steep slope and saw the lodges burning, two hundred of them at once, the flames lighting the hills around, making the cold night look warm, as everything the people had, all their winter stores, burned in the fire.

Mo'é'ha'e looked around her. Beyond her uncle, hunched over his fire, there were mostly women with children, but there were a few warriors sleeping, waiting for dawn and the chance to fight again. These women were singing, too, and if they stopped, the babies began to cry. Some of the infants were wrapped in pieces of robes, and some had only their mother's arms. Near her a woman held her baby tightly to her breast, covering her as much as she could with her body, but the child was not moving. The woman had her mouth right next to the baby's ear and she was whispering. Mo'é'ha'e could not hear the words, but she knew it was a death song.

▲ ▲ ▲

THE SNOW MELTING on the window of the van had turned the world into a blur of dull, wet color. I couldn't stop thinking about Granddad's notes on the Dull Knife massacre. I'd sat three hours by the freeway on ramp in the cold thinking about it, but I could not come close to imagining a whole night in temperatures below freezing without proper clothing. I could not imagine surviving. I could not imagine wanting to. Losing Mom was sometimes enough to make me not care what happened to me, and she was just one person, taken by chance, not deliberate murder. My grandfather's version offered this history as a matter of fact, explained the victims' suffering as the unfortunate casualty of an inevitable process.

A destiny. I thought of the pages turning dryly in his hands. How was it even possible that I grew up here and never heard about this?

A bump in the road jarred me back.

"So whose suitcase is that anyway, your grandmother's?"

I shrugged. "I guess a backpack would've worked better."

A dream-catcher hanging from the rearview mirror swayed slowly as the van made a wide turn. Over my shoulder I could see some deer antlers wrapped in a Pendleton blanket. He noticed me looking.

"You like Native American stuff?"

Oddly, I realized I didn't have an opinion. To be polite I said, "Yeah, sure."

"Maybe you're not the redneck girl you look to be," he said. "No offense."

I wasn't sure if I should even smile. I looked away again.

"So what are you runnin' from? Boyfriend didn't treat you right? Cowboy rode off into the sunset?"

I still didn't answer.

"Pretty girl like you's gotta have a boyfriend somewhere."

"No," I answered, instantly aware that I should have kept my mouth shut.

"Now that's a shame."

I wished he'd stop talking, but he wasn't going to. There was a disquieting dryness to his voice. I stared ahead, trying to ignore him. The empty prairie melted and refroze with every pass of the windshield wipers. There wasn't a sign of human habitation as far as I could see. I just wanted to be left alone; but he kept looking over at me. When I did glance back, he caught my eyes and I looked away quickly. I probably should have reacted, said something, not just froze up that way. If I had laughed, or maybe started some story, loudly and confidently, it might just have been enough to scare him off, derail the fantasy he was developing.

When the van began to slow down, I couldn't help turning toward him. He wasn't looking at me now. The road was empty, the honest-to-god middle of nowhere. My suitcase bounced just at the edge of my reach between our two seats. I tried to decide whether I was going to reach for it or not when he stopped.

"I got a real nice setup in the back here," he said with that dry voice. "First class."

The van had almost stopped, but he was hesitating. I meant to jump as soon as the vehicle wasn't moving too fast, but I reacted too slowly and the van came to a stop and he was shifting it into neutral and setting the parking brake before I started to move. I grabbed for the suitcase and the door, but he got it at the same time. "Where you going?"

I kept moving so that I had both feet out of the door and my arm was stretched full length, holding on to the suitcase. I knew I should let go of it and just run. Then he tried to grab for my arm, letting go of the suitcase to do it, and I fell back with the suitcase on top of me. Underneath the van I could see his boots land by the wheels as he slipped on the slick road and swore.

I got up and started running, the suitcase slowing me down as it banged against my calves.

"Come on, come back here." He stopped at the edge of the road, hesitating again. I ran like hell, crashing through the snow-covered sagebrush. Ahead of me was nothing, a distant horizon and heavy, bruised clouds. It was snowing lightly.

He ran about thirty yards, gaining on me, and stopped to yell again, "Where you runnin' to?"

After what felt like minutes but might have only been a few seconds, something made me look back, some sense that he wasn't following me. A car was coming down the road, and he had turned back. I dropped down on the ground to hide, and the snow felt cool on my warm face. I heard the car passing, and then nothing. I didn't know whether he would come looking again, follow my tracks to where I was hiding, or move on. It felt like a long time passed before I heard him start the van up and drive away.

I didn't get up after he was gone. I stayed there feeling the cold, the freezing ground soaking up into my body.

▲ ▲ ▲

MO'É'HA'E TREMBLED AND shook against her mother. The bleeding had stopped in her leg but had left her weak, and it felt as if the cold had entered her body through the wound and was seeping up the bone of her leg toward her heart.

White Bird had finally been able to start a fire, but the light of it brought shooting from the soldiers camped below, enough to keep them away from the fire. Slowly it died until it was coals, and only two or three people could huddle against it. More fires were built, and the people kept away until the fire dimmed too much to be seen anymore; then they held the rocks it had heated, and sat as close to the embers as they could. It was hard to keep the fires alive this way, but it got some of them through the first night. Those who did make it left the rocks just before light. Mo'é'ha'e scrambled up the ridge behind her mother as best she could with her injured leg. At the top they paused for one last look at the fires still smoldering in camp, the last of their possessions, and then they disappeared into the forest on the other side, headed for the open plain at the foot of the Bighorns.

AT SUNRISE THE Captain and a small force rode up the hill to the rocks that had harbored most of the fugitives from the camp during the previous day's fighting. On the way up they encountered some snipers who yielded under heavy return fire. The horses picked their way single file through the rock ledges that were steep and treacherous with scree hidden beneath the snow. As the Captain came through a narrow gap in the rocks ahead of the group, he was alone. Cold, black fire rings, smaller than two hands together, were scattered for thirty yards and attending them were many frozen bodies, some still sitting. Among these were eleven mothers with babies frozen in their arms.

The Captain stopped. He did not allow the men to enter, and for a long while, as they mumbled behind him, he sat on his horse and stared at the desperate scene. Somehow, despite all of the grisly battlefields he had ever attended, this violence of cold, these frozen bodies, overwhelmed him. He raised his hand and motioned for the men to move back. It was difficult to turn his horse on the narrow trail and he jerked its head around with uncharacteristic roughness.

"Why are we turning back, Captain?" asked the lieutenant behind him.

"There is no way through here," he snapped, though the soldier could plainly see that there was and gave him a questioning look.

"I've seen enough. Now turn about, man!" the Captain yelled. "That's an order."

Chapter Twenty-Seven

THE MOTEL WOMAN had a lot to say, to the sheriff and to Dad, not much of which was useful. She was clearly pleased that her phone call had summoned them both so quickly. She didn't mention that although I had left without bringing her the keys or checking out, she was still two days ahead on rent. Dad stood in the open doorway and tried to tune her out. Everything was just as I had left it—the covers on the bed a mess, towels on the floor. It was as if she hadn't cleaned so the sheriff could see just what she'd had to contend with. The storm outside was building and wet flakes of snow blew on Dad's bare neck through the open door as he took it in. He'd almost made it on time. I had a six-hour lead on him at best.

He noticed the extra blankets on the bed, all the pillows, then the telephone on the bare counter next to the TV, mute evidence that I could have called home at anytime. Below the telephone was a trash can. He walked over and halfheartedly picked it up to check. At the bottom, tucked in the thin garbage bag, was just one wadded-up piece of hotel stationery. He sat down on the bed with it as if he was almost afraid to see what had been written there, afraid to see anything in my handwriting.

The sheriff was just outside the room talking to the motel woman. Dad caught just part of it. "Strange weather for the end of August . . . I've seen it up in the mountains, but not snowing out on the plains like this."

Dad opened the note I had written but had never really intended to send, unfolding it carefully and then straightening it out on his knee. I remember that letter. My usually bad handwriting was an emotional scrawl, and half of what I'd written I had scribbled out to rewrite. He read through the information he already knew, about Charlie and the baby. Then he got to the part that had finally made me wad it up.

> I've been trying to figure out what I did wrong. I remember when I was little girl, and you were the whole world. I remember the things we did together, though I'm afraid you have already forgotten. Now, is there anything we could do like that, together, anything we could agree on? I know what you're thinking, What a shame. What a *shame*—such a strange and terrible word that can be so cruel and so gentle. I'll tell you what the shame is, Dad, the shame is that Mom is a pile of ashes and that has left both of us alone. You said you were sorry about that and I never answered. It seems easy, now, to say, It's okay— I forgive you.

Dad let the letter fall to his lap. He looked down at it without really seeing it.

> Don't worry. I'm not gone forever. I'll run out of money. I'll run out of time. Maybe I'll even be home before you get this letter. I have nowhere else to go.

He sat on the bed for a long time. The sheriff started to poke his head in, to say something, but when he saw Dad sitting there, the letter in his hand, he stepped quietly back outside, and gently shut the door.

Dad didn't look up. I can only guess what he was thinking. He will never tell me. Maybe he realized, finally, in some real way that I was almost an adult, that no matter what the letter said, I wasn't ever coming home. Or maybe, all the anger that had been sustaining him, that gave him the energy to get this far, to find the actual motel room where I had been, simply faded. His own missteps, the things he had done in anger that could have turned out much worse, had to have weighed him down, taken the strength from his arms. I don't know. Maybe he never articulated his thoughts in such a conscious way. It was a hard thing for a man like him, but I think even he sensed that to let me go now wasn't giving up, but something else. But then who knows—how do you ever know what goes on in someone else's head? Especially your own father's.

Whatever he thought, or didn't think, he knew the game was up. He had no idea where to look for me now. He folded the letter, carefully, smoothing its wrinkles and put it in his pocket. He stood up and went to the truck, backed up and drove away without saying another word to the sheriff who was sitting in his squad car filling out paperwork.

As he drove home, he stared through the windshield, through the melting snow. He drove much too fast. I have always imagined his thoughts turning to Mom, a moment from a long time ago, the end of a fight they didn't know I'd overheard. Her eyes were red. She'd been crying. Her hand rested on the counter on a dish with soap suds slowly dripping from it. The water was running; it was the only sound in the room, that and the overflow sucking water and the suds from the top. The thing is, I don't think he would have remembered what he said or what Mom said; I don't think he would have tried. In that memory, there would have only been the intense awareness of her shoulders rising and falling as she tried to control her breathing. That's what he would have re-membered—that she was breathing, and that when he touched her, she was warm.

Chapter Twenty-Eight

I PROBABLY SHOULD have moved back to the road, but something kept me from it, maybe the fear that the guy in the van would come back, or someone like him. Clayton had left some matches in the pocket of the jacket he gave me. I played with them in my wet hands. The wind died, and the snow stopped, but it was still impossible to get warm. I opened the suitcase and dug through it, but there was nothing but summer clothes.

I started with the most useless, a dress. I tried to keep it off the snow to keep it dry as I tied it in tight knots so that it would burn longer. Then, sitting on the suitcase, my feet tucked under me, I set fire to the printed fabric. It wasn't easy; it took three matches before the flames took hold. Some of the sagebrush was dry enough to burn, though it was difficult to break off usable pieces. The branches held on as though they knew what I had in mind for them. Eventually, I had a small, fragrant fire going. I think Dad would have been proud of his Boy Scout. Mom would just have been horrified. I don't think she could have seen burning the dress. You have to draw the line somewhere, even if you're cold. That would be Mom's position. A line for civilization.

I was getting hungry and wished I had something to eat. My stomach growled, but at least I hadn't gotten sick for a while. I looked around. I could see much farther, though it didn't change anything. It was as if you took the same piece of the world and stretched it out, same thing with the same sky. Not even bigger somehow. The sagebrush was a dull green-gray, dusted with snow like powdered sugar, and it stretched out across low hills so they that looked like white-crested ocean waves.

I threw more clothes on the fire. No matter how many escapes I ever imagined for Mo'é'ha'e, I always knew what was waiting for her.

▲ ▲ ▲

SHE WOKE IN the night to an eerie screaming. In the darkness she could faintly make out the shadow of one of the warriors stooping over a horse, which lay on the ground, blowing the last of its air. When the horse died, the warrior cut his gut open and spilled out the entrails onto the snow. Immediately, several of the children who did not have any blankets or clothing, put arms and legs into the mess to melt away the frostbite; the smaller children crawled completely inside the cavity.

The fires were dead, the sky was still black, when she woke again, but she could feel from the light breeze that dawn was coming. Her mother was beginning to stir too. There was a quiet rustling and murmur as they prepared to march. White Bird and two young men had gone ahead to build a fire for the women and children to stop at for a rest. They were sure the army would not pursue them now. Cumbersome and slow, the soldiers were expected to attend to their wounded and then return south to re-provision.

At first the snow was deep; as much as a foot had fallen over the past day, but as they dropped over the ridge and down the northeast-facing slope that fell off to the plain, the snow lessened and then disappeared except in occasional drifts. The ground was frozen under their feet and the dry grass was long because there had been so few buffalo to graze it in recent years. A stiff wind began to blow with the first light. The sky was gray with low sweeping clouds, moving fast, dragging on the hills and mountain peaks. A few black crows drifted by, caught in the wind, but otherwise, there was nothing moving.

They walked deliriously, heads down against the wind, as many as could on the lee side of the horses. Mo'é'ha'e watched her feet take each step. She had to because she could not feel them. She was limping badly on her hurt leg, but there was no place for her to ride. She simply had to walk. Her dark hair whipped across her face and snapped in the wind. Ahead of her, she followed her mother's bare legs. There was no color in anything, as if the world was dying with them.

Mo'é'ha'e tried to think of Henry, where he might be. By a fire, clothed and warm, listening to his own language for the first time in months, and eating. Eating salted pork and beans and foods so heavenly her stomach hurt to think of them.

After they had walked for several hours, someone shouted that they could see the fire. All heads looked up to see it, a vague haze of smoke that quickly disappeared in the wind and melted into the grayness of everything. But it was there, and it gave them hope. At least Mo'é'ha'e knew she would now make it to the first of the fires. She didn't dare think beyond that.

As they walked a magpie appeared above her, flying into the wind, letting it roll him back and then catching up again.

"*Look,*" Mo'é'ha'e said to her mother, pointing up at the bird as it flew back over them again. "*We have a friend.*"

Her mother didn't answer right away.

"*Mother.*"

She turned.

"*Do you see the bird?*"

Her mother looked up and nodded.

"*It's a good sign. We have help,*" said Mo'é'ha'e.

She stopped watching her feet, trusting them to fall right, so she could watch the bird that played in the wind as if delighted to have company.

"*Where are you going?*" the bird chirped.

"*To the next fire,*" said Mo'é'ha'e, and smiled. "*Is it far? Can you see it?*"

The bird lifted up on a gust, and then called down that he could see the fire and that it was big and orange and looked warm.

"*What will you eat?*" asked the bird.

"*I don't know,*" said Mo'é'ha'e. "*We have very little.*"

"*I'm hungry too.*"

"*What will you eat?*" she asked, looking out for a moment at the barren landscape.

The bird did not answer as he did a quick loop and rolled over on one wing, and Mo'é'ha'e looked down at her feet again to keep from tripping.

When they came to the fire, the magpie lit in the top of a wind-ravaged juniper. Mo'é'ha'e sat near the fire, on the smoky side because there was no room anywhere else, and tears ran down her face as if she were crying. She ate her small ration of horsemeat, savoring each bite. When the wind shifted and the smoke was not blowing in her face, she noticed the magpie in the tree. She held out her hand.

"*Here is some meat, if you want it.*"

The magpie dropped down from the tree and hopped a few feet away. Then it hesitated.

"You wouldn't eat me would you?" it asked.

"No. I won't eat you. Will you eat me?"

The magpie looked back at her with a keen, shiny black eye.

"Is that why you're following us?" Mo'é'ha'e asked.

"No, not mostly." He hopped forward and took the meat from her hand. *"I like the company."*

BY THE TIME night came, the fickle magpie had left them. The wind dropped a little, though it hardly mattered. Mo'é'ha'e lay next to the smoldering flames. She could feel her mother's hand on her brow, and her vision was filled with fire. When the fever made her warm it was welcome, the touch of heaven, but then it made the cold even worse and she could not stop shaking.

"Náhko'éehe, I'm hot and so cold."

Mo'é'ha'e saw in her mother's eyes that she already knew. She wiggled her toes trying to feel her feet, but on her left side they would not move at all.

"When we get to Crazy Horse, we'll be okay."

Her mother subtly nodded her head as she tried to think of how to answer.

"I saw him!" Mo'é'ha'e looked back to the fire and imagined him, his great horse, his strange light hair, his body painted with spots. He reached down to the river and scooped up water to drink with his cupped hands.

"Náhko'éehe, I'm thirsty."

THE CAPTAIN USED the heel of his boot to break through the ice. It was thick and he nearly lost his balance. When it finally yielded, he squatted down with a tin cup and scooped it into the dark hole to get a drink. His horse nudged him. He smelled the water, too, and neighed softly. The Captain stood up and the horse pushed by, pulling against the reins and metal army bit to drink some of the cold, delicious water.

The Captain took his watch from his pocket. The seconds ticked by. Seven-sixteen in the morning. It was just getting light, slowly, dully. His face was chafed by the exposure to the constant wind, and the chill of frost clung to his hair and eyebrows.

He listened to the murmur of his small command as they brought their mounts to the water to drink. At his feet he could see where the Cheyenne had left footprints in the snow. One set stood out clearly to him among the jumble—a small child's prints, blood on the left side. He looked up, hearing a strange sound, an animal noise. The source of the grunt was Hoke, who sat nearby carving at a slab of dried buffalo meat he had taken from the Indians' camp.

"Sergeant," the Captain said, and the man looked up, his mouth as full as a greedy child's. "This is not a picnic."

Hoke scowled and stood up, spitting the half-chewed meat into the snow. The Captain mounted his horse and waited a moment for the men. Then he led them across the creek, following the wide swath of the refugees' trail.

As they rode, he thought over the past year, scouting and fighting these Indians. It was over. The feeling of victory had come before the battle, a fait accompli, and though there had been excitement in the fighting itself, now that it was done, the drudgery had begun. His orders were to capture these fugitives, bring them back as prisoners. He did not see any evidence in the trail that he was following more than a handful of warriors. The majority were clearly women and children. The illogic of this pursuit frustrated him; to his idea of military strategy, his next goal should have been to find Crazy Horse. He would not have chosen to tag along behind this ragged band of refugees, and he wished he did not have this contingent of twenty regular soldiers with him either.

Still, as long as he didn't catch up with the Indians too quickly, he thought they might be able to lead him where he wanted to go, though it was becoming almost impossible not to overtake them the way they'd been stopping every few miles to huddle by a fire.

The wild world around him lay on the verge of being tamed. Even in this miserably cold winter campaign, he had never missed the civilization he was fighting to extend. He did not yearn for the gaslights and crowds and warm buildings of the East. The government had given him a gun and ammunition and sent him into the wilderness to track and to hunt and to fight. And though it had been his one goal, the game was almost done. The enemy was reduced and wretched. He'd been sent on this last mission as an assassin.

They rode all day, stopping for short breaks. The Captain did not push the horses but allowed them to walk slowly, heads down. They traveled almost silently except for the sound of iron-shod horsehoofs clattering over rocks and the quieter squeaking of stiff saddle leather. He flexed the fingers of his rein hand to keep them from losing their feeling, and he fixed his gaze on the furthest point of the horizon to keep from falling asleep.

At midday the Captain halted. Perhaps four miles away, he could see the smoke from a fire drifting over the low hills.

"Damn," he cursed quietly to himself. He glanced over at his second, the young lieutenant who was nearly blue in the lips from the cold, despite his heavy buffalo robe. "Lieutenant, hold the command here until I return."

"Sir, what if you are attacked?"

He sighed heavily, frustrated with having to make contingency plans, which were so clearly unnecessary.

"Then reinforce me son, as quickly as you can."

"Yes sir."

The young officer had not lost the pinkness in his cheeks despite the hard winter campaign and engagements with the enemy. He looked tired, almost asleep, but still somehow he gave the impression of one who'd been sleeping in a feather bed, not on the frozen ground. What was it? He looked weak and pampered, and the whole frontier was being overrun with his kind. It almost made the Captain yearn to shift sides. He spit. "Just hold the command here, Lieutenant, unless you are certain we are going to be overwhelmed. Don't come charging over that hill just because you hear a few shots fired."

"Yes sir."

The Captain took his two scouts with him, and quickly rode off. They trotted the horses for a while and then slowed down as they approached the low hill, which hid the fire. The Captain surveyed the area for a way to approach without charging blindly over the ridge. But there really wasn't much of a way around it. The spot had been well chosen. They rode to just below the crest of a closer hill, out of the line of sight and dismounted. The Captain took his brass spotting scope from his saddlebags and walked and then crawled to where he could see the fire.

He adjusted the focus, struggling with the poor optics of the dim scope, then abandoned it for his naked eye. He could see clearly enough. The fire was nearly burned out. And there were only half a dozen Indians left by the fire, stragglers who apparently could not make it any farther. The main group had moved on. He stood up and walked back to the scouts, unconcerned about being seen now. He got on his horse without a word to the Crow and waited for them to get back into their saddles.

As he rode down toward the fire, he tried to make up his mind about the dilemma that confronted him. These survivors were only here because they did not have the strength to continue with the rest of the refugees. He wasn't any more likely to persuade them to walk back as prisoners than his pursuit had compelled them to walk on. The question was what to do with them. He knew the Crow riding behind him would be wondering the same thing.

Two of the Cheyenne ran off as they approached, not destined to make it far. The Captain stopped his horse and got off. He didn't look back at the scouts. He took his carbine out of its scabbard, and he knelt with it as if he were praying. It was less than two hundred yards to the fire. He shot four times, slowly and deliberately, hitting as close to the figures huddled by the fire as he could. His shoulder hurt where the boy had stabbed him; he rubbed it then reloaded and fired again. The few Cheyenne who could limped from the fire into the storm, but several did not move despite the shots which blew apart the frozen ground near them.

The Captain got back on his horse and rode back to the hill, anticipating the Charge of the Light Brigade, and he wasn't disappointed. The lieutenant had the full contingent galloping to his rescue. He turned back to the fire. Off in the distance the refugees were still running into what looked like a white, empty void.

He waited on the hill for his command. About halfway, the lieutenant noticed him standing there and called off the charge. The Captain laid his reins over the saddle horn and filled his pipe. He felt an unfamiliar anxiety in the pit of his stomach, in his arms and in the weight of his shoulders.

For half the day they stayed there, on that hill, despite the wind. The Captain finished his bowl of tobacco and stood by his horse looking to the west. It seemed an arbitrary direction in the heavy overcast. Once it had meant so much—the West, the wilderness. Eventually, he headed off down the trail without saying anything. The men fell behind silently, and they rode down the hill. If he could have, the Captain might have chosen another way. Instead, the whole command filed past the fire, which had died down to a few feeble coals glowing dimly in a wide pile of gray ash, which the wind teased and chased in minute circles. Several bodies lay in the snow as though they had been sitting there until the wind tipped them over, but the girl was not among them. There were black holes in the snow here and there, where the Captain's shots had hit. A whiff of gray smoke hovered just over the ground.

The Captain saw the scene long after he passed it. He saw it in the blizzard before him and in the empty sky, and he heard the killings in the shallow wind. Though he had not drawn blood here, he knew murder well enough. They rode the remainder of the day, slowly so that they did not overtake the refugees, but the Captain did not stop even as dusk neared and the horses' heads dipped toward the snow. Finally the lieutenant rode up to question him.

"The men need to stop, sir; the horses, too." He looked at his pocket watch. "It will be dark within the hour."

"Then halt your command, son."

"Yes sir," he answered, puzzled, and stopped his horse and the column behind. He searched the shallow hills around him for a reasonable spot to camp but the empty landscape offered nothing in the way of shelter.

"Okay, men," he said to those nearest who could hear. "This is camp." The men were quickly off their horses and at the noisy work of unpacking mules and putting up tents. The lieutenant turned back to find the Captain, but he was already two hundred yards away, still riding. One of the other officers rode up next to the lieutenant and dismounted.

"Is he gone mad?" the other officer whispered.

The lieutenant shook his head. "Find some men to follow him."

"His scouts?"

"No. Send soldiers."

"Yes sir."

In a few minutes, grumbling but back on horseback, Lucius and Hoke rode up with the officer.

"Did these men volunteer?" the lieutenant asked.

"In a manner of speaking. It will be difficult to get more— under the circumstances." He didn't say what he meant—better men.

"Fine." The lieutenant cleared his throat and turned to the two unlikely candidates. "Gentlemen, you are to accompany the Captain on a brief scout this evening."

The two sat on their horses, unable to contain their grins.

"Well, get a move on!"

As they rode off to catch up with the Captain, Hoke was laughing.

BY THE SECOND NIGHT, the refugees had made it almost to the Tongue River where it wound north through a long, dry fold in the plains. Six fires. As the sun angled into the horizon, the clouds began to clear and an icy moon rose over the distant Bighorns. Mo'é'ha'e's fever was high.

For a long while she stared into the hallucinatory maze of constellations in the heavens. Her mother leaned over her, and her glowing face filled the sky and replaced the cold stars. She was singing a death song and slipping thimbles onto Mo'é'ha'e's fingers. Mo'é'ha'e questioned her with her fevered eyes.

"So Ma'heo'o will know you were a useful girl, little one." Her mother's eyes seemed already distant, shining, just like the stars she could not reach. Mo'é'ha'e closed her eyes, and the world seemed warm again.

THE CAPTAIN WATCHED the glow of the fire, only a few hundred yards away. He told himself he should turn back, stick to his plan of following them to Crazy Horse. The two men sent to accompany him were about fifty yards behind. His mind raced as he tried to think of how to stop them before they, too, saw the fire. He almost started to turn back, thinking they might not see. He reined his horse and gently urged it with his spurs, but before he could move a couple steps, they rode up next to him. He turned his horse back awkwardly, trying to conceal his indecision— maybe this was better, to put an end to it now, just get it over with. He looked into Hoke and Lucius's eyes. For what? Some kinship perhaps—but he found nothing recognizable.

The men drew their revolvers and checked that they were loaded.

"How many do you suppose there are?"

The Captain shook his head.

"Mostly women and old men," Lucius spit.

"Not much use in taking prisoners, eh Captain?"

The Captain took out his pistol, checked it, and replaced two spent cartridges. He looked back to the men who were grinning and watching him like children.

And then in a second, their horses were running as if they had gone on their own, sensing the anticipation, and the men were shooting into the fire and yelling, and the Cheyenne were falling and running out into the night. The horses ran so fast that they overtook the fire in a moment. The Captain turned his horse hard, nearly causing it to stumble and go down. This bunch was bigger than he had expected, and there were armed warriors among them, firing back. But in the dark it was hard for anyone to see. His shots were wild, meant to run them off.

Hoke turned his horse and headed back to the fire to make a second pass. Most of the Cheyenne had fled, but there was still Mo'é'ha'e and Sweet Rose Woman leaning over her, and White Bird next to her, shooting at Lucius as he rode by the fire on the opposite side. Hoke shot at the warrior from behind, but then his horse stumbled and went down violently. He hit the rocks, breaking a shoulder and a leg.

White Bird was frustrated when his first shot hit Hoke in the gut. He could see the big man fumbling, trying to get control of his revolver. They had so little ammunition left, White Bird hated to waste any. He fired coolly, more the way he would finish off a wounded buffalo than a man. The lead slug hit Hoke in the head and he stopped moving.

White Bird turned back to Mo'é'ha'e, still in her mother's arms, and he leaned close to put his mouth near Mo'é'ha'e's ear. *"You have a good horse—ride fast!"*

He stood up and waited for Mo'é'ha'e's mother. *"We must go,"* he said and tried gently to pull her away. *"She's gone, sister. We have no way to carry her."*

But Sweet Rose Woman would not move, and the Captain was almost upon them again, and Lucius had turned around and seen that Hoke was down, and he, too, was charging in. White Bird's hand was firm, but she bent over Mo'é'ha'e, determined not to leave her.

"She's gone." He pulled hard on her now and she struggled with him. He got her only a few feet away from Mo'é'ha'e before he had to let go and fire at the Captain and Lucius approaching fast out of the darkness. The two veered off but then fired back striking the hard ground close to Sweet Rose Woman, forcing her to scramble away from the fire.

Mo'é'ha'e lay motionless.

"Sister, she does not need us now," White Bird said. *"But others do."* He had to drag her away, but this time she let him.

The Captain turned to attack again, Lucius right behind, but before either of them got there, White Bird and Mo'é'ha'e's mother had disappeared into the darkness, safe for now, in the grim protection of the night.

Three people lay shot by the fire alongside Hoke's heavy body. And Mo'é'ha'e lay there, too. The Captain stopped his horse next to her, and got down quietly. He recognized her. Behind him, Lucius was off of his horse. He had his knife out, already scalping the other victims who lay by the fire.

The Captain stood over the girl. He could see that she was breathing as he slowly reloaded his pistol. Behind him he heard Lucius breathing hard at his work. He held the scalps up in the mad, dancing light of the fire and started to walk over toward Mo'é'ha'e but stopped short.

The Captain cocked his pistol and pointed at Lucius's head. "Get on your horse."

Lucius glared back at him, his eyes black beads of hate. He turned away and picked up Hoke's pistol and took his gun belt, then he got on his horse and rode off at a trot, stepping nimbly over the bodies out into the night. The Captain followed him with his pistol to the edge of the light, his finger resting heavily on the trigger.

When he was gone, the Captain knelt down by Mo'é'ha'e, her face flush and hot. He felt it with a cold, rough hand, and then he put an ear to her mouth to listen for breath. It still came, faintly sweet and warm with the fever. He looked around at the suddenly quiet and empty world, reduced by the snow and darkness to the feeble reach of the dim light of the fire. He lifted her right hand and touched the thimbles on her fingers lightly. They shone in the warm light. Her body looked small and weightless, as though a big wind could blow it away. He took his coat off, discarded the rags that covered her and wrapped her in his wool coat, then picked her up in his arms.

The Captain held Mo'é'ha'e in a swirl of white snow and darkness without moving. After a while the fire died, and the only thing he could see by the light of the moon glowing in the clouds was her face, her eyes gently closed. Finally the snow stopped melting on her skin, and her body felt heavier, made of the earth. He laid her down, and even though she had no use for it anymore, he tucked the coat tightly around her shoulders and pulled it down to cover her bare feet. With his saber and hands he dug a shallow grave. He covered her body with the partially frozen dirt and then with the largest stones he could find.

When he was finished, the Captain rode back toward camp slowly, listening to coyotes chattering balefully in the distance, drawn in by the gunfire. He could no longer see where his horse led him, and in the blackness that caressed his face, he realized that the world had been irrevocably changed, re-created by the fire of his own gun—a place he could no longer live in.

CHAPTER TWENTY-NINE

MY FIRE DIED down to a weak flicker, and the cold, wet snow began seeping into my neck and shoulders. My eyes were red from the smoke, but also from crying. I dumped the last of my stuff out of the suitcase. The fire flared up and was warm for a few minutes again before it finally consumed itself, leaving a few ashes that trembled in the cold breeze. I could not stay. I pushed the wet hair away from my face and used the sleeve of my jacket to clear my eyes. Even though this darkening plain looked empty—it was not. The road lay only a few hundred yards away.

My feet were numb and my shoes soaked, but it was easier walking without that heavy suitcase banging against my leg. All I had left to carry were Granddad's journals, tucked under my arm like schoolbooks. The light faded until I could barely make out the road. I walked that way for some distance, placing each footstep more on faith in the grade of the road than on what I could see. The inch of snow that had accumulated silenced my footsteps, and without a wind it was so quiet that I heard my own breath and heartbeat more than anything else—steady and even and determined—until I didn't mind walking in the dark.

Then, subtly, the world began to brighten in front of me, or not the whole world, not all of it, just the road. It was so faint at first that I wasn't sure I was seeing it at all, and then I could make out my own shadow, stretching out in front of me, awkward and alone in the untracked snow, at first growing, then shrinking to something believable. I realized that there was a car behind me, and when I turned, the light was blinding. The car stopped and the snow danced in the headlights like a swarm of white moths.

I wanted it to be Charlie. But it wasn't. It was an old Indian couple. An ancient man leaned out the window and yelled for me to get in. They were Crow, headed to Hardin.

CHARLIE HAD BURNED up most of his gas money and all he had to show for it was a wrecked car, a few more bruises. He crisscrossed the web of county and state roads that threaded across the rolling prairie, but all his attempts to pick up my trail came to nothing. He drove through the storm until long after dark, and then parked at a spot where he might be able to see some distance at first light and then decide what he should do next.

Eventually, the night began to fade, revealing the sage burdened by the heavy snow, the distant white hills. I've always imagined him sitting on the hood of his car, leaned back against the window, staring out at the too many questions that filled the landscape. He sat there for a long time as the sun rose, until it was as bright and hot as an August sun should be and it burned on his face and chest.

There's a story Charlie told me once, that has always stuck in my head, about a time he and Teddy went to chase wild horses out in the Wolf Mountains. They'd taken Uncle Leonard's best Arabian so they'd have at least one fast horse, and they hunted for them most of the afternoon, before they spooked them out of a clearing that had a small spring. The horses scented them and ran immediately, but Charlie was able to get a rope on a two-year-old stallion. He dallied up and reined his horse to a stop. The colt went wild at the end of the lariat. Teddy held the Arabian while Charlie put on a pair of elkskin gloves and untied the rope from the saddle horn. He wrapped it around himself like a climber belaying and slowly approached the wild horse. It reared back and almost lifted him off the ground, but Charlie kept moving in, talking quietly and steadily to the horse to calm it. By the time he'd got back half the rope, the horse was standing still, its withers trembling, but looking right at him.

"He's going to kill you," Teddy shouted.

Charlie laid his hand on the stallion's neck, and though its skin jumped at the touch and its withers shook, it didn't move.

"You're crazy, Charlie."

Charlie ran his hand along the horse's back.

"Don't do it."

He grabbed the mane and swung up in one lightning-quick move, keeping the rope coiled in his left hand. The horse exploded, but Charlie lay his body low, pulled his gloves off with his teeth and wrapped a fist in its mane. He probably expected the horse to start bucking, but instead, out in the open like that, it just ran. It ran fast. Teddy let his own horse loose, got on the Arabian and took off after him.

They ran for a long time. Teddy stayed close. The Arabian could keep up a good pace though it couldn't outrun the two-year-old. For the first few miles Teddy was laughing so hard he nearly fell off, but then the race got serious. Charlie wasn't planning to let go.

After running almost an hour, he was so tired from holding on, he didn't see that they were coming to the top of a bluff. When Teddy realized where the horse was headed, he started yelling. "Charlie, turn that horse! Turn 'im!"

Almost too late Charlie realized what was happening. He pulled hard on the rope, which was still tight, high up on the stallion's neck, but it didn't change course, it merely ran at the cliff with its head turned sideways so it could no longer see what was coming. Teddy pulled back on the Arabian and yelled again, "Charlie, stop 'im."

Charlie yanked harder and the horse stumbled. At high speed they both went down together, the horse somersaulting right over top of him. The horse got up and limped away about a hundred yards where it stood breathing hard, bathed in lather. Charlie wasn't moving when Teddy caught up. It was a miracle that he wasn't dead. Teddy tried to talk him into getting up and riding the Arabian out, but he couldn't, and finally Teddy had to leave him there to go get the truck. It was hours after dark by the time Teddy got back. Charlie hadn't moved. As he lay there, he said he could feel the ground vibrating like the horse's body as if it were still running and he were still holding on, his heart pounding in rhythm with the stallion's hooves.

I don't think that feeling ever left Charlie. I think he could feel it still, laying on the hood of his car. He opened his eyes. And what he saw, instead of the emptiness of the plain before him, instead of the questions, was the prairie he had known all his life, laid out in sculpted hills and valleys. He saw its promise, a kingdom that he was meant to inherit. He climbed off the hood and started up the Pontiac. He checked the gas gauge; there wasn't much, but it was a start.

I TOOK THE RIDE all the way to Hardin and they dropped me at a gas station by the freeway. I'd come very close to asking them to stop as we passed by Riverview. I'd wiped the fog from the window so I could see it ghosting by. It was tempting. My clothes were still damp, my hair matted to my neck. A warm bath would have been something transcendental. Standing by the free-way again with my thumb out was worse than hell.

I got a ride to Sheridan after a few hours, arriving just as it started to get light, and then I walked all the way out to my aunt's. It took me most of the day, fighting a headwind the whole way. But I didn't put my thumb out. I no longer wanted help, not from anyone. I had passed that point. With each step I knew what I needed to do. By afternoon the clouds had begun to break up and patches of sun drifted by. Cars flew past me, tires ripping at the pavement, tossing gravel around my feet. Somehow they knew not to stop. As I trudged along, weak because I hadn't eaten, I re-hearsed the phone call to Dad, working myself up to telling him that I was not coming home. I wish I had known how unnecessary that was—that he already knew.

When I got to the ranch, instead of going straight to the house, I went out to Granddad's cabin. I sat on the west side where the sun angled in through the cottonwoods and listened to the breeze. There were patches of snow left from the storm but those were quickly melting. It was almost summer warm again.

I waited a long time before my stomach began to hurt too much, and I got up and walked to the house. Aunt Kristine opened the door as though she thought she only imagined hearing the knock. No car had driven up. The dogs hadn't barked. She stared at me until she began to look like she might cry. I could tell that she knew the whole story, or most of it, and when she wrapped her arms around me, they felt warm and strong.

SHE CALLED DAD that night for me so he would know where I was, and that I was okay. And she promised I would call soon, when I was ready. It took a week to get the old cabin straightened out. Mark found a mattress, which we made into a bed up in a loft area at one end. The refrigerator hummed and rattled, but it worked. The dust, which permeated the logs and chinking, would not go away, and the whole place smelled like a musty library from Granddad's books. The old wood stove smoked, and it wasn't safe to use without cracking a window. But at night it was good to be able to hear the leaves scattering in the yard and occasionally the neighbor's cattle bawling in the distance.

Instead of trying to get me into high school, which had already started, Aunt Kristine set me up with a web site on her computer so I could work on my GED. It wasn't going to take much to pass. Her idea was that I could eventually go to some state school and then on to whichever college I wanted. She took it for granted that I would do something like that. Personally, I couldn't think that far into the future. But it seemed like a lot better plan than trying to convince the county school district to let a pregnant girl attend classes.

Then one day Mark came over with a sewing machine and about fifty yards of fleece in earthy shades of blue and green and brown. He'd found a small pine table in the barn, and he set it all up before he explained himself.

"This is a great way to make money."

"What?"

"I've got three different patterns here. Simple stuff." He took an envelope out of his pocket and pulled out some cloth tags. "Make sure you get these sewn in the neckline. Each item is worth ten bucks, alright? Just vary the colors and sizes."

I must have looked stunned.

"Kristine thought it was a great idea." He smiled, but he looked a little uncomfortable, as if he worried he'd made a mistake. "You can sew, right?"

"Yeah, I can sew."

He left me in the cabin staring at the sewing machine and the soft warm cloth on the chair. I took a deep breath. It was something to do.

IT TOOK ME a while to get up the nerve to try to call Charlie. I sat by the phone in Aunt Kristine's house with my hands on my knees waiting for my breathing to calm. When I finally dialed there was no answer, and I was surprised to feel relieved. I let a couple more days pass before I tried again. I hadn't planned for Uncle Leonard to pick up. I'm sure my hello sounded particularly breathless.

"Charlie's gone," Uncle Leonard said.

"Where?"

"Gone to school . . . in Boulder."

"But I thought . . . "

"He didn't tell nobody about it. It was his big secret." Uncle Leonard spoke slowly as ever, despite my obvious impatience. After a long pause he said, "First he went to look for you, you know?"

A long silence filled the space my voice could not. I closed my eyes. "Will you tell him I called?"

"Don't know when I'll see him." He coughed.

I held the phone tight. Even through the mad, buzzing panic of what I so desperately wanted at that moment, I could hear what he was saying. Charlie might not be coming back. Ever. Uncle Leonard waited for me to catch my breath. "If you do see him, tell him I hope he's doing okay."

He didn't answer right away, and I began to assume he'd hung up. I almost set the phone down.

"Don't worry about Charlie," he said. "He has a strong heart."

I set the phone down, but I didn't move. Aunt Kristine was in the other room, typing at the computer. I prayed that she wouldn't hear that I was off the phone and come to find me to see how it had gone, or try to say something comforting. I looked down at my hands and tried to remind myself that Charlie had not disappeared off the face of the earth.

I got up and walked out onto the porch. The air was crisp with the approaching autumn. I sat on the step and looked up at where the sun peeked through the cottonwood boughs. When I stopped to gauge my actual reaction, as opposed to the one I had anticipated, I was disappointed and my heart hurt, but I felt, too, that I'd expected this all along, that I had always known it would turn out this way.

I DIDN'T MAKE it up to Billings to see Dad for a couple of weeks. Aunt Kristine took me so I could pick up Mom's car, which he had agreed to let me have. It felt as if years could have passed since I walked across that bridge over the Yellowstone to meet Charlie on the opposite bank, enough time for the bank to have crumbled into the river, the bridge and Riverview to have washed away. I half expected to find it that way, but it was all still there, unchanged, except that the water was at its annual low. The current pushed weakly at the rock out in the middle.

When we got to the house I hesitated, as though I should knock before walking in, like a stranger. But I didn't. I opened the front door and yelled for Dad. I heard him get up from the dining room table, and as he came into the front room, he looked older. Something about seeing him in that house, with its missing furniture and bare walls, made me feel that I'd been terribly wrong, running away, abandoning him. And though it was all that I might have hoped for once, to see him weakened, now it brought only regret. The few feet across that room seemed vast, but I couldn't just stand there. I walked over to him.

He tried to make a joke. "I wasn't planning to kick you out of the house until you were eighteen, you know."

I nodded and attempted a smile, but he saw the frustration in my face, something he normally would have missed. His shoulders dropped just a little, his face melting into an earnest expression that was unfamiliar.

"Well, the place feels pretty empty. I guess I just got too used to you being around."

I could hear that the *you* meant us — Mom and I.

"You really had me worried."

"It's okay, Dad. I'm okay."

He took my shoulders and wrapped his arms around me. I buried my face in his chest, and tightened my hands into fists to keep from crying. If he had started, I wouldn't have been able to stop. I felt his breath catch for a moment, and he held me tighter. Whatever else there was or was not between us, that hug felt good.

Finally he cleared his throat and stood back from me half a step in the middle of the room. Aunt Kristine rescued us both from a moment we might not have gotten beyond, stuck as we were without words. "Well, Jack, I really like what you've done with the place," she said with obvious irony.

He grinned and shrugged his shoulders. "Want some food?"

We sat in the kitchen and ate the lunch he'd made. Sausages and sauerkraut with onions and applesauce. It was his favorite, and I guessed he was probably living on it, without anyone else around to complain about the monotony. I could picture the empty applesauce jars and sauerkraut cans piling up in the pantry.

As I try to remember that day now, I inevitably experience a strange shift of time. It's not something that I can properly explain. Maybe it's because I grew up at that table, from the time I was an infant until I left home. Always the same table. My memory slips. I cannot organize, without effort, the correct order of things that happened. I swear as I sat there, that day, that Rose

292 ▲ MARCUS STEVENS

was sitting in his lap, three years old. He was so used to her, so comfortable with her, that he talked with Aunt Kristine without looking down, just bouncing her on his knee, keeping a comforting hand on her shoulder. After a minute she hopped out of his lap and tugged at his sleeve until she finally got his attention.

"Grandpa, I want juice," she said.

"Rose, Grandpa might not have juice. We'll have to see," I said, trying to help.

"You bet I do," he said and he walked her over to the refrigerator. As she waited for him to find a cup and pour it, she watched him with adoring eyes. She seemed absolutely satisfied, as if that's all it took to win her heart. Of course Grandpa had her special kind of juice; he knew how to take care of her. It made sense to me, that he was going to be a much better grandparent. She drank the glass in one long drink and gave it back to him. When he turned back from the counter her arms were raised to be picked up. He lifted her with a smile and she wrapped her arms around his neck like a promise.

Chapter Thirty

As I sewed, the cottonwood and aspen leaves turned and fell. They danced in eddies of the cold breeze under the eaves and rested quietly each morning coated delicately with frost. My tummy grew and I got used to being pregnant. Crows gathered in black flocks and beat low overhead beneath V's of migrating geese drawn against the high, flat ceilings of northern fronts. One morning a whitetail buck startled me by staring at me through the window; he moved closer until his wet nose practically pressed against the glass. His big eyes looked familiar. I knew if it weren't for the glass between us, we could speak. At least he seemed to have something to say. Several nights in a row I listened to a bear shake the last few apples from the tree. I heard him sniff around the cabin and rattle the door. Then for a week a great horned owl perched in the aspens where I could see it as I sewed.

So you see, I had company. I was alone, but I wasn't. I wasn't even thinking about Charlie much by the time he showed up.

He came up for the long weekend break without calling and found me at Thanksgiving dinner with Aunt Kristine and Mark and a new couple who had recently moved out from Connecticut. A knock at the door nearly stumped us. We weren't expecting anyone, and it took a full minute for Mark to register the sound, put down the knife and go answer the door. He came back looking even more perplexed. Charlie was right behind him, and I could see each person in the room react. It *was* funny. Here it was, Thanksgiving dinner, and a real Indian had just shown up. Of course we pilgrims felt obliged to invite him to join us in our feast, but he had already eaten at a McDonald's on the way up. There was a long, awkward moment as we all sat looking up at Charlie before I got up and ushered him out of the room.

We decided to drive out to the lake. Kind of a strange thing to do in November, but we knew nobody would be there. We could talk. The sky was flat with gray clouds that hung low, void of detail, almost close enough to touch. A marsh hawk glided over the barbed-wire fence and out across the pasture, tipping its wings to maintain its balance in the light wind. Dust drifted from the gravel road as we dropped down from the bench to the lake. It was a particularly unspectacular day to visit such an unremarkable body of water. Without the mountains visible in the background because of the clouds and hardly a tree to adorn its shores, without a clear sky to blue its water or sun to illuminate its depths, the lake was not much at all.

Charlie turned off at a boat ramp and stopped near the edge of the water. He turned the engine off, leaving a dull quiet, just the faint wind against the car. Bare, treeless hills pressed against the sky. I could hear the blood pulsing through my body like the steady lap of the waves on the gravel shore. We both stared straight ahead.

Charlie was trying to decide how to say that he'd meant to call, without explaining that he didn't have a phone where he stayed in Colorado, that he'd scraped together loose change just to find the gas money to make it up for this trip, and that anyway he hadn't known what to say. He hadn't known if I wanted him to call. I was trying to find the best words to explain why I'd run off, why I hadn't told him everything. We stared out at the slightly ruffled water of the lake, both of us consciously avoiding the curve of my stomach.

"I . . . "

"I . . . "

We both started at the same time and had to stop.

Charlie turned to me. "Go ahead."

"No, you go."

"I don't know what I was going to say."

"Me either."

Something about his face, the furrow of his brow . . . he was trying so hard. It made me laugh, I couldn't help myself. Then he started laughing, too.

"Let's get out of the car," he said.

I grabbed my jacket. It was cold, but not that bad. We sat on the hood, which felt warm under my legs. We managed to get the basic facts out of the way—when I was due, a short version of how school was going for him. Then the conversation faded off again. A breeze caught a strand of his hair and blew it across his forehead. I almost reached to pull it back. I didn't want to lose him, this man, but his eyes gave me courage. "Look, I don't expect anything, you know. I ran off. I . . . "

"It's alright." He pulled the hair out of his eyes. "It's okay . . . I mean, I know." He was sitting close enough to take my hand or touch my shoulder, but he was waiting. I had a sick feeling in my gut that it wasn't going that way.

"Charlie. I don't know what should happen. I mean, not *should* . . . I don't know what I *want* to happen."

He was quiet.

"What about you?" I asked.

He just shook his head and looked down at the gravel at his feet.

"You have to finish school, right?"

"Yeah. I have to finish school."

The breeze dropped on the lake, left it slick, but with nothing to reflect except the featureless sky.

"Maybe we can't figure this out." When I looked over he wasn't looking down. He was looking right at me. My voice was barely working. "Maybe we shouldn't try."

I couldn't tell from his eyes if that hurt him, if he took it to mean that I didn't want him to come back into my life, or if it was a relief and he was happy to be off the hook. Maybe he didn't know either. But he did take my hand, and then he kissed me. His breath tasted like pure oxygen, not something I merely wanted, but something I had to have. The marsh hawk distracted us both by swooping almost directly over the car and then began working up the shoreline. Charlie let go of my hand, which was trembling. I needed to change the subject. "This is an awful lake."

He looked out at it. "Why?"

"I don't know. It's so blah and plain. It doesn't even seem that deep."

"It's probably deeper than you think."

"It must be man-made."

"No. It isn't. It was here before."

The water was as still as glass now. Across the small bay the reflection of the marsh hawk made a second bird, which glided in perfect synchronization.

"There's an old Cheyenne story about this lake."

"Yeah?"

He sat up. "It happened around this day."

"Thanksgiving?" That seemed surprising.

"Yeah, but not Thanksgiving. November twenty-fifth, or actually a couple days later, I guess, a day or two after the U.S. cavalry attacked Dull Knife's camp in the Bighorns."

I looked out across the brooding lake, at its inscrutable surface.

"Actually, there's a couple of versions. I heard it a long time ago. I'd almost forgotten it was this lake. The white army was chasing the Cheyenne after wiping out the camp, destroying everything. They'd broken up into small groups—everyone just trying to get away."

"It was snowing, too, huh?"

"Yeah and really cold. There was no place to hide or get away, and they knew the soldiers were catching up, only a few hours behind them. They got to the edge of this lake and stopped. They had only a few horses; many of them didn't even have moccasins for their feet. They were thinking about their dead, everyone who'd been murdered by the soldiers already." He pointed at the shore of the lake, a line that was hard to define because of the flatness of the water and the diffused light. "They say the whole group, horses and all, walked right into the lake, or under it, really, to escape. They just disappeared."

The lake was silent now, even the waves against the shore seemed to speak—hush, hush—like Charlie's breathing.

"The people who came after knew that's what had happened because they found the tracks that led right up to the edge, and some say they found a colt running back and forth at the shore. He'd been separated from his mother, maybe because he'd fallen behind, but he was afraid to follow, afraid the magic would no longer work."

I thought of that colt, running frantically back and forth at the shore of the lake, which was already forming ice on its edges. "What are you going to do Charlie?" I asked quietly.

It wasn't a simple question. He couldn't answer it with a word.

After a minute I asked a different one. "Would you have gone with them?"

"I don't know," he said.

Charlie stayed two days, but he slept on an air mattress that Mark brought over. It didn't seem like a good idea to have him share my bed, and he didn't suggest it. I lay on top of my covers, only a few feet away, trying to decide if I was in love with Charlie, or if I ever had been, truly in love. I had wanted to be. I know that. He was a song I could not get out of my head, but sometimes I think that there is something that instinctively protects you from letting what you want become what you need, or what you think you have to have. And maybe love is something that must stand on its own feet, and if it is real, must make its own way—like a child, or the answer to a difficult question, a place to live. Whatever was going to happen with us, with Charlie and me, was going to have to wait.

He had nothing to pack, so when it was time to leave, he simply stood up. He looked awkwardly around the room as though he might have brought something. But he hadn't. He put his boots on, stood me up with two hands, held me so I could feel his heart pounding in his chest and then softly kissed my neck.

As he walked from my cabin to his car, he seemed to diminish from being Charlie to an anonymous figure who was simply a man getting in an American-made car and fading away into the dust of the dirt road.

My FIRST WINTER in the cabin felt long. I didn't have Rose yet to keep me company, to occupy my time. I went to town to see the midwife. Sometimes I helped Aunt Kristine with her errands. I sewed, and I did my schoolwork.

It was sometime in those first few months that I learned who built this cabin. I thought about it whenever the cold was so hard outside that everything became perilously fragile, when it seemed that if the temperature dropped just two more degrees, the trees might begin to swell and burst. The Captain, my grandfather's brother, came here because he had been a soldier all his life. He had nowhere else to go. His brother offered him a place on his homestead, and he felled the trees for the cabin on the spot. It's small because it was all he could manage before winter settled in.

The wind lay heavy on his shoulders as he worked. I would imagine him in the evening, his back to the window, the yellow flame of a candle lighting the side of his face, just enough wood in the smoky stove to keep him alive. I'd think of this: the Captain, who had fought so many battles, the barest thread of happen-stance away from death so many times, died alone. He died here, in this room. It was below zero in the cabin when they found him. The black coals of the fire were just as cold. He was sitting in his chair, and I am sure, now, that he let that fire go out.

Chapter Thirty-One

It's been just two weeks since I took Rose to the river to talk. Every once in a while she's come to me with a new question, but mostly she's absorbed it all with remarkable calm. I feel as though I've thought about nothing else.

This morning I'm awake early, ahead of her, which doesn't happen often. Like most six-year-olds, she's usually up with the sun. My mind is racing as I gaze out the window. The glow of the approaching day reaches and rolls across the landscape in a way that seems miraculous. The birds leave their perches in the trees as if to catch that wave of light, as if to confirm an instinct I can barely trust—that I have chosen well. That I know my own heart. I haven't actually made the decisions I had set myself to make. Except this one. Today is the day.

By the time what is left of my coffee is cold, I hear Rose's footsteps coming in from the other room. She pauses at the door, rubbing her eyes. How often I wish I could borrow that sleepiness, which she allows herself so unselfconsciously, and trust everything to someone else again. Sometimes I feel willing to accept even a

USEFUL GIRL ▲ 301

kind of tyranny not to be the one to decide, to guide. She wanders
from the counter with her bowl of cereal.

"Good morning, Rose."

"Mmm MmMm Mmmm," she says, mumbling the syllables
for *Good morning, Mom,* a bite of food already in her mouth.

I watch her eat. No hurry, but big bites. Though I've told her
almost everything, I haven't yet shown her the letter. I pull it out
of my pocket, and carefully unfold it. It is well worn from being
carried so long there, from being taken out and put back so many
times.

"What's that?"

"A letter."

"Is it for me?" she asks brightly. Letters are always good news
in her world.

"You and me, really."

She doesn't ask me who it's from. She seems to know from the
tone of my voice. She puts her spoon down, and I read it to her.

Dear Rose,

It may sound silly to you, but this has been a hard letter for
me to write. I think I must have thrown away five sheets of paper already. Sometimes grown-ups can be afraid of the craziest
things. To tell you the plain truth, I'm afraid that you might be
angry with me. Or maybe I'm afraid that when you meet me, I
won't look like a father to you. You must have some idea about
that, and I may seem pretty ordinary. Dads are just people, after all, I guess. When I last saw your mother, we didn't know
what was going to happen next, and that's a difficult way to
leave things. I know that I never thought it would take me six
years to finish school or that I would end up with a master's degree. But maybe your mother did. Maybe she always knew.

Someday I hope you'll be able to understand what a big thing she did for me. There's something else I've been afraid to tell her. Maybe you can think of a way. Maybe you can tell her that I miss those days when we used to find someplace to go that no one else knew about, someplace out in the prairie where it felt like we could see to the edge of the world. I miss the feeling of not needing anything anymore.

She and I share a lot of secrets. I'm sure she's told you about Mo'é'ha'e. She died so long ago it seems like it shouldn't matter anymore, but it still bothers me that we had to hide her bones that way. The Cheyenne didn't used to bury people under-ground. I don't know, but maybe the reason is that being hidden like that, like a secret, makes it harder for the soul to find its way.

The other secret in my life, the most important one, is you. And I can't stand that anymore. What if we never met, and no one else in my life knew about you?

One day soon, if your mother says it's okay, I will come to see you, and maybe by then she will have told you our story.

— your father, Charlie

Rose is silent when I finish, but she has an expression on her face that doesn't belong. It's too mature. I might have had trouble making up my mind what I wanted but not her.

"Today?" she asks.

I nod, and her eyes light up.

We do our best to kill time the rest of the morning. Rose likes to "help" with my sewing. I give her scrap pieces to cut out and pin, then I sew them for her. She makes a neat pile next to mine. There's no question it would have been easier in a lot of ways to keep things as they had been. To say no to Charlie. I look at her concentrating over her work, easily passing the time as if she's already forgotten that we are waiting. There is still the question, how *should* this child be raised—the descendant of a Cheyenne warrior and a U.S. cavalryman? I guess, in the end, the answer will be Rose's. Not mine.

I hear Aunt Kristine's dogs barking, and Charlie's car pulls up at a perfect angle. I can see it through the window over Rose's shoulder. He gets out as if he had left only a few hours ago on some errand, and Rose jumps up onto her chair so she can see, too. Charlie is halfway to the cabin.

Acknowledgments

I am deeply indepted to the many friends and family who helped me along the way with this novel. I need to mention first my friend Ken Galen York who died a few weeks ago, just as he finally made it back to Montana. We used to fish together, sip scotch and talk late into the night about politics, philosophy and, most of all, writing. He always had a great book in hand that he knew I needed to read, and his thoughts about narrative voice helped guide me through this story.

It's hard to overestimate how important a simple expression of confidence can be to keep you writing; for that I must particularly thank my brother and sister who have always been there to cheer me on. And, of course, I must thank my mother—for all the things you expect from a mother, but also for a dream and the confidence to pursue it.

I am especially grateful to those willing readers who offered insight and suggestions—Deidre Combs, Rebecca McNatt, Tina Buckingham, Corrine Madden and Camille Burkard.

My grandfather, who was never the cantankerous man of this novel, nonetheless made his own contributions by sharing photographs and stories of my ancestors who homesteaded in Utah and Idaho in the mid- to late-1800s. Conrad Fisher, Dean of Cultural Affairs at Chief Dull Knife Memorial College, provided Cheyenne translations and guidance on cultural issues. My gratitude also to Holly Rainey, Nate Naprstek, Michael Speers and Leonard Mountain Chief, whose personal experiences enriched this novel and, I hope, brought to it some level of accuracy. I would like to include a special thanks to Claudia and Kenny Williams of Montana Rose whose music was my original inspiration.

Thanks to my editor, Antonia Fusco, for her heartfelt dedication to this book, and to Sylvie Rabineau and David Hale Smith for their commitment and enduring faith in this story.

Lastly, I want to thank my children Haley, Madison and Wyatt for the brilliant spark they bring to every writing day, and my wife Diana—my partner, my collaborator, my courage and inspiration, my love, my life.